high stakes crime
A SHELBY NICHOLS ADVENTURE

Colleen Helme

www.colleenhelme.com

Book Cover Art by Damonza.com Copyright ©2021 by Colleen Helme

High Stakes Crime/ Colleen Helme. -- 1st ed.
ISBN 9798544925866

Dedication

To my Grandparents
For your amazing examples of love and devotion throughout
your lives. I'm so blessed to have known you!

ACKNOWLEDGEMENTS

I'd like to start off by thanking Don for coming up with the great title for this book. It's awesome and so are you!

I'm so grateful for all of you who love Shelby as much as I do! Thanks for your support, encouragement, friendship, and great reviews You keep me writing.

As always, a big, huge thanks to my daughter, Melissa. You are always willing to listen to my plot ideas and your input is invaluable.

Thanks to my wonderful husband, Tom, for proofing the manuscript and for your insight—and also for believing in me, even when I struggle. Thanks to my awesome family for your continued encouragement, support, and belief in me. I love you all!

A big thanks to Kristin Monson for editing this book and making it better. You are the best!

I am so grateful to the talented Wendy Tremont King for bringing Shelby and the gang to life on audio. Thanks for sticking with me through fifteen books! You rock!

And last but not least, to my Grandpa Chappell, who took me prospecting for gold. It was great fun, and I've never forgotten it!

Shelby Nichols Adventure Series

Carrots
Fast Money
Lie or Die
Secrets that Kill
Trapped by Revenge
Deep in Death
Crossing Danger
Devious Minds
Hidden Deception
Laced in Lies
Deadly Escape
Marked for Murder
Ghostly Serenade
Dying Wishes
High Stakes Crime

Devil in a Black Suit ~ A Ramos Story
A Midsummer Night's Murder ~ A Shelby Nichols Novella

Sand and Shadow Series
Angel Falls
Desert Devil (coming soon)

NEWSLETTER SIGNUP

For news, updates, and special offers, please sign up for my newsletter at www.colleenhelme.com. To thank you for subscribing you will receive a **FREE** ebook: *Behind Blue Eyes: A Shelby Nichols Novella.*

Contents

CHAPTER 1

I held the gun in both hands and pulled the trigger, automatically squeezing my eyes shut. Opening them, I searched the target for a bullet hole and frowned, unhappy that I'd missed it again.

Beside me, Dante Mitchell, my firearms instructor, shook his head and tapped my shoulder to get my attention. I took off my ear protectors, even though I could still hear his thoughts with them on. Of course, he didn't know that I could read minds, but, since he said everything he was thinking, it didn't really matter.

"You can't keep closing your eyes. How can you expect to hit anything with your eyes shut?"

I couldn't tell him that every time I pulled the trigger, the image of the man I'd killed popped into my head. It wasn't the look of surprise on Jameson Beal's face that bothered me. It was the blood. With each bullet that slammed into him, his body had jerked, spraying blood all over the place.

For some reason, I hadn't remembered any of that until I'd fired the gun today. Now that was all I could see. Damn. Before it slipped from my fingers, I set the gun on the counter and stepped away. "Could I take a break?"

I heard his thoughts and tried not to cringe. He could hardly believe I'd ask for a break. Normally he yelled at his cadets for not following his instructions, but I wasn't a cadet, so he couldn't treat me the same way. But this was ridiculous.

What was going on with me? Did I want to fail? Examining my face, he noticed the fine sheen of sweat on my upper lip and the pasty white coloring of my skin. Was I going to faint? He swore under his breath.

Stepping beside me, he picked up the gun and removed the magazine before setting the gun and ammo on the counter. "Hold it together, Shelby. You are not fainting on me."

I blinked before straightening my spine. The command in his tone sent all thoughts of blood right out of my brain. "Of course I'm not going to faint."

Dante shook his head, but gently took my elbow and guided me out of the shooting range to a bench near the locker room. The cadet firearms class didn't begin for another thirty minutes, so we had the place to ourselves. He sat beside me and gave me his undivided attention.

"What's going on?" I began to shake my head, but he stopped me with a dismissive growl. "No. You need to tell me, or I won't be able to clear you to work in the police department—ever again. You understand? Your fate rests in my hands. So spill it."

"Wow... you're kind of bossy."

As the firearms instructor at the police academy, Dante didn't have a soft spot in his body, and I wasn't just talking about his toned physique. Authority rolled off him in waves, and the fact that he was even talking to me nicely surprised me.

His lips twisted, but he smoothed them out and narrowed his gaze, not wanting me to know that I'd almost made him smile. That gave me the courage to look up into his deep brown eyes, taking in his raised brow and pursed lips.

With his dark, creamy skin, shaved head, and taut muscles under a tight black tee, he was more than a little intimidating. But I'd been dealing with a mob boss and a hitman for more than a year and a half, so I was used to macho-men.

Besides that, after listening to Dante's mind, I knew he had a grudging respect for me. When Chief Winder had told him I was coming in for firearms instruction, he'd read up on me and found out that I'd killed a man in the line of duty, even though I wasn't a cop.

Right now, it bothered Dante that I sat beside him, clenching my hands together so they wouldn't shake. "I'm waiting."

"Okay, okay." I wiped the sweat off my brow, surprised that firing a gun had brought it all back. It had been nearly three months since I'd killed Beal, and, outside of my dreams, this was the first time it had truly shaken me. "I don't know why shooting that gun brought it all back."

I glanced his way. "You know I killed a man a few months ago. But it was either him or me." I didn't add that I'd acted out of sheer desperation to save Ramos's life after he'd already been shot trying to save mine.

"What did you see? Just now... in your mind?"

"I saw the bullets hit him and... all the blood. I'd forgotten about that part until I started shooting the gun. It must have 'triggered' the memory." I smiled at my pun, but he didn't think it was funny, so I dropped it. "I'm not a fan of blood... and that was just... the worst."

"So it was thinking about the blood?"

I nodded, but I didn't add that it wasn't just Beal's blood that had gotten to me. There was blood all over Ramos, too.

So much blood had poured out of him, that he'd nearly died. He was fine now, so what was wrong with me? I thought I'd dealt with this, and now it was like it had happened yesterday.

"Hmm..." Dante was thinking that I'd managed to put off coming to the shooting range for at least three, maybe four, weeks since my first appointment. I'd gotten good at pushing that memory away—until today. He'd helped several people who had gone through this before. It took some of them a long time to get over killing someone, and using a gun again was actually part of the process.

"This is what I want you to do," he began. "We're going back onto the shooting range. You will load the gun and get ready to fire. Then I want you to look at the target and think of it as nothing more than what it is—a piece of paper. It has no face, no body, and especially, no blood. It's just a target. If you keep your eyes open and your mind focused, that's all you'll see."

I raised a skeptical brow, but kept my mouth shut, knowing it wouldn't do any good to question him. "If you say so."

"I do." He stood and stepped away, so I had to follow him back to my spot at the shooting range. After slipping on his gear, he took his position beside me and folded his arms across his chest. Letting out a sigh, I slipped my protective glasses back on, along with my ear protectors, and picked up the gun. I loaded it, flipped the safety off, and positioned my feet in the correct firing stance.

I raised the gun to fire and sighted down the barrel at the target, opening my eyes extra wide. I moved my finger to the trigger, slowly let out a breath, and pulled. The gun fired, and I fought against the image of Beal that seemed burned into my brain, instead, focusing on the target in front of me.

"Again," Dante said.

I repeated the action, firing several more rounds until the magazine was empty. Lowering the gun, I emptied the magazine and set it down. Dante pushed the button for the target to come toward us and examined it.

"Well, at least you hit it this time," he said, noting two bullet holes along the bottom edge. "Let's go again."

He sent the target back, and I reloaded the gun, repeating the process. After a few more magazine rounds, I had finally managed to keep my eyes open and my hands steady. Dante brought the target back to us, and, this time, elation rolled over me. I'd actually hit the center circle a few times.

"Better." Dante glanced my way, thinking it had been worth it to continue. "That's enough for today, but I'd like to see you back here tomorrow."

"Tomorrow? So soon?"

"Yes. I don't want you to fall into your old pattern of avoidance, and the more you get used to handling a gun, the easier it will be to keep your head clear. When you pick up a weapon, your mind needs to be focused, or it won't do you any good."

I nodded my agreement, even though I didn't love the idea. Guns meant death, but wasn't that part of the job? Deep down, I knew that I couldn't always count on someone else to protect me, and it was past time I learned how to protect myself.

If that meant learning how to shoot a gun without flinching, it was worth it, especially if it meant saving Ramos, or Dimples, or even Uncle Joey and my family. It was time for me to do my part.

I gave him a firm nod. "Okay. I'll come back tomorrow. Same time?"

"Yes." I followed him out of the shooting range, and he took the gun I'd used. "Do you own a gun?"

I twisted my lips. "Not anymore."

His brows rose, so I told him what had happened to it. "Someone stole it right out of the safe in my bedroom closet. Then they used it to murder a private investigator. Since my fingerprints were on it, and I'd been the one to find his body, they arrested me for murder. It was awful. After I was exonerated, the police offered to give it back, but I told them to destroy it."

His eyes widened, and he changed his mind about telling me to buy my own gun. "Oh. I see. No wonder you have an aversion to guns."

"Yeah. That's probably part of the reason I put off coming here, but now I realize that I need to put all of that behind me. I need to be reliable for my partner if a dicey situation comes up again. But don't ask me to own a gun, because that's never going to happen."

"Sure." He could understand it, but he thought I needed something for protection, since I seemed to get into all kinds of trouble.

"I have this." I pulled my stun flashlight out of my purse and held it out to show him. "It packs a wallop, and I've used it several times. It hasn't let me down yet, and I don't have to worry about killing anyone."

Dante took the flashlight from me, and his lips twisted into a grin. "Not bad."

I put it back into my purse. "Thanks. Well... I guess I'll see you tomorrow."

He nodded, thinking that I was full of surprises, and he looked forward to seeing me again. I left with a smile, grateful my first time on the gun range was behind me, and that Dante had even helped me out. From my first impression of his hard, no-nonsense attitude, I never would have thought that possible.

The police station was just a few buildings over, and I'd told Detective Harris, aka Dimples, that I'd stop by after my mandatory training session. I hadn't seen him for a while, mostly because my husband, Chris, had insisted I take some time off.

A while back, I'd solved a case by nearly becoming the next victim, and it still made me cringe. How had I ever thought I could outsmart a womanizing killer? A few days later, I'd been shoved down a long staircase by another murderer. After those near misses, I was more than ready to agree with Chris. We'd even managed to take the kids camping for a few days, and our new dog, Coco, had gone with us.

We'd had a great time, and I don't even like camping. Just thinking about Coco brought a smile to my face, and I knew he was the main reason I'd recovered from the trauma of the last several weeks so quickly.

Besides helping the police, I'd taken some time off from helping Uncle Joey as well. He was the mob boss who knew my mind reading secret. At first, he'd coerced me into working for him. Now I did it because he'd claimed my family and me as part of the Manetto clan.

Some of that may have been my fault, since I'd been calling him Uncle Joey from the first day we'd met, and that had made it seem true. In fact, I had a closer bond with Joey "The Knife" Manetto than I did with my real uncles, so maybe it wasn't so unexpected.

A year ago, I never would have thought it possible, but now I couldn't imagine my life without him. Of course, that included his hitman, Ramos. He was one of those hot, sexy, dangerous men that women of all ages couldn't help drooling over... me included. He'd saved my life more than a few times, nearly dying in the process, so we had a special bond.

Since I was happily married, and he knew it, he liked to push my buttons. I may have enjoyed those times more than I should, but nothing had ever happened. And... as long as I got to go on long motorcycle rides with him... that was enough to keep me on the straight and narrow.

Dimples also knew my secret, but he was the only person on the police force who did, and he'd sworn to keep it to himself. I told everyone else I had premonitions in order to explain my psychic ability. By now, the whole department believed I was the real deal, so it was nice to have respect, even if some of the detectives gave it grudgingly.

But... the downside of my notoriety was that I was in such high demand. The chief had even asked me to help another police chief in New York while I'd been there on vacation. It just proved that I hadn't learned how to say no, and another reason I needed a break.

Now that my break was over, it was time to get back to work. Too bad firing that gun had brought back the memory of killing Jameson Beal. If not for that, I might be a little more excited about seeing Dimples today.

Since I couldn't help worrying, I decided that from now on, I'd be in charge of my life. I'd call the shots for a change, and things would go the way I wanted, regardless of what everyone else thought. That settled me down, and I entered the police station to find Dimples.

After a quick greeting with the desk officer, he buzzed me into the inner sanctum of the station, and I followed the hallway to the detectives' offices. Dimples glanced up, and his face broke into a huge smile, causing his dimples to turn into little tornadoes whirling around on his cheeks.

Just looking at those dimples brought a grin to my face, and I stepped toward him like he was a long-lost friend. It had only been a few weeks since I'd last seen him, but he came around his desk to give me an enthusiastic bear hug that squeezed the breath right out of me.

"It's so good to see you," he said, before finally letting me go.

"You too. How are you doing?"

"Good. You ready to come back to work?" He smiled extra-wide, hoping to entice me with his amazing dimples.

I chuckled. "Just about, but I have to see your wife at her office first."

Dimples had recently married Billie Jo Payne, a reporter for the *Daily News*. She'd helped me out a few times, and I'd returned the favor. We'd even become good friends, but now she wanted to interview me for a featured article. So far, I'd managed to avoid her, but she'd insisted I come in today. I'd agreed, but only on the condition that there were no strings attached.

"Oh yeah?" he asked. "You're really going to do an interview?"

This time I grinned. "No way. I finally figured out that I have leverage. If she ever wants my help again, then she'll have to forget about an exclusive interview."

"Whoa... that's a change." He thought I'd come a long way from those early days when I'd been so eager to help the police, and just about everyone else, to prove my worth. Now that I was in such high demand, I didn't need to prove anything.

Knowing I was taking charge of my life gave me a feeling of power that I was beginning to like. "I think I like this way much better."

His dimples disappeared. "Yeah, I can see that."

"But don't worry." I patted his arm. "I'll always help you when you need me."

He opened his mouth to ask for something, but I cut him off. "But your wife awaits, and we don't want to disappoint her."

He sighed. "You've got me there. But, just so you know, I wasn't going to ask you to help me right now." At my raised brows, he continued. "Okay... maybe I was, but I can manage." He was thinking that it would sure be nice if I could sit in on a couple of interviews he'd planned for tomorrow.

"That might work... especially since I have to come back for another training session with Dante at the firing range."

"Great. So, about this time tomorrow?" I barely got in a nod before he rushed on. "Thanks Shelby. I'll see you then. Oh... be sure and tell Billie hi for me."

"I will." As I left the station, I shook my head. So much for learning how to say no... but it was Dimples, so I didn't mind. Plus... it was nice to be wanted. A little voice warned me that something bad could happen tomorrow, but I scoffed. What could happen during a simple police interrogation? Thoughts of an earthquake and a freaky ghost came to mind, but I shoved that away pretty quick.

The newspaper office was only a few blocks away, and I parked across the street. Walking toward the building, I caught sight of my reflection in the two-story wall of glass. It reminded me of the day that I'd stopped a shooter right there in the lobby.

That had given me more recognition than I'd wanted. Even worse, Jameson Beal had begun stalking me to prove my premonitions weren't real. Since I'd killed him, he wasn't a problem anymore, but I couldn't help the chill that went down my spine to walk into the large, open space.

I stopped at the front desk, and the receptionist called Billie to let her know I was there. Billie told me to come on up, and I went through security to the elevators, grateful they let me keep my stun flashlight. Stepping out on her floor, I found Billie waiting for me.

"Shelby, it's so good to see you!" She gave me a hug, thinking that she'd missed seeing me, and she was a little disappointed that I'd been avoiding her. She hoped to patch things up, because she liked having me for a friend. And... it didn't hurt that my life fascinated her. I was always getting into trouble, and she hated hearing things second-hand from Drew.

"I know you've been busy," she continued, "and Drew told me you'd taken some time off, so I'm glad you were able to come."

"Yeah, it's been a while. So how are you doing? Still enjoying married life?"

"Yes. Drew's great." She ducked her head. "To be honest, it's been kind of nice to have an inside source with the police, you know?"

I chuckled. Wait. Did she really say that out loud? I wasn't sure her lips had moved, so I asked a question instead. "So how's work going? Any interesting stories?"

"Yeah... but nothing like the chimerism case we worked on together. Did Drew tell you that I got a journalism award for that story?"

I gasped. "You did? Wow. That's wonderful. Congratulations."

She nodded. "Thanks. It wasn't a Pulitzer Prize or anything, but I still got recognized, so that was pretty cool." She glanced over my shoulder. "Oh... it looks like they're ready. Come with me."

She turned toward the conference room, and alarm raced down my spine. "Wait, what's going on?" From her mind, I picked up that this was a surprise just for me. She'd hoped to pull it off, but, from my raised brow and fierce glare, she didn't think it had worked.

Her lips drew up in a saucy smile, and she shook her head. "Man... having premonitions is a bitch. You can never be surprised, can you?"

That brought a chuckle out of me, and a sardonic smile strained my lips. "No, I guess not."

"Just come with me. It won't be that bad."

I rolled my eyes. "Right."

I followed her into the large conference room, a little overcome by all the people who had crowded inside. Michael Lewis-Pierce, the editor-in-chief, stood at the head of the room and smiled warmly at me. "Hey Shelby. We're glad you could make it. Come on up here."

With a sigh of resignation, I made my way toward him. A few people thought I looked unhappy but, since I had premonitions, it was probably hard to act surprised. Hearing that, I tried to imagine serene thoughts and pasted a smile on my face.

Michael beamed at me before he began. "We don't usually do this, but our editorial board and the newspaper owner felt it appropriate. We're just sorry it took so long to get you back in the building."

A few people chuckled, and his lips twisted into a knowing smile. "On behalf of everyone here, we'd like to present you with a small token of our gratitude. Most of us in this room will never forget that fateful day when you kept us from harm by stopping a shooter with your quick thinking and extraordinary powers."

He reached behind him and picked up a beautiful, crystal paperweight, with the newspaper logo etched in gold and my name engraved underneath. With a smile, he handed it to me. "Thank you, Shelby."

"Oh wow. It's beautiful. Thanks so much." After examining it, I glanced around the room, picking up the heartfelt warmth and admiration of everyone there. It filled a part of me that I hadn't realized was empty and made everything I'd been through, lately, worth it.

"Thank you all so much. This is... well, it really means a lot to me." My throat got tight, and I couldn't say another word. Holy hell. Was I about to cry?

"Yay for Shelby," Billie said, and started clapping. The rest of the group joined in, adding a few whoops and whistles. The tightness left my throat, and I even managed a chuckle.

"Okay," Michael called over the din. "That's enough. Now get back to work."

They filed out with good-natured grumbles, and I surreptitiously wiped my nose, grateful that my eyes were dry. Michael turned to me. "That was fun. You even seemed surprised."

"I was. I mean... I knew something was going on, but I didn't know what it was for sure." I held up the paperweight. "Thanks for this. I really appreciate it."

He shook his head, thinking it was nothing after I'd saved several of their lives... well... mostly his life, since he was the intended target. "What do you think about doing an exclusive interview with Billie?"

I chuckled. "Is that what this is about?" I knew it wasn't, but I couldn't help rubbing it in.

Affronted, he raised his chin. "No, of course not." Seeing the twinkle in my eyes, he shook his head. "But you can't blame me for trying."

"Yeah... I get it... but the answer is no. I don't need more attention... and you should know what I mean."

He nodded, expecting as much. He couldn't really blame me, since my fame had brought a killer out of the shadows to torment me. Even worse, that man had gotten close enough that he'd nearly killed me. In fact... Michael's gaze jerked to mine. Hadn't I killed him? He glanced away, feeling a little bad that he'd even asked. "Well... thanks for coming in."

"Sure. And thanks for this." I held up the paperweight.

"Just a minute," Billie said, glancing his way. "Maybe we should ask Shelby what she thinks about the big story tomorrow."

Michael's brows rose. "Oh yeah... she could be helpful." He glanced my way. "What do you say, Shelby? Want to hear about it?"

With both of them ganging up on me, their eyes brimming with hope, how could I refuse? "Sure, I'll listen."

Michael smiled, thinking that deep down I enjoyed what I did, even if it sometimes got a little weird. "Great. I'll let Billie explain while I go back to my office. But just so you know... this story's not something I'm going to invest a lot of time in unless it's true. Right now, that's up in the air, and this newspaper is based on facts, not conspiracy theories."

I picked up that the story was somewhat unconventional, and it piqued my interest. "Makes sense to me."

"Good."

He turned with a wave, and I sat down at the conference table with Billie. Her eyes glazed over with excitement, and my curiosity rose. "The story is all about a journal that was recently discovered. If it's real, it could have huge consequences. Have you heard anything about "The Lost Taft Mine" in the news, or anything about the legends surrounding it?"

"Sure. I've heard of the legend, but I haven't seen anything about it recently."

"Then I'll explain. A few weeks ago, a history professor announced that he had found a journal written by Jeremiah Taft, the man who had discovered the gold mine in the late eighteen-hundreds.

"Before Taft's unfortunate disappearance, he had amassed a substantial amount of gold, which validated his claim, but he never told anyone where the mine was located. When he didn't return from his last expedition, it was rumored that he'd written a journal, with a map revealing the location of the mine, and left it with a woman.

"Dr. Charles Stewart, the professor who tracked it down, is holding a press conference tomorrow about his discovery. But that's only part of the story. Apparently, he's already staked out several claims to different locations in the area where there's a chance the treasure is hidden, but he needs investors willing to help him retrieve the gold.

"That's why this press conference is so newsworthy. There are rumors that Stewart is not the upright person he claims to be, and this could all be a hoax to bankroll a bogus expedition. On the other hand, if the journal is authentic, which he claims it is, he could be sitting on a lost gold mine worth millions."

I frowned. "But letting everyone know about the journal seems like a risk. Isn't he afraid someone will try and steal it from him?"

"Yes. I think that's part of the reason he needs backers who are willing to help him with security and funding for the expedition."

"But if he's already staked a claim, isn't he giving the location away?"

She shook her head. "Not necessarily. He took out at least seven different claims to throw off anyone who might be after him. The legend of the mine basically tells us it's located in the Soapstone Wilderness area of the Rocky Mountain Range, but, without a map, it's a large area to cover."

"Yeah... that makes sense."

"So? You want to come with me? You might know if he's telling the truth or if this is just a bogus claim. I'm sure there will be time for questions, and you can ask as many as you like."

I grinned. She was making me an offer I couldn't refuse. "Okay. I'm in. But it seems like he's going to a lot of trouble with staking claims and the whole press conference thing if it's all a lie, you know?"

"Sure, but it's still worth having you there with your premonitions. It might be the only way to know if he's telling the truth." She was thinking that I was like a secret weapon against all those evil men and their mad plots… kind of like I was a real super-hero.

I held back a chuckle and gave her a nod. "I'll do my best."

"Great. The press conference is at ten in the morning at the State Capitol rotunda, but I want to get there early enough to get a good spot. Let's meet here at nine. I'll have a press badge ready for you, and we'll have plenty of time to get a place right up in front."

"Sounds like a plan."

We said our goodbyes, and I made my way to the elevator. As much as I hated to admit it, this case intrigued me. The excitement of finding a lost gold mine was the stuff of legends, and I wanted to be part of it. Did Uncle Joey know about it? If it was real, he'd probably want to invest.

My sudden enthusiasm for finding a lost treasure brought me up short, and I knew gold fever was real. Of course, it didn't hurt that my grandpa had taken me up into those same mountains when I was a kid to look for that mine. No wonder it excited me so much.

My phone began to ring with the familiar tune of "Devil Rider," which I'd set for Ramos's ringtone, and a little thrill rushed over me. Wow... just thinking about Uncle Joey... and here was Ramos calling me. Was this a sign?

I decided to take the stairs so I'd have some privacy, letting the song play a little longer before I started down. "Hey Ramos. What's up?"

"Babe. You sound like you're out of breath. Is this a bad time?"

"No. I'm just leaving the newspaper offices."

"Then you're not too far away?"

"Nope."

"Good. I need you to come to Thrasher. A guy showed up a few minutes ago wanting to see Manetto. Jackie sent him to Manetto's office, but, before I could ask her who he was, she left the office in a rush. I knocked on Manetto's door and asked if he needed me, but he waved me off. Something's not right, and I'd feel better if you were here."

"Is it about a gold mine?"

"A gold mine? Uh... no."

"Oh... okay." I tried not to sound disappointed. "I'll be there in about ten minutes."

Exactly ten minutes later, I walked into Thrasher Development. With Jackie gone, and no sign of Ramos, I peeked inside the conference room. Finding it empty, I wandered down the hall toward Ramos's apartment, but couldn't see him anywhere.

At the other end of the hall, Uncle Joey's door was closed, but I could hear faint sounds of conversation. Maybe Ramos was in there?

On the way, I stopped in front of my office door and stepped inside, hoping to find a nice spot for my new paperweight. I admired it for a moment before setting it down next to the framed photograph of my family. I opened my door to leave and gasped with surprise.

Ramos stood just outside my door, and his lips turned up into a cocky grin. "Babe. I just came to find you."

"Geez, you startled me."

"Sorry." He leaned against the door jamb, not looking a bit sorry.

"So, did Jackie just go home without telling Uncle Joey?"

He straightened. "Apparently. When I got here, a man was talking to Jackie like he knew her from somewhere. Her face was a little pale, and she seemed upset. She sent him down to see Manetto and then took off. She didn't say a word to me, but I think she had tears in her eyes."

"That's not good. Does Uncle Joey know that she's gone?"

Ramos shook his head. "No. He's been in there with the guy ever since."

"How long is that?"

"Since I called you."

"Is Uncle Joey safe?"

He nodded. "Yes, of course. I opened the door and asked if he needed me, but he said no. That's when I called you."

"So he didn't let you in, but you think he'll let me in?"

"Maybe not if you ask."

My eyes widened. "So you want me to barge in there?"

"Yeah. Tell him you have some good news... or make something up... then see if he'll introduce you and let you stay. Something about this guy is off, and I want to know what it is."

I straightened my spine. If Uncle Joey was in trouble, I'd do just about anything to help him. "Okay." I glanced at my new paperweight. "And I've got just the thing." I picked it up. "The editor-in-chief at the newspaper just gave me this. It's kind of a memento for saving their lives... you know... from the shooter?"

"Right." He glanced at it, thinking it was a nice gesture, and one I probably deserved. "That should get his attention. Let's head on down there."

"You're coming in with me?"

"Of course."

"Sweet." I stepped down the hallway and stopped at Uncle Joey's door. Taking a breath for courage, I readied myself for a show and knocked. Plastering a smile on my face, I pushed the door open and rushed inside.

"Hey, Uncle Joey, I couldn't wait to show you what I got. Isn't it beautiful?" I held it out to him and froze, glancing between him and the man sitting in front of him. "Oh... sorry. I didn't mean to interrupt." I turned toward the stranger. "Hi, I'm Shelby Nichols, Uncle Joey's niece."

Surprised by the interruption, the man gaped at me. He stood a little stiffly and shook my outstretched hand. "Uh... Sonny Dixon. Nice to meet you."

Uncle Joey narrowed his eyes, taking note that Ramos had followed me inside. What was going on? He caught my gaze, thinking I had some explaining to do. Then another thought occurred to him, and he sent me a nod, realizing Ramos must have called me in case Sonny was up to something.

Although he'd spoken with Sonny several times over the phone, this in-person visit had been a surprise, and it was nice to know that Ramos and I were on his side.

He smiled. "Shelby... it's good you're here. Please come in and sit down. I'm sure I mentioned the poker tournament to you before you took all that time off, remember?"

"Oh yeah, I vaguely remember that. When is it anyway?" When he'd mentioned the tournament to me, it sounded so far away that I'd totally forgotten all about it.

"This weekend."

My eyes widened. "That soon?"

"Yes. Is that going to be a problem?"

"Uh... no. Not at all. I just didn't realize it was so soon."

Uncle Joey shook his head. He'd been happy to give me some space, but now it was time to get back to work. "Sonny owns a hotel and casino in Las Vegas, and he's hosting the poker tournament. Since he was in town, he stopped by to discuss the details." He sent Sonny an appraising glance. "I haven't told him I'd be participating for sure, so he's here to sell me on the idea."

"That's right," Sonny said, a congenial smile on his face. "I was just telling your uncle that his friend, Terrence Chatwin, might also be participating." He was thinking that a little competition was the best way to assure Manetto's participation.

"Oh." I smiled at Sonny. "How nice."

Sonny nodded. "I won't bore you with all the details, but I wanted a firm commitment from your uncle before I invited anyone else. The tournament is limited to a select few who can afford to lose, but who are willing to take the risk for a chance to win the ten-million-dollar jackpot."

"Ten million dollars?" My eyes widened. "That's a lot."

"Yes it is." He was thinking that the tournament would lure in some of the biggest gamblers in the country, as well as several high rollers with money to throw around. He could clear at least half that in a week, and it would give him the funds he needed to pay his debts, as well as give him some leverage with his biggest investor.

My brows rose. "So it's a winner-take-all tournament?"

"Yes. That's what I was discussing with your uncle, along with the buy-in amount to play."

"How much is that?"

He shrugged. "I'm asking fifty grand per entry. It's a mere trifle if you win the whole thing, right Manetto?" Uncle

Joey stared at him before dipping his chin. Sonny didn't like it much, but he wasn't going to let Uncle Joey get under his skin. "So what do you think? Are you ready for a chance to win it all?"

"I believe so." Uncle Joey glanced my way, thinking that it would be fun to clean this guy out. "Are you talking to anyone else besides Chatwin?"

"Yes. I've been in contact with a couple of others, Timothy Branigan and Ken Miller, to name a few. I'm pretty sure Chatwin is coming, but Branigan hasn't committed yet. Once I get a commitment from you though, it's between the two of them, since I only have two spots left."

Uncle Joey nodded, thinking Sonny definitely knew the high-rollers around here. If Uncle Joey didn't know I could win the jackpot, he might not go for it. But the lure of beating Chatwin was almost more than he could pass up.

I caught Sonny's gaze. "Are you playing in the tournament?"

Sonny's brows rose. No one had asked him that, and he hadn't expected it. "No. I can't play in my own tournament."

He was lying. He'd already tagged two of his best poker players to participate, with a third in the wings. He planned to win the money, even if he had to cheat to do it.

"But you could hire someone to play for you, right?"

Sonny's brows furrowed. Why was I asking that? "I suppose I could. Not that I would." He glanced at Uncle Joey. "You in?"

"What do you think, Shelby?" Uncle Joey asked. "You want to play?"

It must have been Sonny's last thought about cheating to win that decided it for me. "I think it would be fun. We should totally do it."

Uncle Joey smiled. "All right." He settled his gaze on Sonny. "Put me down... and, while you're at it, I would take it as a personal favor if Chatwin could join us as well."

Sonny's brows rose, then his eyes narrowed. Did Manetto have something against Chatwin? This could play to his advantage. "Certainly. I'll let him know you're in, and if he wants the spot, he's got it."

Sonny glanced my way. He hadn't missed my exchange with Manetto and wondered if that meant I would play in the tournament. I didn't look like the type to spend a lot of time gambling... which could be a good thing for him. "Then it's settled. I only require a small token of five grand to hold your spot. You can pay the rest when you arrive."

Uncle Joey's face turned to stone. What had he said? Leaning forward, he caught Sonny's gaze. "You don't think I'm good for it?" Asking Joey "The Knife" Manetto for a retainer was an insult of the highest degree. It showed a lack of respect, and Uncle Joey wouldn't stand for it.

Sonny froze. He was usually the one calling the shots, and he'd forgotten who he was dealing with. Ramos stepped from his spot at the door to loom over him, and Sonny's stomach tightened. "Oh... I'm sorry, of course you are. Forget I asked. It was a slip of the tongue."

Uncle Joey sat back with a curt nod. "Good to know."

Sonny bit back a sarcastic response. He hated bowing to Manetto, but he had other ways to get to him. It had been a shock to see Jackie after all these years. Now that he knew she worked for the mob boss, he might be able to use that to his advantage. Did Manetto know about her past? There might be a way to exploit that if things didn't go his way.

"Of course." His voice held a tone of compromise, but it didn't fool anyone. "It won't happen again."

"Good. Then we'll see you in a few days."

"I'll send you all the pertinent details." He glanced my way, and I tried not to flinch from the calculating superiority in his eyes. "I look forward to seeing you again as well."

We all stood, and Uncle Joey motioned toward the door. "Ramos will show you out." Ramos ushered Sonny into the hallway and closed the door behind them.

"That was interesting." Uncle Joey sat down, motioning for me to do the same. "Now tell me what he didn't say."

"He knows Jackie, but I don't think he knows you're married to her."

"What? But I've never met him before."

I shrugged. "As he left, he was thinking about Jackie and her past. Now that he knows she works for you, he could use that to his advantage. I don't know what he meant by that, but he—"

Uncle Joey jumped from his chair and hurried to the door. He continued down the hallway, meeting Ramos as he came back into the office. "Where's Jackie?"

"I don't know. She left right after she spoke to Sonny."

Worried, Uncle Joey pulled out his phone and called her. She picked up, and his shoulders slumped with relief. "Jackie... where are you?" As he listened, I picked up that she'd gone home. "Why? What happened?"

I didn't want to eavesdrop, so I glanced at Ramos, but he didn't know any more than I did.

"Okay... yes... I'll be home soon, we'll talk then." He disconnected and turned his steely-eyed gaze on us. "Come to my office."

We followed him down the hall and took our seats in front of his desk. "Shelby, is there anything else you picked up from him?"

I nodded. "Yes. That's all I got about Jackie, but I think there's more to the tournament than he's saying. It sounded like he's got two or three professional poker players entered on his behalf, and he's planning on one of them winning... even if he has to cheat to do it. I think he might be in debt or something, because he needed the money to pay someone off, and that's why he wanted to win so badly."

"That's good to know." Uncle Joey rubbed his chin and looked out of his window, lost in thought.

"How does Jackie know him?"

He shook his head. "I don't know. She said she'd tell me when I got home, but she didn't want to talk about it over the phone."

"Okay... that sounds ominous." I suddenly realized that I knew next to nothing about Jackie's past. I didn't even know how long she'd worked for Uncle Joey before I met her. They'd only been married for about a year now.

Uncle Joey focused on me. "Did you pick up anything else about Sonny?"

"No. But I don't trust him."

"If he's connected to Jackie's past, I'll find out more, as long as she tells me everything." He glanced my way, wishing he had my psychic powers right about now. If he could hear Jackie's thoughts, he'd know if she was hiding something from him. He considered asking me to go home with him, but that was just a fleeting thought he quickly dismissed.

He'd given her a job after her run-in with the law, and now sharp disappointment crashed over him. Had she told him everything? He shook his head. It didn't matter. He'd move heaven and earth to get to the bottom of it, and if that meant Sonny had to die, he'd take care of that too.

CHAPTER 2

U ncle Joey glanced my way, knowing I'd heard that. "Thanks for coming, Shelby. I take it Ramos called you?"

"Yes."

He nodded. "Then I guess we're headed to Las Vegas this weekend."

"Sounds good, but I might need to brush up on my poker. It's been a while."

He smiled at that, and it relieved some of the tension in the room.

"Is Jackie in trouble?"

"I don't know. But with Sonny showing up like this, it seems suspicious." He caught Ramos's gaze. "I'd like to know more about Sonny Dixon. He said he owns the Mojavi Desert Hotel and Casino. Why don't you check him out? I want to know if he's had any brushes with the law."

He glanced my way. "Would you mind taking Jackie's place at the front desk for a little bit? I have a meeting scheduled with Nick Berardini before I can leave. Maybe you can help Ramos with the research until then?"

"Sure."

"Good. Then get started."

He picked up his phone to make a call, and I followed Ramos to Jackie's desk. As I sat down, I realized she'd left so quickly that she was still logged into her computer. To my surprise, Ramos grabbed one of the extra chairs and pulled it right next to mine.

Sitting this close beside him, I found it too tempting to resist inhaling his fabulous, musky scent. I tried not to let my breath out too loudly and give myself away, but his lips twitched, and he leaned in a little closer. "Is that better?"

I smacked his arm. "Maybe. Why are you sitting so close to me anyway?"

He raised a brow. "Manetto said to work together. You complaining?"

I swallowed. "No... "

"Good. Let's see what we can find out about Sonny Dixon." He opened the browser and typed in Sonny's name. It came up on Google, and the search took us to his hotel website, with Dixon Property Management as the owner.

He tapped the screen. "It looks like he bought the place about five years ago and upgraded the hotel and casino from the ground up. You'd have to have some serious money to do that. It would be interesting to know where he got all that money."

I nodded, while Ramos opened another tab and typed in a public police records site. Using the state of Nevada, he entered Sonny's name. Nothing came up, so he went to another website and did a search for criminal records.

This time, after entering Sonny's name, a record came up showing that he'd been arrested for insider trading and securities fraud. The charges weren't dropped, but his sentence only amounted to a short probationary period of ten months.

"Wow. You sure know how to get information off the Internet." I grabbed a notepad to write down the names of the websites he'd pulled up.

"I'm surprised you don't already know this."

"Well, most of the time, I just look stuff up on my computer at the police station. Everything I need is usually there, but I didn't know you could search for criminal records."

Ramos turned his head to look at me, his face startlingly close to mine. "Since they're public records, it's just a matter of knowing which sites to go to. But there is a lot more I could teach you."

"Yeah? I'd like that..." I suddenly realized that only a few inches separated our lips. His eyes darkened, and I gasped. "Wait... you're still talking about research, right?"

His lips turned into that sexy grin that sent heat down my spine and made my brain quit working.

"Of course. Aren't you?"

I snapped my mouth shut and turned my head away to break his spell. "Yes."

With a satisfied grin, Ramos turned his attention back to the computer. "His sentence of probation for the charges indicates that he must have turned on someone, otherwise, he would have gone to prison. Let's see if we can find out which company he worked for at the time of his arrest."

The name, Linaria Investment Management, came up, and Ramos sat back in his chair. "I remember hearing about these guys. They were involved in a big scandal a few years back. The owner and his partners ended up in jail for securities fraud, perjury, and insider trading—all white-collar crimes."

Ramos glanced my way. "Maybe Sonny was the biggest winner of all. If he had access to any of the company's off-shore bank accounts, he may have siphoned all that stolen money into an account of his own, and that's where he got the capitol to buy the hotel and casino. But, even then, he'd need more investors in order to purchase and renovate a hotel that big."

"So you're thinking he took the money the investment firm stole, and put it into buying and renovating the property in Vegas?"

"Yeah. That makes the most sense."

I nodded. "That might explain why he thought about using the money from winning the tournament to pay someone off."

"Maybe. But it doesn't explain his connection to Jackie." He caught my gaze. "Have you ever picked up anything about her past?"

"No. Nothing."

"I don't know a lot, either. When she first came, Manetto hired her on the spot, and it was clear they knew each other from somewhere. It looked like Manetto was doing her a favor, and it earned her loyalty. But she kept her distance until Carlotta showed up. I didn't realize how she felt about Manetto until then. Hell, I don't think she did either. I saw a side of her I didn't know existed."

I chuckled. "Yeah... I'm still a little shocked that Jackie hired that hitman, Mercer, to go after Carlotta. She was pretty upset."

I glanced at Ramos, remembering that day because he'd killed Mercer before Mercer could kill me. It was the second time that Ramos had saved my life. I'd never tallied up the number of times he'd done that, but I knew one thing for sure... I owed him a deep debt... more than I could ever repay. My heart swelled with gratitude and—

"What are you thinking right now?" Ramos asked, his brows drawn together.

I blinked. "What?"

"You've got that look in your eyes... like you want to kiss me... really bad. I'm happy to oblige—"

I sucked in a breath. "What? No. I was just... ugh! You drive me crazy, you know that?"

He chuckled, giving me another grin before standing. "I'll take this information to Manetto. If Berardini gets here before I'm done, have him wait."

"Okay, sure." My shoulders slumped. Thank goodness he broke the spell before I did anything stupid... like kiss him... that would have been a huge mistake.

Sending another grin my way, he stalked down the hall. I felt a chill as his heat left my side, and my traitorous gaze followed his backside all the way down the hall. Shaking my head to clear it, I glanced back at the computer and got busy taking notes on the websites he'd used. These would be great references for my own cases.

While I finished up, Nick Berardini came through the doors. His eyes rose in surprise to find me sitting at Jackie's desk. "Hey Shelby, it's been a while. How are you?"

"Good." We spoke for a few minutes before he asked me about Jackie, and I told her she'd gone home early. "Have a seat, and I'll let Uncle Joey know you're here."

"Oh... sure." He was thinking that Jackie usually just sent him down to Manetto's office, but I probably didn't know that. Still, he hated waiting, especially when he had such good news to share.

Hearing that little tidbit lightened my mood, and I quickly called Uncle Joey's extension. "Nick's here with good news."

"Oh? Nice. Tell him to come on down... and thanks for staying, Shelby. You can leave now. Just be sure to turn off Jackie's computer before you head out. Why don't you plan on stopping by tomorrow?"

"Sure."

"Good, I'll send you a text with the time."

"Okay. See you then." I disconnected and smiled at Nick. He was wondering how I knew about his good news, so I hurried to explain. "Uh... remember that I have premonitions? That's how I knew you had good news... although I don't know what the good news is all about, so you don't have to worry if it's private."

"Oh... right. You can still do that, huh?"

At my nod, he realized he'd forgotten all about my weird quirk. After spending a few days with me and Ramos in Orlando, it shouldn't have taken him by surprise, but it wasn't something he would ever get used to.

After he hurried to Uncle Joey's office, I straightened Jackie's desk, turned off the computer, and stood to go. I hesitated for a minute to see if Ramos would come back out, but Uncle Joey must have wanted him to join their meeting.

With nothing left to do, I walked out of the office and took the elevator down to the parking garage.

I arrived home, opening the door to an excited woof. Coco, a beautiful German Shephard, and the newest addition to our family, rushed to greet me. He snuffled and woofed before licking my face, and I heard, *you here, you here.*

It still surprised me that I could understand him, but since it was mixed up with my mind-reading ability, I just went with it. "Yup. I'm home."

He woofed again, and this time I heard *play.*

"Sure, let me change my clothes first." It was kind of weird to be talking to a dog like this, but I'd learned that most dog owners spoke to their animals all the time, so it wasn't too far from normal.

Now that school had started, I knew Coco was missing the kids, so I hurried to my room and changed my clothes. With him home alone, I was grateful we had a doggy door to the back yard so he could come and go as he pleased. We'd also upgraded the fence around our yard so it was more private.

I stepped outside with a diet soda. Coco brought me his Frisbee, and I threw it several times to help him release some of his pent-up energy. Twenty minutes later, he was worn out enough to rest, and I was more than happy to have a few minutes to myself before the kids got home.

I sat on my deck swing with Coco beside me and told him all about my day. Petting him while I spoke was one of the best therapy sessions I'd had in a while.

My kids arrived home not long after that, and things got busy. Josh's sixteenth birthday was coming up soon, and he was excited to get his driver's license. He could hardly think about anything else, and I wondered if I'd felt the same way at that age.

At thirteen, Savannah was going through puberty, and I never knew what to expect. Luckily, today hadn't been as full of drama as the last few days, but I knew it could change in a heartbeat. It seemed like there was always something going on that required major theatrics, so any day that didn't happen was a day to celebrate.

"Did you talk to Uncle Joey?" she asked me, thinking that Miguel was supposed to come home for a visit, but, so far, it hadn't happened, and she was getting tired of waiting. "About Miguel?"

"Uh... no. But I'll ask him tomorrow."

"Yeah... right. Maybe he's never coming back. He probably loves it so much in New York that he doesn't even miss any of us." She was thinking that he'd forgotten all about her. With all the girls there to choose from, she didn't stand a chance.

"That's not true. He'll come home when he can, you know that. But that's his world right now, and you need to concentrate on your life."

"My life sucks." I caught a brief thought about a group of popular girls who'd made fun of her, before she ran up the stairs to her room and slammed the door behind her.

"Geez, thirteen-year-old girls are the worst," Josh said.

"She's just going through some stuff." I glanced at Josh and realized he hadn't said that out loud. I inwardly cringed, but, since I hadn't technically agreed with him, my comment still made sense.

"I guess." He glanced at the dog. "Come on, Coco, let's go play."

I knew I'd need to talk to Savannah, but not until she'd cooled off. It surprised me that I had no trouble talking to a hitman or a mob boss, but a thirteen-year-old girl challenged me more than either of them.

I wished I could wave a magic wand and erase her infatuation with Miguel. But I knew her dreams of Miguel gave her something positive to focus on, and I'd just have to hope I could talk some sense into her instead.

Since Miguel was Uncle Joey's son, it just complicated everything. At eighteen, he'd moved to New York because he'd gotten the lead part of Aladdin on Broadway. We'd visited New York for his opening night, and Savannah had fallen even harder for him.

I sighed. Tonight, I'd have to spell out the hard facts to her and remind her that, if she wanted to be in Miguel's life, she had to take the time to grow up first. As hard as that seemed, it was the truth. I just hoped she'd listen.

The rest of the evening went by quickly. Savannah came down for dinner more like her old self. She even seemed a little embarrassed by her outburst. Later, I managed to have that talk with her, and she took it all in. "Yeah... I know. You don't have to tell me."

"Oh, okay."

"Are you done now? I've got homework to do, and it's getting late." I picked up that she knew everything I'd told her in her head, but her emotions sometimes got the best of her, and I needed to chill out and quit bringing it up.

I let out my breath and closed her door.

My husband, Chris, waited for me downstairs. "How'd it go?"

I shook my head. "About how you'd expect."

"Oh." He was thinking that boys were so much easier at that age. I wanted to point out that they had their flaws too, but it wasn't worth it.

"So how was your day?" I asked instead.

"Busy. I've got a new client. He's one of Manetto's friends, so I have to take good care of him." Chris had recently become a partner at his law firm, mostly because Uncle Joey was his main client. "But he hasn't committed a crime or anything, so that's a good start."

I shook my head. "Yeah, for sure." I sat down next to him and snuggled against his side. "Every once in a while, I think maybe our lives are normal, but then it hits me how far from normal we really are."

"Well, I don't know about that." He pulled me close. "Our normal is normal for us, so maybe it's not that far of a stretch."

I chuckled. "Yeah... but you haven't heard about my day yet."

He groaned, thinking that he wasn't sure he wanted to— no—of course he wanted to hear all about it. My exploits always spiced up his mundane life, so how could he not want to know?

"Nice save."

"I'm learning. So what's up?"

I began with my lesson at the shooting range, then moved on to the cool paperweight the newspaper had given me. "But while I was there, Billie Jo asked me to help her with a story."

I explained the whole story about the lost gold mine and the journal, telling him about the professor's press conference the next day, and that I was looking forward to asking him leading questions and getting the truth from his mind. "Have you heard anything about it?"

He shook his head. "Not really. I've been too busy at work. All that time I took off is catching up to me. But it sounds intriguing."

"Yeah. I'm actually looking forward to going."

"Good. I can't wait to hear all about it. Is there anything else I need to know?" He knew that I sometimes left my interactions with Uncle Joey until the end, mostly because they had the potential to be bad.

"It's not that bad... exactly."

"I knew it. What's going on?"

"First, let me explain. Uncle Joey had an unexpected visitor with a connection to Jackie. You know... I don't really know anything about her past, but apparently this guy was part of it, and it really shook her up.

"Uncle Joey didn't know much about the guy either, but I'm sure he'll find out from Jackie, and then he'll fill me in when I go back tomorrow. Anyway... Sonny, the guy who showed up, is hosting a big poker tournament this weekend in Las Vegas, and he invited Uncle Joey to participate."

Chris's brows dipped. "Is Manetto going to play?" I didn't answer right away, and he frowned. "You're going to play for him?" At my nod, he continued. "A poker tournament in Vegas? Shelby..."

"It will be fine. It's a winner-take-all-ten-million-dollar jackpot, so I have to win because Sonny is as crooked as they come. He's planning to cheat to keep it, and I don't know what he has to do with Jackie, but we can't let him get away with it."

Chris's mouth worked, but no words came out. Since it was Uncle Joey, he couldn't object, and he didn't want to sound like a controlling husband, but how could he be happy about sending me off to Las Vegas to play in a rigged poker tournament?

"Hey," I soothed. "You don't have to be happy about it. I'm not even happy about it. But I'll be fine."

He shook his head. "But this weekend... wasn't there something we already had planned?"

"Oh... that's right. Josh and I were supposed to train with Lance Hobbs on Saturday." Since Coco was a search-and-rescue dog, and Lance had trained him, we'd decided to learn the job so Coco's work could continue.

We'd already been to Lance's place a few times, but I'd had to put this training session off for a couple of weeks, and I hated to reschedule. "I know... why don't you and Josh go? Then Coco won't be so disappointed."

"Coco?"

I shrugged. "Well... I know he's looking forward to it." That was stretching it, since Coco didn't really think about the future, but if he could think that far ahead, he'd be disappointed not to go. "Okay... maybe not, but Josh is planning on it. Hey... you could take Savannah too. It might get her mind off Miguel for a while."

Chris knew when he was outmaneuvered. "Fine. So how long will you be gone?"

"I don't know, but probably just Saturday and Sunday. I'll know more of the details tomorrow."

"Okay. But I'm not real happy about this." He was thinking that Ramos was probably going with us, but maybe that wasn't so bad, since Chris knew the hitman would risk his life for me. Still, he hated sending me off to play poker in Vegas... geeze... I might even have fun.

I chuckled. "Ha! Not likely. I'll probably get the worst headache ever."

Chris shrugged. "Maybe so... but I wish I could be there to watch you win."

"I'm glad to hear you say that... since I'm not so sure I can."

"What? Of course you can. I have no doubt about it. And what about that jackpot? That's a lot of money." Naturally, he was thinking that Uncle Joey should be willing to share the profits if I'd gone to all the work of winning it.

"Chris. Uncle Joey's not going to let me keep ten million dollars."

He shrugged. "Hey... maybe not all of it. But it wouldn't hurt to ask. I mean... you do a lot for him, and winning that much money... he's bound to feel grateful."

I shook my head. "I'm sure he will, and he'll probably make sure I'm compensated."

"Good, because I want to buy a new car. I think maybe a red sports car would do the trick." At my frown, he continued. "But I'd settle for you, back home safe and sound." He thought a couple million wouldn't hurt, but he kept that to himself and kissed me soundly as a distraction.

Soon, I couldn't remember what we'd been talking about, especially after he spoke some of my favorite words. "Oh baby, oh baby."

The next morning, I arrived early at the newspaper offices. Billie had a lanyard with my name on it and PRESS, in capital letters, all ready to go. A man stood beside her with a camera, and she introduced us. "I don't know if you've met before, but this is Jeff Allred."

He was thinking that he'd taken that awesome photo of me right after I took down the shooter in the newspaper lobby. I really liked that photo, since it made me look like a superhero. He thought about offering me a copy, and I nodded with enthusiasm.

His gaze narrowed, and I realized my mistake, so I quickly told him how much I loved that particular photo. As we took the elevator down to the parking garage, he offered to send me a copy, and I eagerly accepted. I was more careful after that, since Billie hadn't missed a thing, and I knew she'd figure out my secret if I wasn't more vigilant.

We drove to the press conference together and even managed to be the first to arrive. Billie jumped at the chance to get front-row seats. The place filled up pretty quickly after that, and I was surprised to find a few national news outlets there.

Several men entered the room and headed straight to the podium, standing behind it like bodyguards. Everyone took their places and quit talking while the whir of camera clicks filled the air. Following behind the bodyguards, a man carrying a black binder came in.

He wore a dark gray blazer over a white shirt and jeans, and his sandy brown hair curled slightly around his head. His round glasses added to his academic persona, and, with his understated good looks, he reminded me of Indiana Jones.

Another man followed behind him, and I took an instant dislike to the polished veneer of his slicked-back hair and high cheekbones. He was tall and slim, wearing a dark blazer over his blue shirt and jeans. But something about him set me on edge.

He stepped to the podium and smiled. "Thank you all for coming. My name is Ian Smith, and I represent Professor Charles Stewart, head of the historical society and history department of our esteemed university.

"He has graciously offered to hold this press conference to address all the rumors concerning his significant discovery. After his statement, he will leave plenty of time open for questions. Dr. Stewart."

The man wearing the glasses stepped to the podium. "Thank you, Ian." Dr. Stewart glanced over all of the reporters staring at him and ducked his head, clearly not enjoying all the attention. "Good morning. After years of meticulous research and study, I am officially announcing a find of historical significance, the lost journal of Jeremiah Taft."

A soft murmur filled the room, and several reporters raised their hands. Dr. Stewart held his hands up before continuing. "I'm sure you have many questions, but I'd like to finish, if I may." He paused for the room to quiet down.

"The journal was not in the best shape when I found it. Many words had faded, and several pages were torn or lost. Though we had the use of several special technological resources, it has taken us many painstaking hours to recreate the missing words into a narrative that made sense. That said, I am now announcing my intention to find the lost mine. If anyone is interested in backing this expedition, please contact my representative, Ian Smith." He motioned to the man behind him. "Now... I'll take a few questions."

He pointed at a journalist in the back who stood and introduced himself. "Isn't it true that you've already searched for the lost mine with no results to show for it?"

"We've scouted out the area, but there's a lot more we can do."

"Aren't you taking a risk by announcing your expedition? Couldn't someone follow you to the area?" he continued.

Dr. Stewart pursed his lips. "Yes and no. Word has already spread about the journal. Because of that, I decided to make my intentions clear so I could proceed with the expedition. I have all the necessary paperwork filed with the government, and my claims are all legal. I do have need of a few more investors, so, if you're interested, please let me know." He said that with a smile, and a few chuckles sounded in the room.

I zeroed in on Ian Smith and picked up his hopes that this press conference would do what he'd intended and get them some much-needed cash. Things hadn't gone as easily as he'd thought, and they were already in debt up to their eyeballs. This press conference was a last-ditch effort to get the ball rolling, and he hoped Dr. Stewart's reputation gave the journal enough credibility to pull it off.

Credibility? Did that mean the journal could be a fake?

As the questions continued along the same vein, I sensed a growing edge to Dr. Stewart's nerves. He hated publicity, and he was ready for this to be done, so I raised my hand high and smiled to catch his attention.

He finally called on me, and I stood. "Shelby Nichols with the Daily News. Dr. Stewart, is it possible that the journal could be a forgery? Has it been tested for authenticity?"

Surprise washed over him. That was the last question he'd expected. He knew he couldn't show any anger, and he tried to calm his indignation. "Yes... of course we've tested it, and I'm confident it's authentic."

"That's encouraging, but is it still possible someone could make a forgery of it and pass it off as authentic?"

"The forger would have to be a master at his trade to fool the testing process we put it through. With all of the tools at our disposal, I don't believe it's possible."

I wasn't about to let it go. "So you're saying that it's not likely, but there's still a possibility? Then... is it also possible that a master forger, with the right kind of tools and attention to detail, could pull it off?"

He didn't like the doubt I'd thrown into the equation. The whole room had gone quiet waiting for his response, and he knew his answer was critical to his success. Sounding too confident either way could backfire, but he didn't want to leave anyone in doubt that the document was real.

"The testing process we have put the journal through makes the probability of such an occurrence less than one percent. Given those statistics, I would say that we are ninety-nine percent certain that the document is authentic."

Satisfaction that he'd shut me down rolled over him, and he hurried to call on someone else. I caught a spike of anger directed my way and met Ian Smith's gaze. He didn't like my line of questioning, but Dr. Stewart's response had been perfect.

He'd made the odds sound pretty good, which shouldn't dampen a potential investor's enthusiasm. That was the thing about investors. They knew right up front that they were taking a chance, so if it didn't pan out, they couldn't scream for their money back.

What did he mean by that?

The press conference continued for another ten minutes before Dr. Stewart thanked everyone and stepped away from the podium. As they left the room, Ian Smith happened to glance my way. Our gazes met, and he sent me a polite smile, thinking that he was more than ready to take me on any time.

It was a challenge that didn't make sense. If Dr. Stewart was telling the truth, then it wouldn't matter what I said, so they had to be hiding something, but what? I needed more time with them to figure it out. Between Ian Smith and Dr. Stewart, I pegged Ian as the bigger threat. Why was that? Did he have something on Dr. Stewart, or was there something going on that Stewart knew nothing about?

The room began to clear out and Billie turned to me. "That was a great question. Did you get anything from him?"

I nodded. "Yeah. But it's a little confusing." I waited for more people to leave before I spoke. "I think Ian's the one we need to watch. He's got something up his sleeve, but I don't know what it is exactly. It almost feels like he's fooling Dr. Stewart, but that doesn't make sense."

"What about the journal? Do you think it's the real deal like they said?"

"I don't know. I need more time to figure it out, but something's going on."

Billie's enthusiasm for the story rose about a hundred percent. If I had doubts, that meant we were on to something big. If the journal was real, she wanted to document the whole thing. If it wasn't, she wanted to be the one to expose them. Either way, it could be the story of her career. "We'll just have to figure it out. You and me. If anyone can do it, we can."

"I like your optimism." I smiled, knowing that, with Billie on the story, we were bound to find the truth. "Whatever his motivation is, Ian's planning on making a lot of money, and I don't know if it's from discovering the gold or profiting from the investors."

"So that's the reason for all this?"

"I think so, but I'm not one hundred percent sure." I wiggled my eyebrows. "Probably more like ninety-nine percent."

Billie chuckled. "I think we need a sit-down with them. Maybe I can get an exclusive interview. If not, I'll ask them if I can come along to document the expedition."

"Ooo... that sounds intriguing. I wouldn't mind tagging along myself."

"Really? You don't seem like a person who likes roughing it out in the woods."

I chuckled. "That's because you don't know that my grandpa used to go prospecting for that very same mine. He even took me with him a few times when I was younger. It's given me a touch of gold fever, if you know what I mean."

"Are you kidding me? That's insane. We should totally do it. I'll see if I can get Michael to approve my part, and maybe you can see about getting some backing." She was thinking that being so close to Manetto might give me some sway... maybe he'd even invest in the venture and send me along to represent him.

"I can see where you're going with this... and I kind of like it."

She grinned, happy we were on the same page. I wasn't so sure it was a good idea, even if I wanted to make it happen. It could end up being a waste of time and money, and the odds of finding a mountain of gold were pretty slim. Still, who knew? Would Uncle Joey go for it? Did I even want to bring it up?

We made it back to the newspaper offices in time for me to head to the academy for my shooting lesson. At least I wasn't late, and shooting at a target would definitely help me work out some of my latent excitement.

I didn't think Dr. Stewart was a bad guy, but I wasn't so sure about Ian Smith. My first impression of Ian wasn't good, but why was that? I had nothing concrete to go on except for a feeling. Of course, he had stared at me with distrust a few times, but that was because I'd questioned the journal's authenticity. Still, if it was real like they said, he had nothing to worry about, so why the anger?

I needed to find out more about their plans to know what to do. But... was it something I really wanted to get involved with? Probably not. Still, the lure of going prospecting for the lost gold mine my grandpa had looked for all of his life, was a lot bigger incentive than I thought.

Billie had been thinking that Uncle Joey might want to invest, but what about me? Maybe I could mention it to Uncle Joey and use my share of the tournament winnings to invest? That way, I wouldn't have to use my own savings for it.

Either way, if I picked up that the journal was the real deal, I'd go for it. Finding the Lost Taft Mine would be like fulfilling my Grandpa's legacy, and I couldn't say no to that.

CHAPTER 3

I spent the next half hour on the shooting range with Dante. He noticed a big change in me from yesterday. At first he thought it was because of his awesome pep talk and teaching skills, but that didn't quite fit the focus and determination I'd suddenly acquired. I'd obviously had a change of heart. So what had happened?

He brought the target back in to take a look and rubbed his chin. I'd hit it in all the right spots with only one bullet hole out of the circle. "You're hitting the target without even flinching. What's changed since yesterday?"

"You mean besides your awesome pep talk?"

That caught him off-guard, and his mouth dropped open. I rushed on to explain. "Well... besides that, I received a keepsake from the newspaper for stopping a shooter and possibly saving lives. I think that helped me put things in perspective again."

He nodded. "Good to hear."

"Plus... if it comes to defending my partner, or someone I love, I want to make sure I won't let them down."

"That's a good attitude to have. In this business, it's easy to get overwhelmed by the negative, because you see a lot of it, so I'm glad you're doing better."

"Thanks."

"Want to go again?"

"Sure."

Ten minutes later, the target was full of holes, and I was done shooting. "Thanks," I told Dante. "I guess this could be considered therapeutic, right?" Dante nodded, sending me a smile. "So when should I come back?"

"You still have a few hours left for your training, so you can come back anytime. In fact, you're welcome to come back tomorrow if you want."

"Really?" At his nod, I continued. "I just might do that."

"Good. And Shelby... keep up the good work."

"Thanks."

After washing up, I hurried to the precinct, ready to see Dimples. I wasn't sure if he was ready for me or not, but that didn't matter since I wanted to look at the police database for anything I could find about Ian Smith. I doubted that he'd have a police record, but it never hurt to check.

I found Dimples sitting at his desk, engrossed with something on his computer. Seeing my chance to sneak up on him, I slid into the seat beside him. He jerked with surprise, and I laughed. "I haven't done that for a long time. It felt good."

He shook his head. "I'll bet."

"So what have you got for me?"

He grimaced. "Well... I have this case that's going nowhere, and I don't have any resources to help me."

"You have me."

That brought his dimples out in full force, and they rolled around on his cheeks, sparking joy in my heart.

"Tell me what's going on."

"The victim is a mortician by the name of Troy Hudson, and he was killed in his funeral home. There was no sign of forced entry, so he must have known his killer, and he was struck from behind with a blunt object. It happened during the night, and the security cameras were off line, so it looks like somebody turned them off on purpose. But that's not the crazy part."

"What is?"

He shook his head. "There was a body in the crematorium... well... what used to be a body. Only ashes were left, so there's no way to know who was in there. So now it's been classified as a double homicide, and all we have is the fact that Troy lived in an apartment at the mortuary. We think Troy cremated the body, since he's the one with the code to operate the crematorium. But why would someone kill him?"

My brows drew together. "To keep him from talking?"

Dimples shrugged. "Maybe. We've already spoken with the family and the other employees. We came up empty-handed. But now that I've got you, I'd like to talk to them again. You game?"

"Sure." I checked my watch, finding it close to eleven. "I have an appointment at one, so I'm free until then." Uncle Joey had sent me a text this morning, asking me to come to his office at one, and I was eager to find out what was going on with Jackie.

"Great. Let's go." As we left, Dimples wondered if my appointment was with Manetto, but he quickly dismissed it, knowing it was a sore spot between us. "So... how did the press conference go with Billie?"

I told him all about it on the way to the mortuary. "Can you believe it? Finding the Lost Taft Mine would be a major discovery, but I'm not sure it's all on the up-and-up. I think

Ian Smith has something up his sleeve, but I don't know what it is yet."

"Well, I'm sure between you and Billie, you can figure it out."

"That's the hope." A tinge of guilt ran over me since I'd left out the part where Billie was hoping to join the expedition, along with the other part where I might back it with my poker winnings so I'd have a way to join too. But, since it wasn't a sure thing, why borrow trouble?

We pulled into the nearly empty parking lot, and I followed Dimples to the door. "Have they opened for business?"

"Not yet, although I think the victim's funeral is tomorrow."

Dimples opened the massive front door and we stepped inside. The entryway and parlor were painted in a calming blend of beige and cream, with artfully arranged flowers on the coffee tables and landscape paintings on the walls. Dimples led the way down the hall to the office, and we came upon a man sitting at a desk going over some papers.

He glanced up, and his face tightened. "What's going on? Have you found something?" The sight of Dimples reminded him of the hours he'd spent answering all his stupid questions. Did the detective still consider him a suspect?

"Hello Barry. We just need a few minutes of your time," Dimples began. "This is my colleague, Shelby Nichols. May we sit down?"

Barry pursed his lips and gestured to the chairs in front of his desk. "Go ahead." He was thinking that his brother had left him in a bind, and he'd just discovered that a big chunk of money was missing. What had Troy been up to? Whatever it was, it had gotten him killed.

"What can you tell us about Troy in the days before he was killed?" I asked. "Did he seem nervous or anxious about anything?"

Barry shook his head. "I've already told you everything I know. He seemed distracted, but that was nothing new. To be honest, he hated the business. He tried a few other things, but he always came back because he needed a job.

"A few months ago, he said he was back for good, and he'd pull his weight around here. For the most part, that's just what he did. I thought he'd turned his life around, you know?"

I nodded, picking up that Barry had given Troy another chance, but now he regretted it. "What about your finances? Did he have access to the business's bank accounts?"

Barry's eyes narrowed. How did I know? He might as well answer truthfully. "Unfortunately... yes. I added his name to the accounts so he could help with paying the bills."

He pointed at his computer. "I just found out a bunch of money is missing. He must have taken it, but I don't know why. He was really making an effort, and I was... well... I thought he'd turned over a new leaf. But I guess he fooled me."

I nodded. "Do you think he might have been involved with the wrong kind of people before he came back to work for you?"

Barry shrugged. "I don't know. He didn't tell me anything, but it seems likely now. He was always trying to get rich quick, you know? But he'd never taken money from the business before."

"Do you think he was the person who cremated the body that night, or could it have been his killer?"

"To be honest, I think Troy must have cremated the body, but I guess I could be wrong." Since there were safeguards in place for the operator that only he and Troy knew, it didn't seem possible, unless Troy was coerced. But that didn't make sense. The killer would have just put Troy in there too.

"Do you think he may have done something like this before? Could Troy cremate a body for someone without your knowledge?"

That was something Barry had tried not to think about too hard. But with everything else he'd discovered, Troy probably had, especially given the fact that he lived in the basement apartment. Hell, he could have done anything.

"He could have. Now that I think about it, the gas bill's been a lot higher than it should be. It increased right after he came back to work. That means it could have been going on for several months. I just never put it together."

"How much money is missing?" I asked.

Letting out a resigned sigh, Barry glanced at his computer. "He's been taking a few thousand here and there, but if I added it all up, it's probably close to thirty grand. The last withdrawal was about a month ago, but nothing since."

I glanced at Dimples. "Have you questioned Troy's friends?"

"Yeah, but I think we'd better speak with them again."

I turned back to Barry. "Is there a friend that Troy could have been working with?"

He shook his head. "I don't know. He didn't share a lot of his personal life with me. After our father died, I took over the business. Because of that, I became more like a dad to him than a brother, so we didn't have the best relationship."

Barry was thinking of all the times he'd chewed Troy out for being irresponsible. Maybe he was partly to blame for Troy's death. If he hadn't been so hard on him, maybe he'd still be alive. But dammit, all that money was missing because he'd given Troy a chance. Anger boiled inside of him. There was nothing he could do about it now.

"I think you could help us figure out a few things," I said. "You could dig into your bank records and see when the money was withdrawn, and if it was transferred into a different account. It might help us track down his killer."

Barry's face cleared. "Yeah... I can do that."

"Good. I was told he lived in an apartment here that you rented to him. Do you mind if we take a look at his room?" I knew the police had confiscated his computer and anything of value to the case, but it wouldn't hurt to look again.

"Oh... uh... sure. Let me get the key." He rummaged through the top drawer of his desk and pulled out a key hanging from a chain with a skeleton head attached. Noticing my raised brows, he shrugged. "That's Troy's sense of humor. After he moved in, he insisted on installing a deadbolt on his door... for privacy."

"Oh... right."

As I followed him to the staircase, Barry was thinking that living in the basement of a mortuary could be disconcerting, even to those in the business, so it made sense that Troy wanted a deadbolt on his door.

Besides the apartment, the basement was also the place where they did the embalming and prepared the bodies for burial. It didn't bother him so much anymore, but Troy had always seemed a little more sensitive to those sorts of things, and the deadbolt had helped him feel better. Still, realistically, it wouldn't stop a ghost.

Holy hell! I'd thought it was an upstairs apartment. Living in the basement sounded horrible. Dread rolled over me, and I stopped in my tracks. Did I really want to go down there? Nope. Given that I sometimes 'heard' dead people, it shook me up even more. "Uh... maybe we don't need to see the apartment."

Barry and Dimples had already gone down the stairs to the basement, leaving me at the top of the staircase. Barry glanced back at me before unlocking the door. "Did you say something?"

Dimples raised his brows, wondering what was wrong. Then it hit him, and he couldn't hold back a smile, which turned into a cough as he tried not to laugh. Was I scared? Given that this was a mortuary, it made sense.

The last time I'd heard a dead person had been at the precinct while interviewing the dead man's killer. It had scared the crap out of Dimples, although he hated to admit it. But since this was different, it shouldn't be too bad. It wasn't like we were there alone in the middle of the night.

He smiled real big so his dimples did that happy dance in his cheeks. "Come on Shelby. It won't take long."

Letting out a breath, I hurried down the stairs, noticing the chill immediately. Goosebumps broke out on my arms, and I rubbed them.

Noticing, Barry frowned. "Oh... sorry it's a little cold down here. We keep the temperature around sixty-two. It's better for the bodies that way."

Why did he have to say that? "How many bodies do you have here now?"

"Just Troy's, but I usually have two or three a week."

What was I supposed to say to that? That's nice? How lovely? I just nodded and tried to turn my lips into a smile.

Barry unlocked the door and pushed it open. Before any of us could step inside, a small, furry object came barreling out of the apartment with a high-pitched yowl. I jerked back, stepping on Dimples's foot and smacking him with my arm.

Dimples stepped sideways, putting him right in the cat's path, and it ran up his pant leg and all the way up his chest to his shoulder. Dimples yelped, and his arms spiraled before he lost his balance. As he fell back against the hallway, the cat jumped off of him and ran up the basement stairs.

"Oh my gosh!" Barry said. "That was Lola! I had no idea she'd been locked up in there." Barry took off after her, hoping to find his poor kitty before she destroyed the curtains in the foyer. If she was as mad as she looked, there'd be hell to pay before he could catch her. At least his wife would be happy to know the cat wasn't lying dead in a ditch somewhere.

Dimples sat sprawled against the wall, his hair slightly mussed from trying to get Lola off him. He rubbed his shoulder where the cat had dug him with her claws, and I noticed the trail of puncture marks going up his shirt. Was that a drop of blood staining his white shirt? "That was crazy... are you okay?"

"That damn cat ran up my leg."

"Yeah. It... it sure did." Slapping my hand over my mouth, I began to shake with laughter. I tried hard to keep it in check, but the more I held back, the harder I shook.

Swearing under his breath, Dimples slowly rose to his feet. Before he straightened to his full height, I burst out laughing. I laughed so hard I doubled over. Tears leaked from my eyes, and I couldn't catch my breath. I leaned against the wall, laughing hard enough that my stomach cramped.

Every time I tried to get under control, the vision of the cat running up his pants to his shoulder set me off again, and I could barely stand.

"Come on..." Dimples took my arm and tugged me into the apartment.

Following behind him, I made it to the couch before I had to plop down, while another gale of laughter burst out of me. "Attack... of the killer cat." I laughed harder. "Put that... in your... report." Just thinking about it sent me into another bout of uncontrolled mirth.

Dimples rolled his eyes and managed a chuckle or two, but it wasn't anywhere close to my hilarity. Since I couldn't seem to stop, he finally left me there and began to search through the apartment on his own. After a few cleansing breaths, I calmed down enough to take in my surroundings.

The apartment was bigger and nicer than I'd imagined. Of course, the mortuary was a big building, so even taking up half of the basement amounted to a lot of space. A kitchen and dining area took up the corner side of the room and opened into a living room, with an entertainment center along the wall.

From what I could see, a short hallway led to a large master bedroom and bath. The apartment was painted in shades of blue-green with a darker blue-green accent wall. The kitchen had white cupboards with green, white, and gray tile and countertops, reminding me of ivy and spring.

It wouldn't be such a bad place to live if it weren't for the dead bodies across the hall. At least it didn't smell bad like the morgue. Just thinking of dead body smells dried up all of my laughter, and the chill in the air settled around me, clinging like a second skin.

I glanced around the room, looking for clues about Troy's life. He obviously had something going on. If he was getting rid of dead bodies for someone, there had to be a clue here somewhere. Of course, if he disposed of the bodies, then why was he taking money from his brother? Shouldn't he be getting paid for doing that?

I wandered to the kitchen and found the regular junk mail sitting on the counter. Finding nothing more, I stepped into the bedroom where Dimples searched the drawers and under the bed. "Find anything?"

"No." He sounded mad, but I picked up that he was still smarting about the cat. Plus it hurt where the cat had clawed through his clothes into his skin.

"Ouch... I bet that's painful. I wonder how long the cat was locked up in here."

"Probably a couple of days."

"That's too bad. Poor kitty." I pursed my lips together, but it didn't stop my body from shaking with laughter. Before I lost it in front of him, I retreated into the master bathroom and leaned against the wash basin until I got under control.

Noting the bottle of expensive cologne on the counter, I picked it up to take a whiff. It smelled amazing, like cedar and musk with a bit of pepper and nutmeg. I pulled out my phone and took a picture so I wouldn't forget the name, knowing I'd have to get some for Chris.

"You find anything?" Dimples asked.

"Uh... not exactly." I pulled out the drawers and looked through them all, just to make sure I did my job. Dimples moved into the closet, so I left him there and followed another short hallway that branched off the living room.

I found two doors, one at the end of the hall, and another along the hallway. Taking a breath, I opened the hallway door to a small office with a desk and filing cabinet. The desk was clear of papers, and there wasn't a computer, so I figured the police had taken it.

I turned to the door at the end of the hall and found it slightly ajar. I flipped on the light before pushing it open and came upon a storage and laundry area. Clean clothes had been hung on a stand, and a laundry basket sat on the floor.

A box of kitty litter sat in the back of the room, answering any questions about why the cat was there. With nothing more to see, I turned out the light and stepped into the hallway.

As I took another step, the light in the room came back on. I froze. Did I push the switch wrong? I stepped back to the room and reached inside to turn out the light. The scent of the exact same cologne I'd just smelled wafted over me, and my breath caught.

Holy hell. Was it Troy trying to get my attention? I glanced at the light switch, finding it in the on position, so maybe I hadn't turned it off all the way. But that didn't explain the smell. Swallowing, I stepped inside for a closer look.

The tops of the washer and dryer were clear, so I turned to the clothes hanging on the stand. They were all shirts, and I ran my hands over them but nothing stood out, so I moved on to the laundry basket. It was full of dirty clothes, and I began to sort through them.

Coming across a pair of slacks, I picked them up and felt something hard in the front pocket. With my heart fluttering, I reached inside the pocket and pulled out a small burner phone. Excitement raced over me. This was it. The clue we needed.

Leaving the light on, I hurried down the hall and found Dimples looking through the kitchen drawers. "I found something." I held up the phone. "I found it in the dirty clothes basket."

Dimples took the phone, his eyes shining with anticipation. "This is great." He turned it on, but nothing happened. "I guess we need to charge it up. I think I saw a charging cord in the bedroom."

A few minutes later, the phone had charged enough to turn on, and we found several texts to the same number.

"They're mostly times and dates," Dimples said. "And the times are all late at night. But that's it." He glanced my way. "I'll bet it's when the bodies were brought here for Troy to cremate."

"That makes sense."

"I'll have to see if I can track down the number, but if it's a burner phone, it's probably untraceable." Dimples sighed. "But it might lead us to someone." He was thinking about texting the person as Troy's brother and threatening to expose him if he didn't return the money Troy stole... or something like that.

"That's a possibility. But first I think we should find out what Troy was doing before he came back to work for his brother. Barry obviously doesn't know, but maybe one of Troy's friends or former employers will."

"That's true," Dimples agreed. "And even if they don't tell us anything, you could pick it up."

I grinned. "Right."

"Okay. This is good. Is there anything else we should do before we leave?"

I glanced back down the hall to the laundry room and realized the light wasn't on anymore. I knew I'd left it on, and a chill ran over me. "Not right now. I think we should go."

"Okay."

I followed Dimples to the door, and we stepped into the hallway. He locked the door behind us and glanced across the hall. "Do you think that door goes into the preparation room?"

"You mean for the bodies? Probably."

He'd always been curious about this part of a funeral home. He thought that, since all of us would end up there at some point, it might be interesting to take a look. Before I could stop him, he pushed the door open.

It was dark and spooky in there, and I had no desire to step inside and take a look around. The only time I wanted to be in a room like that was after I was dead. "Wait. I don't want to go in there."

"But aren't you curious?"

"No."

"But... what if you can pick up something from Troy? His body's in there, so it might be worth a try."

"I already did."

"What?"

"That's how I found the phone." I explained what happened with the scent of Troy's cologne, along with the light switch. "So I don't need to go in there."

"Why didn't you tell me?" It surprised him that I didn't start out with that when I brought him the phone. Weren't we partners?

I shrugged. "I don't know. I'm not used to talking about that sort of thing." At his hurt expression, I continued. "But I'll try and do better."

"That's okay. I didn't mean to give you such a hard time, and this phone is a great clue." He let the door close behind us, and I sprinted up the stairs, so ready to get out of there. Getting a nudge from beyond the grave might be helpful, but it still gave me the willies.

We stepped back to the main office, but Barry was gone, so Dimples left the key to the apartment on Barry's desk, and we stepped outside. Back in the sunshine, I breathed in the fresh air and shook off the chill.

Climbing inside the warm car, I relaxed against the seat. "Well... we made some progress, right? It looks like Troy was getting rid of bodies for someone. He must have decided he was done, and his partner in crime killed him for it."

"Yeah. That's what it looks like to me. Whoever needed bodies to disappear had a good thing going until Troy had a change of heart, for whatever reason. So our next question is what kind of person needs to get rid of bodies?"

"I guess killers... so gangs, or criminals."

"Right." He was thinking that group included the mob and Manetto, but he didn't want to say that part out loud. Then he thought that maybe I should ask Manetto if he had something to do with the murder.

It would sure make things easier if we could eliminate him right off the bat. But what if someone in his organization had, and they'd killed Troy. That seemed way too sloppy for someone like Manetto. He glanced my way... had I heard that?

"Yes I did, but don't worry, I don't think that's Unc...uh...Manetto's style either."

He easily picked up my slip and thought I should just call him Uncle Joey, since he was used to it by now. Nothing could change the fact that I worked for a mob boss, no matter how he felt about it, so he might as well accept it.

He glanced my way, knowing I'd heard that, too. "I'm trying not to let it bother me anymore, but it's easier said than done."

"Yeah, I get it. But it might help if you'd look at the positive side of things. I mean... just think of all the times he's helped us out. And it doesn't hurt that he can do things a police officer can't."

Dimples shook his head. "You're dreaming if you think a mob boss would help the cops. Don't you know that every single one of those times Manetto got involved was to help you?"

"Hey... I know that, but you have to admit that, by helping me, he's also helping you, so it's all worked out."

He thought the way my mind worked was fascinating. Somehow, I always seemed to make the mob boss look good. It was a real talent, but he couldn't fault me for it. I was a good person, and I needed to believe I was making a positive difference in the world, no matter how I did it. So far, I'd succeeded, and he hoped to God it continued.

I hoped so too, because nothing about my situation with Uncle Joey was about to change.

"I can't wait to tell Billie about the cat," I said, wanting to change the subject. "The look on your face..." I paused to snicker. "It was priceless. Dang... I should have taken a picture." Just thinking about it again sent gales of laughter tumbling out of me.

Dimples shook his head. "Before you get too carried away, let's get back to the case. I've already contacted most of the people from Troy's phone. I was looking through his latest emails when you came in. I haven't found anything new, but why don't you take a look? Maybe you'll see something I missed?"

Still snickering, I checked my watch. "Sure. I only have about forty-five minutes before my next appointment, but I'll look through it."

"Thanks."

A few minutes later, we pulled into the precinct and headed inside to Dimples's desk. As he pulled up the files he'd obtained from Troy's computer, I stopped by my desk and sat down.

My chair didn't list to the side, and my desk had a placard with my name on it. That was real progress. I sat down, realizing that, for the first time, I felt like I belonged. I'd come a long way from the early days, and a sense of satisfaction rolled over me.

While Dimples was busy, I quickly booted up my computer, so I could look up Ian Smith. A few keystrokes later, his name came up without a record of anything but a traffic ticket. Dang.

"Shelby?" Dimples called.

"Coming." I flipped off my computer and hurried back to his side. "What have you got?"

He showed me the emails he'd flagged, and nothing seemed off. "I even checked his spam folder, but I couldn't find a thing that seemed out of place."

"What about his deleted emails? Did you look through those?"

"No." Dimples quickly clicked on the trash icon, and a bunch of emails came up with several from the same email address. He clicked on the most recent email, and a food order of crispy chicken sliders came up.

"Hey... look at that." I pointed to the logo on the food truck. "It's called The Burnt Food Truck. Burnt... get it? Maybe that's the connection."

Dimples's brows rose. Just because the truck had a name that fit with a crematorium didn't mean the two were related. But it wouldn't hurt to check it out. "Let me see if I can find it." Dimples put the food truck into his search and came up with a schedule of truck stops and a phone number.

"Is it the same number that's on the burner phone?"

He quickly checked. "No. But I think I'll call and see where the truck is today."

"Good idea. You could even get some lunch."

While Dimples called, I checked the time, finding I only had a few minutes before I was supposed to be at Thrasher. He hung up and smiled. "They're not too far. Want to get some lunch?"

"Sorry. I wish I could, but I've got my appointment right now. Tell me about it later?"

"Sure." He didn't think he'd get far without me there to listen to anyone, but he'd check it out anyway.

Glancing my way, he wondered if my meeting was with Manetto. If it was, he hoped I'd do him a solid and ask Manetto if he knew anything about using a certain funeral home that disposed of bodies on the sly.

Seeing my pursed lips, he shrugged "Hey. It doesn't hurt to ask."

I shook my head. "I'll see what I can do, but no promises."

His eyes widened... so I was meeting with Manetto. Knowing I'd heard that, he broke out in a big smile. "Thanks, Shelby." He thought it was about time he started using my resources. Since I wasn't going to quit working for the other side, he might as well get something out of it for the good guys.

I rolled my eyes. "See ya."

I quickly left the precinct, knowing that it wasn't his fault I was stuck between two opposing forces. Only now it bothered me that he was starting to think like Uncle Joey, and it put me in a bind. But what could I expect? It was a good move on his part, and he probably knew I'd try to help him if I could.

CHAPTER 4

I stepped out of the elevator and hurried into Thrasher only two minutes late. Jackie wasn't at her desk, so I rushed down the hallway to Uncle Joey's office and knocked before opening the door.

Inside, Uncle Joey sat at his desk, and Ramos sat in his regular seat. They'd been talking, but stopped, and Uncle Joey smiled at me. From the tense set of his shoulders, I knew he was struggling.

"So what's going on?" I asked, slipping into my chair. "Is Jackie all right? I didn't see her."

"She's fine, but she didn't want to come in to work today." Uncle Joey pulled a can of diet soda out of his small office refrigerator and handed it to me.

"Thanks. This is great."

"Sure." After offering a can to Ramos, who declined, he popped a can open for himself and took a swig. "It's funny how things work out. If Sonny hadn't gone through a mutual friend to contact me, Jackie wouldn't have been left out of the loop, and she could have warned me about him."

He shook his head. "You're probably wondering what Sonny Dixon has to do with Jackie." At my nod, he continued. "He's her ex."

Horror filled my heart. "Holy hell. No wonder she was so upset yesterday."

"Yeah. Seeing him again was pretty awful, especially after what he did to her." Lost in thought, Uncle Joey quit talking.

"What did he do?" I prompted.

Uncle Joey leaned forward in his chair, glancing between Ramos and me. "Ramos knows most of this, but I'll start at the beginning to catch you up. I met Jackie through her family's business. Her brother, Bruce, took over after their father died and ran Linaria Investment Management.

"Around that time, Bruce approached me about investing a big chunk of money into their company for a highly lucrative return. It sounded almost too good to be true. Turns out it was. Luckily, Jackie told me that I might want to reconsider.

"We'd met at a party at Bruce's mansion. Jackie was acting as Bruce's hostess since his wife divorced him. We hit it off at that party, but she was married, so it never went anywhere. Still, we ended up forming a relationship and we got pretty close. She told me she wasn't happy in her marriage, but she refused to consider ending it. I had no idea why, and I never met her husband.

"Anyway, it turned out that Sonny was a partner in her family's company, and that alone kept her tied to him. When the bottom fell out, I was more than grateful she'd warned me away from investing. I would have lost a lot of money.

"With the company falling apart, a federal investigation began, putting Jackie, her husband, and her brother, all under the list of indictments the prosecution was bringing against them. Bruce took the brunt of it, but Sonny, and plenty of other employees, weren't far behind.

Uncle Joey let out a breath. "It was a mess. The feds were after them for all kinds of white-collar crimes. During the investigation, the feds froze all the company's assets, as well as all of their personal bank accounts.

"In the months that followed, Bruce and Sonny both worked to clear their names. Sonny claimed he didn't know a thing about the crimes and blamed Bruce for everything. Jackie wanted to believe him, but it was hard when Bruce told her that Sonny had been in on it all along.

"The indictments came down, and both Bruce and Sonny were arrested. Once the dust settled, both of them managed to get out on bail. Jackie urged them both to make a deal and turn over the remaining money for lesser sentences. But, for some reason, Bruce fled the country, leaving Jackie and Sonny in the lurch.

"That's when Sonny made a deal. In exchange for probation, he'd give them the offshore bank accounts and draw Bruce out of hiding so they could arrest him. But when they opened the offshore accounts, all the money was gone, presumably drained by Bruce. Sonny continued to work with them, promising Bruce's capture in exchange for staying out of jail.

"After several months, Sonny managed to draw Bruce out of hiding. Bruce was arrested, and Sonny got off with two years of probation, while Bruce is spending the next forty years in prison."

Uncle Joey was thinking that there had to be more to the story. Jackie hadn't said it in so many words, but it sounded to him like Sonny was the guilty party, and he'd set her brother up so he could stay out of jail.

Uncle Joey sighed. "I don't know all the particulars, but Jackie filed for divorce during that time. Her husband had betrayed the family trust, and she was left with nothing and nowhere to go. That's when I offered her a job here, and, after thinking it over, she came to work for me.

"It wasn't until Sonny showed up yesterday that Jackie realized he'd contacted me about entering his poker tournament, and I never put it together that he was her ex."

"She never told you his name?"

"She probably did, but she never called him anything but 'the ex.' I think using his name was painful for her, and, for some reason, I thought he was in jail, so it never occurred to me."

Uncle Joey shook his head, remembering how upset Jackie had been last night. It had brought up all of the fear and anger she'd spent the last several years working to overcome.

He glanced my way. "Jackie was so fragile back then. It wasn't until my ex, Carlotta, came back into my life that Jackie let down her guard. She'd been so hurt by Sonny that she'd put a wall around her heart, and I didn't know if she'd ever let me in.

"She also had second thoughts about getting married again. She insisted on a prenuptial agreement before she would consider it. Even then, she didn't want anyone to know. I think she wanted to protect me from her past."

He rubbed his forehead, thinking that she had it all wrong. It was him she needed protection from. Still, she'd admitted that his job as a mob boss had made her more willing to marry him instead of less. It didn't make sense until he considered her trust issues.

She knew he had the power and means to keep her safe, and it didn't hurt that he'd come to her rescue when no one else would.

"So what now?" Ramos asked.

"Now we kill the son of a bitch."

I sat up straight, alarm tightening my stomach. "Uh... it's understandable that you'd want to do that... but maybe it's not a good idea."

Uncle Joey's brows rose. He was thinking I was taking a chance going against his wishes. "What are you saying Shelby? That I should just let him go? After everything he's done to Jackie?"

"No... absolutely not. I just think there are better ways to make him suffer."

His eyes narrowed. "Like what?"

My mind went blank. I hated being put on the spot, but I had to stop him. "Well... if you give me a minute to think, I'm sure I can come up with something."

"Huh." He dismissed me and glanced at Ramos. "What about you?"

"I think his death could be arranged."

I gasped. "Ramos." I glanced between the two of them and shook my head. "You guys. I get that you want him dead, but let's at least look at all our options." I listened to both of their minds, hoping they were just teasing me, but instead, I found this was no joke.

I huffed out a breath. After all the time I'd spent with them, I thought I'd made a difference. Well, maybe I had, but it wasn't enough. That meant I'd just have to come up with a good alternative.

"Okay. But before you go too far down that road, just remember that there's a poker tournament coming up with a ten-million-dollar jackpot. You know Sonny wants that money, so winning it out from under him would be great, right?"

They both nodded, and I caught a hint of willingness from Uncle Joey to listen to what I had to say. "Great. And we also know that Sonny's in debt to someone. He needs that money, so he's got to be desperate.

"We all know that desperate people do stupid things, so I think we should capitalize on that. We need to find out who this person is, and what other vulnerabilities Sonny might have. Wouldn't it be better to see him suffer for a while?"

Uncle Joey was thinking that I had a point, but it wouldn't give him the same satisfaction of putting a bullet in his head. "I know you mean well, Shelby, and you're right, I would like to see him suffer before I kill him."

I just about threw my hands up. "Um... before that happens, we should find out all we can about Sonny and his plans for the tournament. After that, we can figure out a plan to make him suffer once we get there. Who knows? Maybe there are a lot of people who want him dead, and you won't have to do it."

He was thinking oh... *but I want to.*

I tried to ignore that and moved on to a different strategy. "There's something else we need to discuss." That took them both by surprise, so I quickly continued. "After I win the poker tournament, we'll have ten million dollars to play with, and I've come across something that I might want to invest in."

Uncle Joey's brows rose. He was stuck on the phrase, *we'll have ten million dollars,* and wondering how the hell I'd thought it was a 'we' thing.

"Well... because I'll win it?" At his deepening frown, I quickly continued. "Hear me out. I just came from a press conference about the Lost Taft Mine. You've heard about that in the news, right?" Uncle Joey nodded. "Good. Well... they're looking for investors, and I thought it might be a profitable thing to consider."

"Wait," Uncle Joey said. "You're talking about the legendary mine that people have been searching for, with no success, for decades?"

"Well... yes, but they just discovered a journal with all the details about where it is. Jeremiah Taft wrote it himself."

"And you believe it?"

"Well... mostly. After the press conference this morning, it looks like there's a ninety-nine percent chance that the journal's real. That's pretty high if you ask me."

Uncle Joey shook his head. "So what are you saying? That you want to use the jackpot money to back these charlatans and lose it all?"

"No... just my part of it. That way I'm not dipping into my savings account. I know it's a long shot, but finding all that gold could be worth it. In fact, the gold could be worth a hundred times more than the initial investment."

Uncle Joey had never seen this impractical side of me. What was going on? It was like an obsession. "Why are you so interested in this?"

Obsessed? Me? I was as level-headed as they came... wasn't I? "I guess it's because my grandpa spent a lot of time looking for that mine, and he took me with him a few times. We found a lot of pretty rocks, but we never found the mine. Now that there's a real chance of finding it, I thought it might be cool to try and... you know... fulfill my grandpa's dream."

Uncle Joey sat back in his chair, wondering if I meant it was my grandpa's dream, or my childhood fantasy. Since I was so intent, he decided to give me a chance to explain. "All right. Tell me about it."

"Sure." I explained all about the press conference, the journal, Ian Smith, and Dr. Stewart, who happened to be a shoo-in for a forty-something Harrison Ford.

After I finished, Uncle Joey rubbed his chin. He was thinking that it was a huge risk, and he could see how the men could run out of money. There weren't a lot of people willing to sink money into something with absolutely no guarantee of a return. It was like throwing money down a sinkhole.

But... when I won the tournament, and then used some of that money, what would it hurt? It would be my money after all. Still, he didn't want them to take advantage of me. "Since you're so set on it, why don't you let me help you? You can call this Ian Smith character and tell him I'm the one interested in a meeting with both him and Dr. Stewart.

"My reputation will ensure that they won't try anything, and we can talk to them together. You can hear their thoughts, and, depending on what you pick up, you'll know how to proceed."

My eyes lit up. "Really? Okay. I'll give him a call. When's a good time?"

"I've got time tomorrow... or even this afternoon if they're free."

I nodded and pulled out my phone. "Sweet... I'll be right back." I hurried down the hall to my office. Since I had no idea how to get in touch with them, I put a call through to Billie.

She picked up right away. "Hello?"

"Hey Billie. It's Shelby. Do you know how to get in touch with Ian Smith or Dr. Stewart?"

"I sure do... I have a number right here. Just a sec." I heard papers shuffling around before she came back on. "Does this mean you're getting some backing?"

"Well... I'm thinking about it." I didn't want to tell her it was me doing the backing. She'd probably think I was nuts. Better to let her think it was Uncle Joey.

"Oh wow. I spoke with Michael, and he's not convinced that it's anything but a waste of time; but if you're involved, I think he might change his mind. So what's the plan?"

"I'm going to call Ian and set up a meeting with him and Unc... uh... Manetto. I'm hoping to pick up something that will help me know if this whole journal thing is for real, or just a hoax. If there's any real possibility that we could actually find the gold mine, I think I can convince Mr. Manetto to invest. I'm sure if he does, Ian won't object to me going along."

"You really think so?"

"Sure... with my premonitions, it will be a real advantage since I'll know if we're headed in the right direction... if you know what I mean." I knew that was stretching the truth, but it didn't stop me from saying it.

"Okay. I found it. You ready?"

"Yes." I listened as she rattled off the number, jotting it down on a notepad. "Thanks. I'll let you know what happens."

"You'd better."

We disconnected, and I put the call through. Ian answered, and I quickly explained who I was. He remembered me, so I jumped right in. "I might have a backer for you, but he wants to meet with you before he commits. I told him I'd set it up. Is that something you're interested in?"

"Yes. I'd be happy to meet anytime."

"Great. Do you have time this afternoon, or would tomorrow work better?"

"I'm free today."

"Okay. What about Dr. Stewart? Could he come too?"

"Uh... just a minute. Let me ask him." He spoke to someone, and I waited for his response. "Sure. We can both be there."

"Nice." I checked the time. It was just after two, so I asked if they could come in half an hour. He replied that they could, and I gave him the address to Thrasher Development.

Now that it was set up, excitement, along with a patch of worry, settled in my stomach. Was I a sucker for wanting this to work out? Maybe. But I wasn't committing to anything, so meeting with them was the best thing. I'd know if they were trying to scam me... so this was the perfect way to do it.

If it ended up that they were the real deal, then I could get excited about heading back into the mountains and finding the lost gold mine.

I slipped back inside the office, interrupting Ramos and Uncle Joey's discussion about taking Sonny down. Maybe I shouldn't have left them alone, because they both quit talking and shuttered their thoughts before I could pick up anything important.

"I got ahold of Ian. He said they could be here in about thirty minutes. Is that okay?"

"Yes. That's fine." Uncle Joey turned back to Ramos. "What do you think about sending Ricky ahead of time? Maybe he could scout out the place and find someone we could get information from."

Ramos nodded. "That works, but it would be better if we had a contact there. Does Jackie have any friends who might be willing to meet with Ricky? He could get more information about Sonny that way."

"That's a great idea. Let me ask her." Uncle Joey lifted his phone from the receiver and pushed her number.

Ramos turned to me, noticing I still held my can of soda. "Want some ice and a glass to go with that?"

"Uh... sure." I picked up that he wanted to give Uncle Joey some privacy, and asking me to head to his apartment was a surefire way to accomplish it, since he knew I couldn't resist spending time alone with him.

I rolled my eyes, and he sent me that sexy, half-smile of his that did me in. Naturally, I followed him down the hall to his apartment. Inside, he handed me a glass, and I filled it with ice before pouring in the rest of my soda. It didn't amount to much, so Ramos pulled out another can and handed it over.

"Thanks." I sat on a bar stool and poured the drink, letting the fizzy sound roll over me.

Ramos pulled a bag of roasted almonds out of the cupboard and sat beside me. After ripping it open, he offered some to me. "So what's going on with this mine thing?"

I studied his face and picked up that he was intrigued by my intense interest in gold. "What? You think I'm getting carried away?"

"Maybe a little, but it seems more personal. Is that because of your grandpa?"

"Probably. Have you ever gone prospecting for gold?"

"Uh... that's a big no. Wandering around the hills for hours doesn't hold a lot of appeal for me."

"Yeah... I see your point. I guess I forgot about that part. But it wasn't ever boring for me. I just remember my grandpa showing me all sorts of rocks. He even knew their names. I loved the quartz ones the most. I even brought some of them home. I think I kept them in a shoe box for a while, but I don't know what happened to them. One time we found an arrowhead though. That was pretty cool."

"Hmm... I'll have to look up the mine's mythology on the Internet and see what I've been missing."

"There are lots of stories about it. I'm sure most of them aren't true, but they're still fun to think about."

"Like what?"

I shrugged. "I don't know a lot, only that it was rumored to be there long before Jeremiah Taft discovered it. He took as much gold as he could carry, but, before he could return, he came down with a mysterious illness. After a woman nursed him back to health, he went out again and never came back."

I leaned closer to Ramos. "There's another rumor that the gold is cursed, but I have no idea why. Maybe it's because so many people have died looking for it." I shrugged. "But that's just a story."

Ramos shook his head, thinking it was probably one of those legends that got into men's heads and made them do crazy things. "And you think this professor really has a journal with the location of the mine spelled out in it?"

"Yeah... it sure seems that way. But talking to them should help me know for sure."

"True, and I have to admit that I'm curious." He checked the time. "We'd better get back."

I wasn't finished with my drink, so I took it with me and stopped to wait at Jackie's desk. "You go on down. I'll wait here for Ian and Stewart."

"Okay."

I sat down in her chair and finished off my drink. A few minutes later, the elevator doors opened, and Ian and Stewart both stepped toward the office. As they came inside, I stood to greet them. "Hi again. Thanks for coming. I'll let my Uncle know you're here. I'm sure he has a lot of questions for you."

Stewart's brows rose. He hadn't known Manetto was my uncle, and he never expected me to become a friend, rather than a foe. He'd spent the last twenty minutes checking Manetto out, and what he'd discovered hadn't exactly reassured him. But money was money, and he needed a lot of it, so he couldn't be too scrupulous.

I used Jackie's phone to call Uncle Joey, and he told me to bring them down to his office. After a quick knock, I ushered them in, and Uncle Joey stepped around his desk to greet them. After I made the introductions, he motioned to the table and chairs at the other end of his office.

"Please have a seat." He indicated where they should sit, while he sat at the head of the table.

I wasn't sure how he did it, but he seemed just as intimidating there as he did behind his desk. The men sat on one side, and Ramos and I sat on the other, facing them.

"Shelby's quite taken with your project." Uncle Joey began. "She's thinking of investing a nice chunk of money, so I told her I'd meet with you and see what you have to say."

"That's wonderful," Ian began, surprised that Uncle Joey was being so magnanimous with me. It shocked him that it was my money we were talking about, especially since I'd seemed so distrustful at the press conference.

"We've spent a great deal of time making sure this project is solvent. The last thing we want to do is risk taking a loss, so rest assured, we truly believe we can find the mine." He glanced at Stewart. "With all of his research, Dr. Stewart is the expert on solving this mystery, so I'll let him explain."

"Thank you Ian." Stewart caught Uncle Joey's gaze. "How much do you know about the Lost Taft Mine?"

"Just that Taft found it and disappeared before he had a chance to stake a claim."

Stewart nodded. "From the research I've done, the mine was first discovered by Spanish conquistadors, who mined the gold at the expense of the Native Americans who lived there. After they left, the remaining tribe members decided that only those who pledged to keep the mine a secret would be allowed to use it.

"They made a few deals with trappers and settlers, but word of its existence began to circulate far and wide.

Because of that, the tribal chief rescinded his permission to let anyone take the gold. He set guards around the mine, and anyone venturing too close was killed on the spot.

"Years later, the mine's whereabouts were lost to legend. That's when Jeremiah Taft stumbled upon it. Of course, he'd been searching for it, but it was quite the surprise to actually find it. He took as much gold as he could carry, but, by the time he came down from the mountain, he was deathly ill.

"He took a room at a widow's home and asked her to nurse him back to health. In his desperation, he showed her his saddlebags filled with gold nuggets and promised to share the bounty with her if she helped him get better.

"Under her diligent ministrations, he began to improve. After a few weeks, he felt well enough to head back to the mine to get more gold. He left the gold from his first trip with the widow, who promised to keep it safe for him. She waited months for his return, but he never came back. Once the winter storms began, she figured he was dead. She cashed in the gold, and it was enough to set her up for life."

He was thinking that it was a terrible tragedy, mostly because it sounded like the two of them had fallen in love. "As word got out, the widow claimed that he never disclosed the location of the mine. She did say that it was north of town, up in the Rockies, and it had taken him two days to get to her house, which put it somewhere in the Soapstone Range.

"After Taft's death, there was a literal rush to find the mine. People set out on a daily basis. A few came back with stories of ghosts, but no gold. A few years later, there was a group of three men who set out. Only one of them came back. He carried a few gold nuggets, but he refused to speak about what had happened to the others. That's when the rumors started that the mine was cursed."

I nodded. "I've heard that."

"So have I," Uncle Joey agreed. "So... where does the journal fit in?"

"Since I'd always found the mine fascinating, I did some research and discovered that the widow had only two descendants, a grandniece and a grandnephew. But, get this... the niece lived in her great aunt's house, and had taken care of her in her old age.

"By the time I met her, Irene was in her nineties. After I told her of my interest in the mine, she was happy to tell me what she knew. She even told me that she'd found several of her great aunt's journals in an old cedar chest in the attic.

"Naturally, she'd read through them all, but never found any mention of the gold or Jeremiah Taft. Irene always wondered if there was more to it, since her great aunt had once hinted that Taft had hidden a journal with a map to the mine somewhere on the property.

"She'd searched everywhere, along with the rest of her family, but they never found a thing. I asked her if I could look around, and I spent the next few weeks searching everywhere I could think of, but it wasn't there.

"Later, she asked me if I'd like the journals for their historical value, since she had no living children, and her brother's family had long since moved away. You can imagine how excited I was to receive them. In return, I promised her that I would let her know if I ever found anything.

"There were five journals all together, and I read through them during the next couple of weeks. Like Irene, I didn't find anything about the gold mine or Jeremiah Taft. It was disappointing, because I really thought there might be something.

"I did find several entries about a cabin in the woods and discovered that the widow spent a lot of time there in the summers. I visited Irene and mentioned it to her, and she told me all about the place. She'd gone there a lot as a kid, but it had been over thirty years since her last visit.

"She'd inherited the property and still owned it, but she didn't know what condition it was in. She asked me if I'd like to take her to see it, so I agreed. We found it in pretty bad shape, and I think it depressed her to see it like that. I offered to buy it from her and fix it up, which seemed to make her happy."

He stopped for a minute, and I picked up that his main reason for offering to buy it was because he hoped to find a clue that would lead him to the mine.

"After I got the deed, I went up there a few times and began to clean it up. It needed a lot of work, and I couldn't spend as much time there as I would have liked, but I managed to fix it up a little. During that time, Irene passed away. She left the old house to her brother's family, and they sold it to a couple who now run it as a bed and breakfast.

"I went back to the cabin this last spring, once the snow had melted, and took the journals with me. As I read through them, it hit me that the summer of Taft's visit coincided with the summer the widow had been at the cabin. That's when I realized that Jeremiah Taft had recovered from his illness there, and not at the widow's house back in town. That meant he'd actually found the gold in a different place than everyone thought.

"In one of her journals, the widow mentioned briefly that she nearly ran out of firewood to keep the place warm because a digger was lost. I didn't understand that at first, but, after reading more of the entries, I realized that she used digger as short for gold digger... and she was talking about Jeremiah.

"Later, she wrote that the digger never returned, and it broke her heart. The next entry was about locking up the cabin and leaving the warming rocks to hold their secrets. That's when I knew Jeremiah's journal was in the cabin, probably behind the rocks in the fireplace.

"The stone fireplace was still intact. After an intense search, that's where I found his journal." He pursed his lips. "I've kept most of this story a secret, and I'm only telling you because I think you'd make a good partner."

He was thinking that he hadn't wanted to split the gold with anyone, and that had been the reason for his reticence. Still, as much as he hated asking for money, he knew he had to sell the story, and with Manetto's backing, he could move forward with his plans and tell all the other interested parties he didn't need them.

"That's an interesting story," Uncle Joey said. "If it's true." He glanced my way, ignoring Stewart's grimace. I sent Uncle Joey a nod, and he turned back to Stewart. "Let's say I believe you. If it's all true, then why haven't you found it? I would imagine that you've been looking for the mine for the last several months. Am I right?"

Stewart ducked his head. "Yes. You're correct. I know we're close, but I've run out of money, and I need better equipment and supplies."

"Tell me what you've done."

"Well... first of all, from the journal, we figured out the area we need to concentrate on. We went through the whole process of staking out our claims and filing all the paperwork. We've been up there several times with no luck, so we decided to create a grid that would help us see where we've been."

He'd thought they would have found it by now, so something was off. Either Taft had gotten turned around, or they weren't reading the map right. Still, he refused to give up. The only problem was that the temperatures were dropping, which gave them only another few weeks at best before winter set in up there.

"Time's running out before the cold sets in," he continued. "And I'd like one more run at it. There are a couple of places left where I think it could be, so that's where I'd like to concentrate our efforts."

He didn't want to believe that he wouldn't find it, not when he'd gone to so much work. The journal was the key, and he was so close. It was within his grasp. He just knew it.

Yikes. He sounded a little crazy... like he had gold fever. It was kind of how my grandpa was at first, but, after a few years, I think he kept going because it gave him an excuse to be out in nature. Still, he didn't seem quite as obsessed as Stewart.

I turned my attention to Ian, who wondered if this was a lost cause after all. When Stewart had first approached him, he'd been excited for the opportunity. Now it wasn't looking so good. They'd funded the project themselves, and now it looked like they'd lose it all.

That's why he'd convinced Stewart to go public and ask for a backer. He'd wanted to recoup his losses, and, with enough money, he could put some of it in reserve to pay for all of the expenses and bills they'd already accumulated. That way, even if they didn't find the gold, he wouldn't be out a dime, and they could use some of the money to pay themselves for their time.

Oh boy... maybe this wasn't such a good idea. I glanced up to find Uncle Joey studying me. He could tell that my enthusiasm had waned, and reality had set in. Did I still want to do this? I didn't nod yes, but I didn't shake my head either. Instead, I shrugged. Maybe?

His lips quirked up, and he turned back to Stewart. "How about this... I'll fund your last expedition as a favor to my niece. If you don't find anything before winter sets in, I'd like the option of continuing, but only with certain stipulations that we can agree to later. If you do find the gold, I'd like a share of the mine... say twenty percent. Is that agreeable?"

Stewart's eyes widened. Twenty percent was more than he liked, but since he didn't think Manetto would actually settle for any less, he quickly agreed. "Yes, sure." He glanced at Ian, knowing he'd answered for both of them. "Is that okay with you?"

Ian slowly nodded. He hadn't wanted to share the gold either, but it didn't look like they'd actually find it anyway, so what did it hurt? Having a lot of money at their disposal was totally worth it.

"Good." Uncle Joey smiled. "Get me a list of the items you need, and I'll provide them."

"What?" Ian's head jerked up. "Uh... I can take care of all that. It would be easier for us if you just invested a set amount. I can keep track of all the expenditures so you don't have to do the work, and, I assure you, the money won't be squandered. I'll keep an accurate accounting of it all."

He could see that Uncle Joey wasn't sold on the idea, so he quickly continued. "Seriously, it's my job."

Uncle Joey slowly nodded. "All right. How much do you need?"

Stewart swallowed, thinking this was the tricky part. He wanted to ask for at least fifty grand, but he wasn't sure Manetto would go for it, so he started a little low. "Between thirty and fifty grand? I know that sounds like a lot, but it would help us get out from under our debt and still have enough money left over to buy some good equipment and find the mine."

Uncle Joey studied them with narrowed eyes, using his hardened gaze to intimidate them. They both stiffened, and I picked up their sudden worry that maybe this wasn't such a good idea.

"Before I agree," Uncle Joey began. "I have some ground rules. First... I don't suffer fools. If you try to cheat me, or double-cross me, I get back every last penny... with interest. If the mine isn't found, and I'm satisfied that you've explored all avenues to find it, I'll take it as a loss, and we'll part ways. But try and cheat me out of my twenty percent, and your lives are forfeit. Now... do you still want to make the deal?"

Stewart licked his lips, thinking that, if he agreed, he could very well end up dead. Manetto wasn't someone you bargained with. He glanced at Ian, who was thinking much the same thing. Ian was more cautious than Stewart, and he was about to refuse, but Stewart spoke first. "Agreed." The lure of the gold called to him, and he gave in to his greed, despite his better judgement.

"All right. Come back in the morning, and I'll have a money order for fifty grand ready for you." He didn't mention the contract he'd also have prepared for them to sign. If they thought he'd just hand over the money, they were in for a rude awakening.

Stewart nodded, relieved and surprised that Uncle Joey had agreed to the entire amount. "You won't regret this." He didn't even think about a contract, too happy about having a backer, and a way out of his accumulated debt, to know better.

Ian wasn't quite so naïve, but he was willing to do most anything for that much money, already thinking about how to use it to pay the bills and get the supplies. They both stood to leave, shaking Uncle Joey's hand to seal the deal.

"One more thing," Uncle Joey said, before glancing my way. "I'll be sending my niece up the mountain with you." He didn't mention that he wanted Ramos to come as well, since he didn't like laying everything out for them.

Stewart's startled gaze landed on me. "Oh... all right. As long as you know we'll be roughing it."

"Yeah... I got that." Did he think I was an idiot? Still, it surprised me that I didn't have to beg Uncle Joey to let me go. It was almost like he'd read my mind. I glanced his way, sending him a big grin. He grinned back before turning his attention to Stewart and Ian.

"Come back around nine tomorrow morning for the fifty grand."

Stewart's eyes lit up, and I figured he'd do just about anything Uncle Joey wanted. "Wonderful. We'll see you then." He ushered Ian out ahead of him, and they left the office.

Uncle Joey turned to me. "How did I do? Fifty grand wasn't so much, so I figured, why not? You know? And just think... you can go with them."

I smiled. "I know. For a minute there, I thought you'd read my mind."

"See Shelby. I'm not so bad." He was thinking that, even though he wanted to kill Sonny, he still had a big heart. "But just remember that the fifty grand is coming out of your share of the jackpot."

"I thought you had a big heart."

He grinned. "I do, but I also have an image to uphold."

I shrugged. "Fine. But if that's the case, then I get the twenty percent of the mine you bargained for."

"Oh yeah. I forgot about that. How about we go fifty-fifty?"

I grinned. "That sounds more like it."

"Good." His heart warmed with proud satisfaction that I'd stood up to him. "Now I'd better call my lawyer so he can draw up a contract. Is there anything you picked up that I should know?"

"I think a contract is a good idea, since Ian was already thinking of ways to use the money to pay off all the debts they've incurred. I guess if you have everything spelled out, he won't get away with squandering it on a salary for him and Stewart."

"That's right, and you'll get to go prospecting with them. So it's a win-win." He thought it would be something if we really did find that lost mine, but he wouldn't bet on it. Still, if it made me happy, it was worth it, especially since I was going to all the work of winning a high stakes poker tournament for him.

"I sure hope I can win."

"Of course you can. You can read minds, it'll be easy."

I just nodded. That was easy for him to say, but I knew there was more to it, mostly because Sonny was planning on cheating. How he planned to do that wasn't something I could prepare for. I hoped I was up to the task, because not only did I need to win the poker tournament, I also needed to figure out how to keep Uncle Joey from killing Sonny before we came home.

CHAPTER 5

I left Uncle Joey's office while he put the call through to Chris's law firm about the contract with Stewart and Ian. Ramos volunteered to walk me out, and I readily agreed.

"If there was any doubt that Manetto has a soft spot for you it should be long gone. I've never seen him put down a big chunk of money like that against such terrible odds. It's like throwing it away."

I huffed out a breath. "Hey. Half of it's my money, you know. Are you trying to make me feel guilty?"

"Do you?"

I shrugged. "Uh... not really. I guess I'm a good rationalizer, because, compared to ten million dollars, fifty grand is just a drop in the bucket, right? And then there's the lost gold mine. Seriously, how awesome would it be to find that?"

He shook his head. "If you say so."

"What's that supposed to mean?"

He folded his arms over his chest and leaned in close. "Babe... I think you've got gold fever."

"No I don't." His right brow lifted, and I sighed. "Okay... maybe a little."

He let out a breath. "I get it. Finding a lost treasure is something we all dream about. Just don't let it cloud your judgement. And just so you know, I'll be coming with you." He was thinking that, knowing my track record with trouble, there was no way I was going without him.

I couldn't help the smile that crossed my lips. "I'm sure I'll be fine, but... I'm glad you're coming."

"Yeah... somebody needs to watch your back." And who knew? Maybe he'd get lucky... those long, cold, dark nights out in the woods... I might get scared and climb into his sleeping bag with him... and he could...

"Stop that." I smacked his arm.

He snickered. "You realize that tomorrow's Friday, right? And the tournament's on Saturday?"

"Oh yeah." Between Jackie's troubles, wanting to stop Uncle Joey from killing Sonny, and finding a lost gold mine, I'd lost track. "What's the plan? When do we need to be there?"

"We were just talking about that when you came in. The tournament starts at one in the afternoon and goes through the night until there's a winner. So we'll probably need to leave around eight on Saturday morning."

"Do you think we'll be staying there overnight?"

"Maybe." He was thinking that we would if he needed to kill Sonny before we came home.

"Ugh! Don't think stuff like that."

He shrugged. "Okay... I'll try not to think about it."

I shook my head and pushed the call button. "Oh... before I go, there was something else I was supposed to ask you."

"What's that?"

"Do you know of anyone who might use a mortuary to cremate dead bodies? You know... the kind they want to get rid of? I mean... not you, but maybe someone else who would need to do that sort of thing?"

His eyes narrowed. "What's this about?"

I shrugged. "Just a police case I'm working on with Dimples... I mean... Detective Harris."

Ramos huffed out a breath. He didn't like my close relationship with the detective. The last time I'd helped the cop, I'd nearly gotten killed.

"This isn't the same as that. And I've learned my lesson. I'm not ever going to be so stupid again." It had been a stupid move to take the killer on all by myself, and I still felt bad about it.

His lips thinned, and he straightened, ready to lecture me on the subject. Did I have any idea what I put him through? The elevator doors swished open, so I stepped inside before he could let me have it. Most of the time, he refrained from chewing me out, so this was unexpected.

At the last minute, he blocked the door with his arm. "I don't know of anyone specifically, but I'll ask around."

"Great. Thanks. I'll see you tomorrow?"

"Yeah." He stepped back, and the doors slid shut.

Whoa... he usually didn't get so upset with me, but I'd obviously stepped into that one. It reinforced how much he hated getting those desperate phone calls from me. He'd never complained much, but now I knew that he probably held a lot of it inside.

Maybe I should tell him to yell at me for a while, so he could get it off his chest? Either that... or he'd just have to stop caring about me so much. Hmm... I think I'd rather take the yelling.

I made it home in time to take Coco on a walk. The last days of summer were shorter and cooler now, but it could still get hot. Up in the mountains, I knew that the leaves had changed and were probably falling to the ground by now. If Stewart wanted to head up there before the first snowfall, it would probably have to happen next week.

That meant I had a lot to do before then, but I could do it, I'd just have to take things a day at a time. My phone rang, and Dimples's name came up, so I quickly answered. "Hey... how's it going?"

"Good enough. The food truck people are legit, but I couldn't pick up anything else about them. Did you find out anything about getting rid of dead bodies from... anyone?"

"Nope. But I'll keep checking."

"Okay. Maybe you can come with me to talk to the truck people tomorrow. I mean... nothing seemed suspicious, but what do I know?"

"Yeah... sure. When do you want me?"

"Probably around lunchtime."

"Was the food good?"

"Yes. I'll buy your lunch."

Now that was an offer I couldn't refuse. "Okay. I'll be there around noon." We said our goodbyes and disconnected.

Before putting my phone away, I thought about calling Billie to tell her I was going prospecting with the guys, but I decided to hold off, since there was still a possibility they wouldn't sign the contract. No need to get her hopes up.

The kids came home from school, keeping me busy for the rest of the evening. Chris texted me that he had to stay late, and I wondered if it was because of the contract for Uncle Joey. If it was, he'd know all about Uncle Joey's plans to finance the mine.

At least it gave me an opening to tell Chris I was going prospecting with Stewart and Ian if they signed. I wasn't sure he'd like that much, but what could I say? It wasn't anything dangerous, and besides, Chris had agreed to support my career, so I hoped he'd be okay with it.

Chris got home a couple of hours later and told me all about Uncle Joey's plans. "I had to get a contract written up for Manetto's meeting in the morning. Did you have something to do with that?" He was thinking that, with my interest in the lost mine, it probably had everything to do with me, so I'd better spill it.

"Uh... yes I did. They seemed legitimate, so, with all the winnings from the poker tournament, I figured it might be a good investment."

"So you're telling me it was all your idea?"

"Maybe... but you can't blame me. I think, with the missing map, there's a real chance of finding the gold mine."

Chris waved my explanation away. "Yeah... I got that, but Manetto drives a hard bargain. Those guys are nuts if they sign the contract." His worried gaze caught mine. Since it was my idea, he knew I'd want to go with them. Maybe it wasn't so bad, but he still didn't like it. "Are you hoping to go with them?"

"If they sign, I probably will, but only for a couple of nights. I think they'll want to go next week, but guess what? Billie's coming with me." That wasn't quite true either, but it might be after I talk to her, and it was better than telling him Ramos would be there.

Chris's eyes widened. "What? Why?"

"She wants to do a story on the mine, and she told me that, if I end up going, she'll be able to go too."

Chris shook his head. Something about this didn't seem right. "So it's all set up?"

"Not exactly. I'll know more after we meet tomorrow morning. They have to sign the contract first."

Chris blew out a long-suffering breath. "What did you have to promise Manetto so he'd agree to back the project?"

"Nothing. He knew I'd like to go, that's all. So he was being nice."

"Yeah... right." Chris frowned. "How do you get into these things? No... don't answer that." He shook his head. "So, besides leaving for the weekend, you might be gone next week too?"

"If they sign the contract... yes, but it might only be for a couple of days."

He didn't think a couple of days would be long enough, so why didn't I just tell him that? He knew I was trying to sugarcoat it so he wouldn't be upset, but just the fact that I did that upset him. He wasn't an unreasonable person.

And now... I'd just heard everything he was thinking. He groaned. "Shelby... you know I love you, and I'm here for you. I may not like everything you get into, but you can level with me. I can take it." That was mostly true, but there were times he wished I'd ask him for his opinion before I went ahead with my plans.

And there it was... the reason I didn't tell it to him straight. "Would it make a difference?"

"What?"

"If I asked for your opinion?"

"It would to me." At my frown, he continued. "Just because I give you my opinion, it doesn't mean you have to change anything. I'd just like to be included in these decisions of yours. I feel like I'm always playing catch-up after the fact, you know?"

He might have a point. "Okay. So, what do you think about my plans to go prospecting?"

He didn't hesitate. "I'm not sure it's such a good idea. I mean... I know it's a dream of yours, so that makes sense, and I suppose you'll be okay, as long as these guys aren't bad people. I have to admit that it makes me feel better to know Billie's going with you, especially since I imagine

Manetto will send some of his people along... one of which is probably Ramos, since you haven't mentioned that."

He rubbed the back of his neck, wondering if he was crazy. He wanted to support me and my career, just as I supported him, so how could he object? "So... I guess if it's something you really want to do, I'm not going to hold you back. I just want you to be safe." He narrowed his gaze at me. "How was that?"

My heart melted. "You're the best." I threw my arms around his neck and hugged him tight. He trusted me, and I vowed to never take that for granted. "Thanks honey."

Our lips met and I kissed him hard, wanting him to know how much he meant to me. All those pent-up feelings led from one thing to another, and soon, I smiled to hear him whisper some of my favorite words.

The next day, I made it to Thrasher close to eight-thirty. I'd decided to get there early so I could tell Ramos to go ahead and yell at me if he needed to. After last night, I'd learned it was important to get things out in the open and clear the air. Not that it was the same with Ramos... but he had seemed frustrated with me, so it couldn't hurt.

Jackie wasn't there again, and I wondered if she'd ever come back. Should I call her? Before I could decide, Uncle Joey's office door opened, and Ricky stepped out, with Uncle Joey and Ramos following behind.

Ricky was thinking that it was nice to have Uncle Joey trust him enough to send him to Vegas ahead of our visit. He looked forward to meeting Jackie's friend, who could fill him in on her ex-husband, and he relished the idea of snooping around Sonny's casino and hotel.

Catching sight of me, he smiled, thinking that he looked forward to watching me play in the tournament. He hoped I'd win, like Manetto wanted, and he was glad it wasn't him under all that pressure. "Hey Shelby."

"Hi Ricky. You heading to Vegas?"

"Yeah. Ramos is taking me to the airport now, so I guess I'll see you tomorrow."

"Sounds good." After they left, I turned to Uncle Joey. "So, Jackie isn't here today?"

He shook his head. "No... she needs some time." He worried that she'd ever come back to work. Sonny wouldn't be back, so she didn't have to worry about seeing him again, but that didn't seem to matter. Maybe if Sonny was dead, she'd feel better. Even then, he wasn't sure.

He arched his brows. "I take it you heard that?"

"Uh... yeah. Sorry. Do you want me to put up my shields?"

"No... it's okay. I'm just not sure what to do. Maybe you could talk to her?" He wasn't sure Jackie was telling him everything... but maybe, if I spoke to her, I'd pick up what she wasn't saying, and I could help her out.

My brows rose. I'd caught an underlying hint that he wanted me to fill him in... kind of like a spy. "You really want me to do that?"

He shuffled his feet. "I think it would help her to have someone besides me to talk to, since you're not so close to the problem. Not that I'd expect you to tell me her thoughts... like you were doing it to spy on her or something."

"Right." That was exactly what he was hoping for, but that didn't mean I'd have to follow through. Still, I couldn't refuse. Jackie was my friend, and I was worried about her. "Sure. I'd be happy to talk with her."

He gave me a relieved nod. "Good. Maybe after these guys sign the contract, you could head over there."

"Okay." I had to be at the precinct at noon, but that could still work.

"The contract is in my office. Why don't you show Stewart and Ian into the conference room when they get here? Let me know when they arrive, and I'll come down."

"Sure." I sat in Jackie's chair to wait. After a minute, I began to straighten her desk. Not much was out of place, but I had to do something while I sat there. Fifteen minutes later, the ding from the elevator sounded, but, instead of the two men, Ramos stepped out. He came into Thrasher with a lop-sided grin, just for me. It sent warmth through my heart.

I smiled. "That was fast."

"You missed me?"

"Well... uh... sure, but that's because there was something I wanted to say to you before the meeting."

His brows rose. This sounded serious. Curious, he pulled a chair next to mine. "What is it?" He sat down, filling the space with his warm presence and clean scent.

My brain malfunctioned, and I couldn't remember what I was going to say. How did he do that? Just having him close made me a bumbling idiot. Ugh.

"Is this about the dead bodies in the crematorium?" he asked.

"Uh... no. It's something else. I was just..." I glanced away. "Well... I just wanted to tell you that it's okay if you need to yell at me..." I dared to catch his gaze. "...for doing something stupid. I can take it."

"Why would I do that?"

"Because I can be an idiot, and it probably drives you crazy." He still didn't answer, so I continued. "You know how I do stupid things, like try to take on a killer alone, and you have to come to my... aid." Aid sounded better than 'rescue,' so I went with that. "You never have a chance to chew me out, so I thought it might be helpful to get it off your chest."

"You mean, right now?" At my shrug, he narrowed his eyes. "How would that help, exactly?" He was thinking that no amount of yelling was going to change the fact that I got into trouble without even trying. I also wasn't someone who changed my mind once I set it on something.

"That's not true. I change my mind all the time."

He let out of huff. "Okay... but I still don't understand why I should yell at you now."

"Well... yesterday, after I got on the elevator, it seemed like you wanted to yell at me for getting into trouble... so I thought that it might help you feel better if you did, that's all."

His lips quirked up, but he smoothed them out and nodded. "I see. Well... I guess you're right, I did think about yelling at you, but I didn't like the odds."

"Huh? What odds?"

He leaned toward me, his voice low and sultry. "That we could kiss and make up... but if that's where you're going with this, I'm all in."

My breath hitched, and my mouth dropped open. The ding of the elevator sounded, startling me. I jumped to my feet, sending my chair rolling. Off balance, I stepped back and tripped over a power cord.

As I went down, Ramos reached for me. He managed to snag my arm, but my falling weight pulled him off his chair and down to the floor. He managed to catch himself before completely crushing me under him. Still, his weight pinned me down, and mere inches separated his face from mine. Our gazes met, and his eyes darkened, sending my pulse racing.

"Uh... you two okay back there?"

I pulled my gaze from Ramos and glanced over his shoulder to find both Ian and Stewart leaning over the desk to study us. Stewart's lips twisted, and he coughed to cover a laugh, thinking that was the funniest thing he'd seen in a long time.

"Uh... yeah. I just tripped." I glanced back at Ramos, who seemed quite content to stay where he was. With clenched teeth, I pushed at his chest. "You can get up now."

A slow smile spread across his face before he finally moved off me. Getting to his feet, he held out a hand to help me up. After pulling me to my feet, we stood toe-to-toe in the tight space, and I couldn't get around him.

Taking his time, Ramos picked up his chair and carried it out of the way.

Letting out a breath, I faced the men and pushed my unruly hair from my eyes. "Hello. We're... uh... meeting in the conference room. It's just through there." Trying to smile, I swept my arm toward the door. "Go on in, and I'll let Uncle Joey know you're here."

Ian took in my embarrassed flush and held back his amusement. What was going on? Were Ramos and I a thing? I was a beautiful woman, and the way my eyes flashed was alluring. As if hearing him, Ramos came to my side and directed a glare his way. With a start, Ian realized he'd been staring at me, and Stewart had already gone into the conference room without him.

Ian quickly stepped away, and I caught my breath. After he entered the conference room, I pinned Ramos with a glare. "Well, that was embarrassing. And it was all your fault."

Ramos snickered, thinking I looked cute when I got rattled, and I should know it just made him want to tease me even more. "I'll get Manetto."

I opened my mouth to reply, but he was already halfway down the hall, so I shook my head instead. As I pushed Jackie's chair back toward the desk, it got caught on the offending cord, and I stooped down to fix it.

By the time I got things sorted, Uncle Joey and Ramos stood in front of the desk, waiting for me. "Everything okay back there?" Uncle Joey asked.

I listened real hard, but couldn't detect any sarcasm in his tone. "Yes, just a loose cord."

I straightened, smoothing my hair back and grabbing a notebook and pen. Uncle Joey nodded and stepped into the conference room. Ramos waited for me to go in first before he followed me inside.

We sat down at the table, and Uncle Joey spoke. "Gentlemen. Thank you for coming. I have the money order here for you, but I'd like you to look over something first." He explained the contract and gave them each a copy. "Take a minute to read through it."

As Ian scanned the document, his nostrils flared. What the hell? He'd never expected a formal contract like this. What was Manetto trying to prove? He got to the part about splitting the profits, if they found the gold, and blanched. Not only did Manetto want his twenty percent, but, once the mine surpassed five million dollars, he expected his share to increase to fifty percent.

"Why the increase from twenty to fifty percent?" Ian glanced at Uncle Joey with a scowl. "That's not what we agreed on."

"I'm a business man, Ian, so I look at the bigger picture. Finding the mine is only part of the process. Digging the gold out of the mine and taking it down the mountain will be costly. After that, the gold must be purified and refined.

"Then there's the matter of security. I have the means to pay for it all, which leaves you with the better deal. You must see that I need to be compensated for all of my expenses, and this is the most effective way to do that."

Ian shook his head, unhappy with the terms, but at a loss to know how to argue with Uncle Joey's reasoning.

Stewart was still reading through it, but he wasn't as bothered by that part. He'd seen working contracts like this before, and it wasn't anything out of the ordinary. He glanced at Uncle Joey. "I'd like a clause added about the future of this venture."

"I believe you'll find that on the next page," Uncle Joey replied.

Stewart turned the page and began reading about the terms of any future opportunities. "So this says that if nothing is found within two years from today, the contract is null and void, and our partnership is dissolved?"

"Yes, that's correct."

Stewart nodded and glanced at Ian, thinking that, if they found the mine, they could just wait a couple of years before actively pursuing it. He knew that Ian would hate waiting, but he hoped he'd agree once he explained why. He was greedy enough to go for it, but patience wasn't a virtue he possessed.

I picked up a thread of distaste toward Ian from Stewart. He'd never wanted his nephew's involvement in the mine, but, after his sister got wind of it, she'd insisted that Ian was worth his weight in gold, and Stewart would be paid ten times over for bringing him aboard.

Stewart had to admit that Ian had been helpful, but his flashes of underlying greed still unnerved him. But, in this one thing, Stewart was sure Ian would see the wisdom in waiting until after the two years were up. Manetto might think he could get away with such an outrageous contract, but there were ways around it. "Could you give us a moment to discuss this?"

"Of course."

The three of us left the conference room and waited by Jackie's desk. "What did you pick up?" Uncle Joey asked.

I told him about Stewart's plan to wait Uncle Joey out. "There's something else. It looks like Ian is Stewart's nephew, and he's a bit greedy."

"Good to know." Uncle Joey rubbed his chin. "Is Stewart still convinced that the mine is real?"

"Yeah... I guess. Why go to all this trouble if it's not?"

A few minutes later, Stewart opened the door. We followed him back inside to hear his verdict. Of course, I already knew they were going to take it. Ian hadn't been as hard to persuade as Stewart thought, and they were both eager to get back up the mountain.

"We will agree to the terms of this contract," Stewart said.

"Good. Then let's sign it." Uncle Joey glanced my way. "Shelby, will you be the witness?"

"Sure."

Uncle Joey pointed at the tabs with arrows on them, showing where each signature needed to be placed. A few minutes later, we were done. Uncle Joey gave them their copies of the contract and kept the other for himself.

He pulled a white envelope from his jacket pocket and handed it over to Stewart. "Here's my initial investment of fifty grand."

"Thank you." Stewart took the money, and it was easy for everyone to pick up his excitement.

"When will you be ready to go?"

Stewart turned to let Ian answer. "We should have everything ready by Monday. I know it's soon, but, with the weather turning, we don't want to wait. Will that work?" He glanced my way, knowing that I was supposed to go with them.

"Will we be back in time?" I asked Uncle Joey.

"Yes." Uncle Joey turned back to Ian. "What's the plan?"

Ian opened the briefcase he'd brought with him and spread some papers out on the table. He placed a map of the area on top of the others and pointed out some landmarks. "We've been using the cabin as a base camp, so we'll meet there." He explained that it was a two and a half hour drive from the city. "Shall we meet at the cabin by noon on Monday?"

I nodded. "Sure."

He went on to show us the areas they'd already been over and what they needed to concentrate on next. "We've staked out claims here, here, and here." He pointed at the map. "With an additional two more here and here."

My eyes widened. That was a lot of land to cover, but it was in the same area where I used to go prospecting with my grandpa, so at least we weren't that far off. Ian explained the places they'd already explored, which cut down the area by quite a bit.

Stewart let Ian take over the discussion, while he tried to see the map in a different light. He knew Taft's map of the area by heart, but he wondered if they'd misread it somehow. His gaze was drawn to an area he'd dismissed as being too far north. But what if he'd miscalculated? Wasn't there a small ravine along a ridge there?

He stepped to the map, ready to mark it with a pencil, but stopped. No need to give away his secret before he checked it out himself. A surge of excitement ran over him. Taft had said the mine was near a ridge, but the entrance was below it. That might be just the place they'd been looking for.

I stepped closer to the map to get a better look at the area Stewart had been thinking about. It was on the tip of my tongue to mention it, but I held back. What I really needed was a map of my own. "Could we have a copy of the map? I'd like to have my own to keep track of the places we go."

"Of course," Ian said. "I'll provide a map on Monday, and we'll go over the plan again then." He had no intention of giving me a copy of his map with all of his notations on it, but it was easy enough to buy a map of the area for me.

Stewart was thinking the same thing, even though he'd just signed a contract saying everything he found would be shared with us. He'd wait until we were gone to look in that direction. Then, if he found the mine, he wouldn't have to tell us.

With Ian in charge of buying all the food and supplies, including tents and sleeping bags, the only thing that I'd need was a daypack containing my personal items. At that point, Uncle Joey mentioned that Ramos would be joining us as well, so to add enough food for him, too.

Now was probably the best time to mention that Billie wanted to come along for the story. I didn't think they'd go for it, but it might keep Stewart and Ian honest, which I was beginning to doubt.

"There's one more thing." Everyone turned to me. "Uh, remember that reporter from the *Daily News* I was with? Billie Jo Payne? She'd like to come up for a day or two and do a piece for the paper. I told her I'd ask."

Their surprise turned to annoyance. How could I even ask? "Before you say no, I think it's a good idea. I'm sure she'd sign a contract, or agree to whatever kind of secrecy you want, but it would be nice to document it, especially if we find the mine. She'd be like a silent observer, with nothing to gain but a story."

I heard thoughts of *no* and *hell no* from everyone but Stewart. He actually considered it, thinking that having someone to keep me busy, and out of their way, could be a plus. It would be boring as hell for her, and two days of that would be enough to send her back to civilization. As a bonus, she might even take me with her.

"I'm happy to think about it," Stewart said, surprising everyone but me. "As long as she signs a non-disclosure agreement, limiting what she can report on, I'm okay with it."

Uncle Joey nodded. "I'll discuss it with Shelby and take care of the details. I'll get back to you later this afternoon." He wondered why in the world I'd want Billie to go, but he thought there must be a good reason, so he was willing to consider it.

After a final discussion about everything we needed, Ian and Stewart left directions to the cabin and hurried to the bank to cash the check.

With them gone, Uncle Joey and Ramos both turned to me. Uncle Joey raised his brows. "Why is Billie really coming?" The other question he didn't ask out loud was why hadn't I mentioned this earlier?

"That's a good question. But first, let me tell you what Stewart and Ian were thinking. It's kind of important." I explained everything I'd heard, including Stewart's idea of where the mine could actually be.

I continued with telling them why Stewart was amenable to Billie joining us. "He wants to keep me out of his way, and if I'm with her, that works. But he doesn't know Billie that well if he thinks she'll stay out of his way."

"What about you?" Uncle Joey said. "Why did you ask if she could come?"

"Well... that's another story. We just kind of talked about it at the beginning, and I thought it would be nice to have her along. But now that we know what Stewart's planning, it could work out better if she was there. I mean, he couldn't just get rid of me so easily with her as a witness."

"Get rid of you?" Ramos said. "What makes you think he'd want to do that?"

"I don't know. Maybe if I found the mine, and he wanted to keep it a secret?" I shrugged. "You know... something like that?"

Uncle Joey shook his head. I was certainly looking at all the angles and already thinking about how this could backfire. "Okay. Talk to her. If she's coming, I'll get Chris to come up with a non-disclosure for her to sign. Do you think she'll come?"

"It all depends on her editor. If he doesn't think it's a good story, he won't send her."

"Okay. Let me know right away. In the meantime, we've got to have everything ready to leave for Vegas in the morning. Why don't you give Jackie a call, and tell her you're stopping by?"

"Oh... yeah, sure."

He watched me expectantly, so I quickly pulled out my phone and put the call through. "Hey Jackie, it's Shelby. Can I stop by for a minute? There's something I need to tell you... yeah? Good. I'll be there in a few minutes."

I put my phone away and stood. "All right. I guess that means I'm going now. I'll let you know what Billie says."

Uncle Joey knew he'd pushed me into talking to Jackie, so he couldn't complain too much about Billie, even though he wanted to.

Ramos was thinking that I was getting in too deep, and something was bound to go wrong. Why would I ever think that having a nosy reporter along was a good idea? And now I was talking to Jackie? It was obvious that it was Manetto's idea. He must want me to read Jackie's mind and tell him what I found. That was just wrong. It crossed a line, and he thought I was better than that. Wasn't I her friend, too?

I opened my mouth to tell him I had no intention of doing that, but, with Uncle Joey standing there, I couldn't say a word. Still, it cut me to the quick that Ramos thought the worst of me. With my head down, I hurried out.

CHAPTER 6

I drove to Uncle Joey's house, wishing I could turn around and go home. Instead, I decided that I'd just have to keep my shields up, so I wouldn't be tempted to tell him anything. He never should have asked me to do this, so if anyone was to blame, it was him.

That still didn't get me off the hook. I should have just told him I wouldn't spy on Jackie for him. Now, here I was in this awful predicament. Why did I do things like this? Now I understood what Chris meant when he said I was too helpful. Not only that, but I was letting my power get the better of me. Just because I could listen in, didn't mean that I should.

Maybe I could start the conversation by leveling with Jackie. I could tell her that Uncle Joey was worried about her, and that's why I was there. I could encourage her to tell him what was bothering her, so I wasn't in the middle of it.

Yeah... that should work. If I happened to pick up anything I shouldn't, I'd just keep it to myself and let them work it out. That would work this time... and if Uncle Joey ever asked me to do something like this again, I'd tell him no.

I pulled into the circular driveway and got out of my car. My stomach churned, and I couldn't seem to step toward the house. Maybe I should just go? I could still back out and tell Uncle Joey I didn't feel right about it.

Before I could get back in my car, Jackie opened the front door. "Are you coming?"

"Oh... uh... yeah." Seeing her reminded me that we'd been through a lot together. We were friends, and there was nothing wrong with visiting her. In fact, I was concerned about her too, and talking to her was perfectly normal. Sure, she didn't know I could read minds, but she understood my premonitions just fine.

In fact, I suddenly wanted to tell her everything that was going on with me. She might be able to give me some inside advice on the poker tournament and Sonny's methods. And none of this had anything to do with Uncle Joey. We greeted each other with a quick hug.

"Let's go out back to the deck," she said. "It's real nice out there right now."

"Sounds good to me."

"You want a Diet Coke?"

"Yes. Thank you." I followed her into the kitchen, and she filled up a glass with ice before handing me a can of soda. "Thanks, this is great."

"Sure." She got one for herself, and we went through the French doors to the beautiful patio that overlooked her amazing backyard and swimming pool. She sat in a lounge chair, and I took the one beside her.

"Sitting out here is nice. No wonder you'd rather be here than at the office."

She nodded before glancing my way with a raised brow. "I imagine Joe sent you."

"Well... uh yeah, but I wanted to see how you're holding up, too. It must have been a real shock to see your ex like that."

She huffed out a breath. "Uh... yeah. It was like a punch to the stomach." She'd always known that running into Sonny was a possibility someday, but she'd never thought it would be here, on her own turf. "At least he had no idea I was here, so he hadn't tracked me down like I first thought."

"Oh. Yeah... that's good. It was probably quite a shock to him, too then."

"Yes... probably, but since he doesn't have a conscience it would be hard to tell."

"You know he's long gone now. So why haven't you come back to the office? You are coming back, right?"

She turned to me, and her face softened. "Yes. But just not yet. I need some time away from all that... you know?"

"Sure do. It's why I've been missing for the last few weeks. Now that I'm back, it's like I never left. But I know my time away helped... so it should help you, too." She nodded, but her lips thinned. Joe was trying so hard to give her some space, and she appreciated it. But she just wasn't ready to go back to the business.

Having Sonny show up at the office had unbalanced her, bringing back the past to settle over her heart like a black cloud. She'd thought she was over it, but now she couldn't get it out of her mind. The way he'd used and betrayed her hurt almost as badly now as it did all those years ago.

"You know what surprises me the most, is how much it still hurts." She shook her head and worked hard to tamp down the anger. "Now I'm afraid that Joe might kill him, and part of me would be okay with that. But if Joe got caught..." She sighed. "I don't want that to happen, either."

I nodded. "Makes sense to me."

"I can't tell Joe not to kill Sonny, even though I should." She caught my gaze. "I'll just have to leave that up to you." She trusted me to talk him into doing the right thing.

My lips thinned. If only it were that easy. "I'm working on it, but you know Uncle Joey and Ramos, they both want him dead. I'm hoping that winning the tournament will ruin Sonny. We know he owes someone big-time, and he needs that money to get out from under his obligations."

Jackie nodded. "Yeah... Joe mentioned something about that. Can you win?"

"Of course." I put conviction into my tone, even though I wasn't completely sure.

"Good." She took a sip of her drink. "Did Joe tell you what happened... with my brother's company?"

"Yes."

She took another sip of her drink before replying. "I knew they were breaking the law, but I ignored that gut feeling. I thought that denying it meant it wasn't happening. That was pretty stupid. Then Sonny made that deal with the feds. He told me he wouldn't go to jail if Bruce came out of hiding and took the fall for their crimes. But someone had to lure him out. That someone was me."

Guilt swamped her. "I couldn't tell Joe that I helped Sonny bring Bruce out. You know how important family is to Joe. I told Joe that Sonny lured him out... but I did it. I betrayed my own brother."

She glanced off into the distance, remembering the day Bruce got caught. "After Sonny got off so easily, I discovered that he'd drained all of the off-shore accounts, leaving Bruce with nothing to negotiate with. Instead of facing eight years by returning all the money from those accounts, Bruce got the maximum of forty years, which means he'll die in prison.

"Sonny should have gone to prison too, and all of that money should have gone back to the investors. To think he used it to buy a hotel and casino makes me sick."

"That's horrible," I agreed. "But I don't think Uncle Joey would blame you for anything that happened. He loves you, and he's worried about you. You should tell him everything. He can take it."

She nodded. "You're right, I should... and I will." She thought getting over the hurt would be easier if Sonny was dead, but she didn't want Joe or Ramos to risk getting caught. She couldn't bear to think of either of them ending up in prison because of her.

She leaned toward me. "Shelby... promise me that you'll do everything you can to keep them from killing Sonny. There's got to be a better solution. I'm sure there are plenty of other people that want Sonny dead. Joe needs to let one of them kill him."

"I couldn't agree more. I'll do my best. I promise."

"Thanks."

She sat back in her chair, thinking that her heart wasn't as heavy now that she'd spoken to me. "So tell me about this gold mine. Joe mentioned it last night. What's that all about?"

I spent the next few minutes telling her the story, including the fact that I'd invited Billie to come. Instead of thinking it was stupid of me to do that, she actually agreed.

"It makes sense to me," she said. "It would be nice to have another woman there. Have you talked to her yet?"

"No... but I need to." I checked the time, finding it close to noon. "I've got to go, but it's been good to chat. Thanks for the soda."

"Sure. I'm glad you stopped by, even if it was Joe's idea." She grinned. "I feel much better now."

"Good. Me too."

We left our chairs, and Jackie walked with me to the front door. "I almost wish I could watch you kick Sonny's ass, but I'll just have to hear about it when you get back." I smiled, and she gave me a quick hug before continuing. "Thanks Shelby... I know you'll do your best... with everything. Good luck."

I thanked her and hurried back to my car. It had been great talking to her, and I was glad I had, especially since it wasn't anything so bad that she and Uncle Joey couldn't figure it out together.

With my heart a little lighter, I pulled into the precinct parking lot twenty minutes early. It gave me time to call Billie, so I pulled out my phone and put the call through.

"Hey Shelby," she answered. "What's up?"

"I'm going prospecting." She squealed, and I had to pull the phone away from my ear. "You still want to come?"

"Of course! I need to ask Michael first, but I think he'll agree. When are you leaving?"

"Monday morning. It doesn't give you a lot of time... and there's something else." I took a breath before continuing. "You might have to sign a non-disclosure agreement. I know that sounds like it defeats the purpose of you coming, but it would mostly relate to the location of the mine... you know... stuff they want to keep secret? If you're still interested, they will have the agreement drawn up for you to look over. Can you let me know soon?"

"Sure. I'll talk to Michael right now and call you back."

"Great." We disconnected, and I headed into the station. As I spotted Dimples sitting at his desk, I realized that I'd just invited his wife to go prospecting with me. It could be dangerous, and he might not approve, especially if he knew the whole endeavor was backed by Uncle Joey.

Hmm... how was I going to tell him about that? Of course, if he knew Ramos would be there to watch over us, maybe it wouldn't be so bad... or... would that make it worse? I knew Chris might not like it, but, if Billie was there with me, he'd be okay, right? Or... maybe I just shouldn't tell him Ramos was coming?

Dimples glanced up, and I sent him a little wave.

"You made it." He stood, pulling his jacket off the back of his chair and shrugging into it. "The truck isn't far today. In fact, I think we can walk over. It's at the Galloway Center."

"Great. I could use the fresh air." The small park with shade trees and decorative benches sat beside a circular drive in the middle of the downtown district, only a block away. "Find out anything new with the case?"

"Not really. There doesn't seem to be any connection to former employers, and I found out from Barry that Troy only did odd jobs here and there before coming back to the mortuary. Barry didn't know more than that, and, if Troy got paid, it was probably in cash, so there are no records of who these people were."

"Dang... that's not helpful. Well... maybe we'll find out something at the food truck. By the way... how are your cat wounds?"

He shook his head. "You're not going to let me forget about that, are you?"

I snickered. "It's just that... every time I think about it, I burst out laughing." I chuckled, even though I tried not to. "I'm sorry... I don't mean to laugh so much. It's just... so funny."

"Yeah... I guess it's funny now, but feeling those sharp claws puncturing my skin was awful."

I winced and nodded, but still couldn't hold back a chuckle. "I'll bet. Did you tell Billie what happened?"

"I had to after she got a good look at the marks. She didn't laugh as much as you, but she still laughed pretty hard, only instead of captioning a police report, she made it into a headline."

"Oh yeah? What was it?"

He raised his hand to shoulder level and swept it to the right. "Missing Cat Mistakes Detective for Tree, Climbs to Safety."

Laughter bubbled out of me. "I love it." My phone began to play *here comes the bride*, the tune I'd made for Billie when she got married. "Oh... speak of the devil." This was the worst timing, but I had to answer now. "Hey Billie. What did he say?"

"Michael said yes!" Her enthusiasm was hard to miss. In fact, I was pretty sure Dimples had heard her voice. "But he only said I could go for a couple of days. I can come Monday and Tuesday, but I'll have to leave Tuesday night, or Wednesday morning at the latest. At least it will give me a taste of the experience. And, if you end up finding the mine after I leave, I want first dibs on the story."

"Of course. And you're okay with the non-disclosure agreement."

"Absolutely."

"Great. I'll let them know so they can get it ready for you."

Dimples stepped closer to get my attention, and his brows drew together. What was going on? I raised a finger. "Hey... I'm actually standing next to your husband. He's wondering what's going on, do you want to give him the news?"

"Uh... no. That's okay... you go ahead, but call me back with the details. What time do we need to leave on Monday?"

"Probably around eight in the morning."

"Okay... call me back."

She disconnected, leaving me with my mouth hanging open. Damn. I still held the phone to my ear, so I kept it there, to stall for more time, and risked a glance at Dimples. The scowl on his face wasn't as bad as the thoughts running through his mind.

He shifted his weight and glanced skyward. "I know she hung up, so you can stop pretending."

Oops. I put my phone away, but found it hard to talk.

He let out a breath and began to calm down. "Okay. What's going on?"

"Well…" I sent him my biggest smile. "You'll never guess what happened. You remember the press conference Billie and I went to? Well… I got invited to go prospecting with the professor and his crew. Naturally Billie wanted to come too, and Michael just gave her the okay. But it's only for Monday and Tuesday."

"Next week?" At my nod, Dimples rubbed his chin. "And who exactly is backing the venture?"

I swallowed. He was daring me to tell him it was Manetto, and that I'd orchestrated the whole thing. Since he had that right, how could I deny it? "Uh… yeah… that's mostly right, but it was Billie's idea to begin with… you know… to ask Uncle Joey?" I knew it wasn't nice to throw Billie under the bus like that, even if it was true.

He sputtered out a breath. "Okay. So what's the non-disclosure about?"

"Well, they can't have Billie telling everyone where the mine is, right?"

His eyes widened. "So they've found it?"

"No… but if we do find it, she can't tell anyone where it is. I don't think they'll want her to tell anyone where they're searching for it either, you know?"

Dimples sighed. "Yeah, yeah, I get it. So is there a whole crew going up there or what?"

"Uh... sort of. But we're keeping it small... you know... because no one wants the location to get out?"

"Sure." He wondered how I'd persuaded Manetto into backing the venture. And now I was taking Billie with me? "It's not going to be dangerous, is it?"

"I'm sure we'll be fine. Nobody's out to get anyone, and, if they were, I'd know... so it's all good. You don't have to worry about a thing."

He sent me a half-hearted nod, knowing how easily I managed to get into trouble. And now I was dragging Billie into it too. Between the two of us, we'd probably be okay; either that, or it was a recipe for disaster.

I tried not to be offended and motioned to the truck. "Uh... should we order lunch?" The line had thinned in front of us, and the woman at the window waited for us to order.

"Oh... right." He stepped up to the open window and ordered the mini two-slider combo of a pulled-pork and a cheeseburger slider with fries. I just ordered the cheeseburger with fries. After she wrote down our orders, Dimples asked her about Troy. "Hey... do you know Troy Hudson? He was friends with someone here. Was it you?"

She froze, staring at Dimples and taking in his suit coat and tie. "Who are you?"

"So you know him?"

She shook her head. "No. Your order will be ready in a minute. Pay at the next window." She motioned to the next person in line, but Dimples wouldn't budge. Exasperated, she spoke. "Look... you need to get out of the way."

Dimples held up his badge. "You want to come down to the station, or come out and chat?"

Letting out a big sigh, she stepped away from the window and spoke with someone behind her before returning. "My boss will come out once it slows down. Now please move."

Dimples stepped to the next window where an older woman stared him down. "That'll be seventeen eighty-five," she said.

He handed her a twenty and waited while she made the change. I picked up the unease she tried to hide behind her sullen expression. She wondered why the police were here, and did Alberto screw it up? She handed Dimples his change, and we stepped away.

Dimples motioned to a small, outdoor table and chairs nearby, and we sat down to wait. "Did you pick up anything?"

"Yeah. The older lady was wondering if Alberto had screwed up, and that's why we were there. That's all I got."

He nodded. "Let's hope he comes out to talk."

"Yeah. Hey... I'm going to make a quick phone call, but I'll be right back."

"Sure." Dimples nodded, thinking that I was probably calling my 'uncle.' Why did I even call Manetto that? It made no sense.

Stepping away, I quickly called Uncle Joey's cell. "Billie's coming, so you'd better have Chris write up the non-disclosure."

"Okay. What about Jackie? Did you speak to her?"

"Yeah. She's good. Hey... can I call you back in an hour or so? I'll explain everything then." He agreed, and we disconnected.

I hurried back to Dimples, and our wait stretched on and on. Several people, who'd been in line behind us, got their food before we did. Dimples was getting angry. A minute later, he'd had enough and stood to confront the worker. Before he took a step toward the truck, a man hurried out with a tray of food.

He caught sight of Dimples and marched over, placing our food on the table with a flourish. "So sorry for the delay. I had to wait for a break before I could step out. My daughter said you needed to speak with me. What's this about?"

Dimples motioned for him to sit down, and he slid into the bench across from us. "I'm Detective Harris, and this is my partner, Shelby Nichols. We're hoping you can help us with a case we're working on. We have reason to believe you know a man who was murdered not long ago, Troy Hudson?"

Shock rippled through him, but he kept his expression blank. "What makes you think I know him?" He kept a puzzled expression on his face, feeling a moment of panic. Troy was dead? Who would kill him?

I smiled to put him at ease. "You're Alberto, right?"

He pinned his gaze on me, and his eyes narrowed. "Yes. So?" He'd never used his name in his side business, so how did we know that? Troy was the only one who knew his name, and, if he was dead, he couldn't have told us.

"We know Troy used his crematorium for... uh... getting rid of bodies," I began. "We think you transported them to his mortuary in your truck, but this last time, something went wrong. Did you have a disagreement? Did he want out of the arrangement, so you killed him?"

"Of course not. I don't know what you're talking about, but I would never do such a thing." Alberto relaxed. If we thought he was behind it, we were fishing, and there was nothing to tie him to Troy's death. Troy made all the arrangements and he just followed instructions.

Hmm... now I'd have to try a different approach. "Okay... so let's say, hypothetically speaking, that you worked with Troy in a little side business he orchestrated, and the last delivery job you did is connected to Troy's death. Would you have any idea who that delivery was for? I think that person could be Troy's killer... so again, hypothetically speaking, who did Troy know who'd want him dead?"

Alberto shrugged. "I have no idea. If I were helping Troy in this so-called business, he knew the value of secrecy, and he would hardly tell me anything about it." He was thinking that Troy arranged everything so no one knew who anyone else was.

"Okay... so you know nothing about Troy's business— only that you were the pick-up and delivery guy?"

"I didn't do anything like that. I am just a food truck manager. I think you'd better eat your food before it gets cold."

"Sure... but one more thing. Do you know anyone who was close to Troy? Did he have a girlfriend?"

Alberto stood, thinking that Troy might have confided in his old girlfriend, Rayven. "Like I said, I don't know what you're talking about. I need to get back to work. Enjoy your meal."

"Thanks." I watched him walk away and turned to Dimples. "He was thinking that Troy's girlfriend might know something. Her name is Rayven spelled with a y... R-A-Y-V-E-N. That's weird, isn't it? That I picked up the spelling in his head?"

Dimples shrugged, not overly impressed. "I guess... anything else?"

"Alberto didn't exactly think it in so many words, but I got the impression from him that Troy was using the crematorium to pay off a debt of some kind. He owed someone a lot of money, and this was his way of getting out from under his debt."

"So—kind of what we were already thinking." Dimples pulled a slider from the bag and took a bite. After swallowing, he continued. "I guess we need to find this girlfriend, even though this is the first time we've heard of her." He checked his watch. "Hey... she might be at Troy's funeral. I think it started at one, so they should still be there. Let's go."

We rushed back to the precinct and took Dimples's car to the mortuary. Troy's service had already begun, so we slipped into the back of the room. There weren't many people, so I began to scan their thoughts, starting at the front with Barry's family.

His wife was there, along with several family members, none of whom had any idea who killed Troy. I picked up a few thoughts that Troy's death wasn't a surprise, given how wild he was. I moved on to a few other people until I came to a woman on the other side of the chairs opposite the family.

Her hair was so black that I knew she'd colored it, and it was pulled into several knots all over her head, with long strands left out to frame her face. I could only see her profile, but she had the whole goth look going for her with a whitened face and black eyeliner around her eyes. She was also completely dressed in black, even wearing black lace gloves on her hands. She had to be Rayven.

A wave of sorrow and grief, tinged with regret, radiated from her. She was thinking that Troy had gone too far this time, and he was a stupid idiot. Why hadn't he listened to her? Now he was dead.

I caught Dimples's gaze and motioned my head her way. He nodded, thinking that we'd wait to talk to her after the service. I nodded back and listened to her some more in case I could pick up anything else.

A few members of Troy's family sent her suspicious glances, and she grew uneasy. Maybe it was time to leave so she wouldn't have to talk to them.

"Get ready," I whispered to Dimples. "She's going to bolt." As soon as the service concluded, she hurried out a side door. We followed right behind her, and she sent a worried glance over her shoulder.

"Rayven, wait!" I called.

Shocked that I knew her name, she slowed to a stop. Taking in Dimples's attire, her eyes narrowed. Were we cops? We reached her before she could outrun us, and she gave us a haughty stare. "Do I know you?"

"We just need a few minutes to talk," Dimples said, showing her his badge. "We're looking into Troy's murder, and we were hoping you could help."

"I don't know anything. I can't help you." She began to walk away.

"Wait. We know what Troy was doing. He was trying to pay off a debt, but something happened, and he was murdered. Please. We want to find the person who did this."

She stopped and glanced around us, noting that we were still alone in the parking lot. "Look. I don't know a lot, only that he got in with some bad people. When they found out his brother had a mortuary business, they made a deal with him to get rid of a few bodies."

She shook her head. "If I tell you who they are, they'll come after me, and I can't risk it."

"If we track them down, are you sure they won't come after you anyway?" I asked.

Her gaze met mine before she pulled away. "I don't think so."

Since I'd already picked up a name from her mind, I had to warn her. "It's a vigilante group called The Punishers... right? They target people who've crossed them, and, with Redman in charge, they've gone off the rails. But it wasn't him who Troy dealt with... it was someone under him. Who was it? Jinx?"

She sucked in a breath. "How did you..." Glancing around, she stepped close to me. "Look... Jinx had clients of his own. Clients who wanted people dead without getting their hands dirty. It didn't have anything to do with Redman, so don't go poking around him, or we're all dead. All I know is that Troy owed Jinx, and something must have happened that Troy objected to, otherwise, he'd still be alive to do his bidding."

She stepped away. "You didn't hear any of this from me, got that?"

"Yes. Got it."

She whirled toward her car, swearing in her mind. Her fingers shook so badly, she could hardly get the car door unlocked. Without a backward glance, she pulled out of the parking lot and took off down the street.

"Holy hell," Dimples said. "I guess we got our answer."

I glanced his way, dread pooling in my stomach. "I think we just stumbled into a hornet's nest."

"Could be." Dimples led the way to his car, and we both got in.

After slipping on my seat belt, I turned his way. "Have you ever heard of them? The Punishers?"

"Yeah some, but I don't know much. They keep a pretty low profile. Some say they're assassins for hire, but I've also heard this Redman person deals with guns. Now it sounds like Jinx, whoever he is, is Troy's killer."

"Yeah. But why kill Troy? I'd imagine Troy was pretty useful to their business."

"True. Maybe he objected to his part in it?"

"But that doesn't make sense. Even if he'd finished paying off his debt, it seems like they would have compensated him for his services. It would be a nice side-business for him. So why object?"

Dimples shrugged. "Maybe Troy recognized the dead person, or maybe he was tired of working for Jinx and wanted out? Who knows?"

I nodded. "I think Jinx knows. Now we just need to track him down."

"That shouldn't be too hard, now that we know the gang we're dealing with. I'm going to check the police records for missing people around the time of Troy's death. Maybe one of them will be the body in the crematorium. At the same time, I'll try to find more information on Jinx. Maybe someone working in vice will know more. This is a great lead. Thanks Shelby. I think we're onto something."

"Good deal."

"While we're at it, maybe you could ask Manetto about Jinx, too? Or maybe Ramos would be better, although either of them would do."

"Yeah... Ramos would be the better person to ask, because if I went straight to Uncle Joey, you know what would happen, right?"

Dimples's brows drew together. "No. What?"

"You'd have to reciprocate. A favor for a favor. That's how it works. Are you ready to do that?"

"No way."

"That's what I thought."

"Okay... you've made your point... unless..." We pulled into the precinct parking lot, and he glanced my way, wondering if I'd already passed information to Manetto. Was it something I'd been doing all along?

I drew in a sharp breath. "What? How can you say that? Of course I wouldn't do that."

He closed his eyes, regret rolling through him. "I'm sorry, Shelby. I didn't mean it like that."

I met his gaze, but I couldn't hold it for long, mostly because there had been a few times when I'd done exactly that. But it was because Uncle Joey was innocent, so I didn't feel too bad about it. "It's okay. I don't blame you for wondering." I pulled on my door handle to get out, but Dimples grabbed my arm to stop me.

He dropped his hand. "Why do you call him your Uncle? You never told me, and I've always wondered." I shook my head, and he continued. "I'd like to know."

I let out a sigh. "Okay, but you're not going to like it."

He shrugged. "We're partners Shelby, you can trust me."

I searched his gaze and knew he meant it. Taking a breath, I began. "Well... it all goes back to the beginning. Do you remember Kate Cohen? She was the lawyer who worked with Chris at his firm?"

At his nod, I continued. "Well, she's the reason I got involved with Manetto in the first place. She called him Uncle Joey, so I called him that too, mostly to bug him. Anyway... it became a habit until now it's like... the truth. You know the saying... the road to hell is paved with good intentions; then, before you know it, you're in too deep to ever get out."

He shook his head. "Uh... I think you've got some of that mixed up. I mean the last part doesn't normally go with the first part."

"Yeah... you're probably right, but you get the gist of it." I raised my gaze to his and caught his lips twitching. I smiled back. "I really am trying to do the best I can. You know that, right?"

"Of course. I get that you're in a tough spot." He understood the fine line I was walking, and he appreciated that I cared enough to help him at all. He just wished I didn't care so much about Manetto. But he could understand it. Hell, he'd been around Manetto enough to be on a first-name basis with the mob boss himself. Who would have thought that would ever happen?

"See what I mean? You're not so different."

His eyes widened. "Uh... yes I am."

I sighed. He was right. "Okay... that's probably true. Anyways... I'd better get going."

"Wait. So this whole prospecting thing... when are you going... and who's going with you besides Billie?"

"There's Dr. Stewart, his nephew, Ian Smith, me, and Billie. I think Uncle Joey's sending a few other guys for protection... so probably Ramos and maybe someone else. I'm sure Billie and I will stick together with our own tent and everything."

Dimples shook his head, inwardly sighing. Even though he'd told me he didn't mind that I called Manetto my uncle, it still made him wince inside. He sucked in a breath, knowing I'd just heard that. "Sorry... I'll try and get over it."

"It's okay. I'll try not to call him that in front of you."

He shook his head before catching my gaze. "No... just... forgetaboudid."

His mob accent was so bad that I couldn't help laughing. "Okay." I climbed out of the car and sent him a smile. "See ya."

"Thanks for your help. Hey... could you come to the station tomorrow if I bring in Jinx?"

"You think you can find him that fast?"

"Probably not, but with you gone next week, I'll have to try."

I pursed my lips. "Well... I can't come in tomorrow. I'm going out of town, but I'll be back on Sunday."

"Oh? Where are you going? Some place fun?"

"I'm not sure how much fun it will be. I'm headed to Las Vegas to play in a high-stakes poker tournament."

His mouth dropped open, and I realized I should have kept my mouth shut. Now he'd want to know all the details, and it wasn't a good idea to mix my two worlds together. Damn... why did I do these things?

He opened his mouth to ask who I was going with, but decided it was better not to know. Still, he was having a hard time wrapping his head around me playing in a poker tournament... in Las Vegas of all places.

When did I start playing poker? Reading minds probably had something to do with it... along with Manetto. He shook his head. Would I ever learn my lesson? Or... maybe he didn't want to know.

"I'm sure I can help you next week, after I get back from prospecting. I might even come back with Billie Tuesday night. You never know."

He just stared at me, thinking I had to be joking. I was probably just saying that to make him feel better. "Okay... let me know... and... uh... maybe I'll see you Monday morning before you and Billie take off."

"Yeah, maybe so. I don't know all the details yet, but I'm sure we'll have it figured it out by then."

"Okay. Well... good luck with the poker tournament."

"Thanks. See ya."

Poor Dimples. He had no idea how complicated my life was. I knew it was better that he didn't know more about my involvement with Uncle Joey, since it might put him in a tough spot. But lately, he seemed to accept it more. At least he wasn't telling me how to take Uncle Joey down.

I sighed. It was a balancing act, and I hoped that someday it didn't come between us, because if I wasn't careful, it could easily ruin our partnership.

CHAPTER 7

There was a lot to prepare before I left in the morning. Not only did I need to get ready for my trip to Vegas, but I also had to get everything settled before I left on Monday morning to go prospecting.

But before I did anything else, I needed to talk to Uncle Joey about the details of the trip and settle things about Jackie. With apprehension, I put the call through, and we exchanged pleasantries before he got right to the point.

"So what's going on with Jackie?" he asked. "Anything I need to know?"

"Uh... well, she is keeping something from you, but it's not a big deal. You should talk to her."

"I've tried. Why do you think I sent you? I think she lied to me about something, and now she won't come clean."

Needing to be diplomatic, I took a calming breath. "Look... you and I both know that she loves you, so if she's not telling you everything, it's probably because she's worried that she'll disappoint you. You're kind of a... well... a hard man to please... not that that's bad, but you do have certain expectations that can make it hard for someone to tell you something they think will upset you... you know?"

I waited for his response, but he didn't say anything. It made me nervous, so I continued. "But she wants to tell you, so just give her a chance. Okay?"

He let out a sigh. "You're right. I'll try not to be such a hard-ass."

A smile tilted my lips, and I was grateful he couldn't see it. "That should do the trick." Oops... did I just say that out loud? "So... where are we meeting in the morning? Should I drive to Thrasher?"

"No. I'll send a car to pick you up at seven-thirty sharp."

"Oh... okay. Thanks. Anything else I need to know?"

"Yes. Pack an overnight bag, and make sure to bring a couple of nice dresses. This is a formal affair, and you need to look the part."

"Okay, I can do that."

"Good. See you in the morning." He disconnected, and I worried that I may have hurt his feelings. Oh well... at least he didn't insist I tell him Jackie's secret, so that was a win, right?

After several calls to work things out for my kids' schedule, I had recruited my best friend, Holly, for most of the stuff Chris couldn't do, along with my mom as a back-up, in case the kids needed her.

Telling Holly about my trip to Vegas was a lot easier than telling my mom. By now, my mom was getting used to all the trips I took, but going to Vegas to play in a poker tournament was not something she'd expected. "And you'll only be there for the tournament?" she asked.

"Yes. Then I'm coming right back, but Chris and the kids will be fine for the weekend. It's next week that I might need your help."

"Why? What's going on next week?"

I explained the news of the Lost Taft Mine, and the opportunity I had to go prospecting with the group. I included that Billie was going too, so she'd feel better about it. "You remember how I used to go up there with Grandpa, right? When the opportunity came along, I couldn't pass it up."

She sighed. "Yes... it was always a dream of his to find that goldmine, and I can understand the pull to go, but I think it was an excuse for him to get away from everything for a few days. Do you really think there's a chance you'll find it?"

"Well, Dr. Stewart has Jeremiah's journal, so that will narrow it down, but I'm not holding my breath. Anyway, I'll only be gone for two or three days, so it's not a big deal."

"Sure, dear." She paused, and I could imagine her resignation that my life was one adventure after another. She wasn't always happy about it, but she'd learned to accept it. "I'm sure Chris can handle most everything, but if the kids need me, I'll be happy to help. You just be careful. It's easy to get lost up there."

"I will. Thanks, Mom."

With those things taken care of, I packed an overnight bag with the essentials, along with two of my favorite dresses. I hated the thought of playing poker all dressed up, but I didn't have a choice. Still, I decided that, if I ever had to play in a poker tournament again, I'd specify that I could wear whatever the heck I wanted.

I figured that, with Chris drawing up the non-disclosure agreement for Billie, he probably already knew I was going prospecting by now, so that would make it easier to tell him my plans.

My kids didn't seem too bothered that I was leaving for a day or two. They thought heading to Las Vegas in Uncle Joey's private jet was pretty awesome. As long as nothing bad happened to me, but, since I was with Uncle Joey, they trusted that I'd be fine. He was a big, bad, scary dude who no one dared cross... so they wouldn't worry.

Hmm... should I be worried they thought that? I shook my head. As long as they weren't worried about me, I should count it on the plus side, right?

Out of everyone, Coco surprised me the most. He picked up my anxiety and kept sniffing at my bag. Once I had it packed, and placed by the door, he sat beside it and woofed *you go?*

I knelt down beside him. "Yes. I have to go, but it's just for a little while and I'll be back."

He whined *I come.*

I let out a breath. "Sorry, buddy, but you have to stay here so you can watch over Josh and Savannah while I'm gone."

He let out a moan and lay down beside my luggage. Placing his head on his paws, his eyes took on a mournful look that melted my heart and sent guilt into the pit of my stomach. Damn... that was not fair. "I'll be fine, Coco. I promise. I'll be back before you know it."

He sat up and woofed *back you come?*

"Yes. I'll come back. How about we go for a walk?" He woofed *yup*, and the tension drained from my shoulders. I didn't have time for a walk, but did that matter? Nope. I cared about my dog, and this was the best way to prove it.

The next morning came too fast. Wearing comfy jeans, a t-shirt, and a hoodie, I stood beside the door, waiting for my ride to show up. Chris got up to say goodbye, and Coco stuck to me like glue. "He's not happy I'm leaving."

"I understand that." Chris ruffled Coco's fur, knowing exactly how the dog felt. "Don't worry, buddy, she'll be back."

The car pulled up, and I gave Chris a quick kiss and a tight hug. "I'll call you when I get there."

"Okay. I love you. Be careful... and try to stay out of trouble."

"I will. Love you."

I picked up my bag and opened the door, closing it on the sound of Coco's whine. There weren't words to describe what that whine meant, but it came across as a feeling of sorrow that I was leaving him. I shook my head. It didn't make sense. I left him every day to go to work, so why was this different?

Did he have a sixth sense that something bad was going to happen? No... of course not. It had to be the bag that did it. So how was I going to handle leaving on Monday to go prospecting? I'd have to put my pack in the car, when he wasn't watching, and just pretend like it was another day at work.

Hey... maybe I could take Coco with me? It might be nice to have him around. On the other hand, I didn't want him to get in the way or make a mess of things. Still, it wouldn't hurt to ask.

Surprising me, Uncle Joey stepped out of the car and popped the trunk for my bag. I got into the back seat and found that Jackie was driving. "Oh... hey Jackie. Are you coming after all?"

"No. I'm just taking you guys to the airport to see you off." It was Uncle Joey she really wanted to see off, but knowing that didn't bother me.

He slid into the car and sent me a smile.

"Where's Ramos?"

"He's meeting us there." Uncle Joey buckled his seatbelt, and Jackie began the drive to the private airstrip. Several minutes later, she pulled into the cargo bay that held Uncle Joey's private jet. As we retrieved our luggage, Ramos pulled up on his motorcycle with a small bag strapped on behind him.

I got out of the car, and Jackie stepped to my side, stopping me before I boarded the plane. "Good luck, Shelby... and... don't forget your promise." Since Uncle Joey still wanted Sonny dead, she knew it was up to me to stop him if I could.

"Thanks Jackie. I won't."

She nodded and hurried to Uncle Joey's side, giving him a hug and a kiss goodbye. I tried not to eavesdrop, but I picked up enough to know that she'd told him everything, and it had brought them closer together. I couldn't help the smile that widened my lips.

Ramos came to my side, wondering what I was smiling about. "Them." I motioned my head toward the couple. "Don't worry, I didn't tell Uncle Joey anything that Jackie was thinking. They worked it out themselves, so I didn't cross a line."

Ramos sent me a nod, knowing that I'd picked up his disapproval yesterday. Still, hadn't I told him he could yell at me anytime he wanted? He raised a brow. He hadn't voiced his disapproval out loud, but, since I could hear it anyway, it should still count. Now came the true test... were we going to kiss and make-up?

"That's not... you are so full of... argh."

His smile widened and he shrugged, thinking it didn't hurt to try. "After you." I boarded the plane, and he followed behind.

This was the fourth or fifth time I'd been on the jet, and it still boggled my mind to be part of the jet-set. The six-seater had four seats facing each other, with two in the back facing forward. Ramos sat facing me, his back to the front of the plane, and Uncle Joey took the seat across the aisle from me.

After take-off, Ramos lowered the small table between us and pulled out a deck of cards. "I thought you might want to brush up on your poker skills."

"Oh my gosh! That's right." For some reason, I'd forgotten all about actually playing poker, and now panic washed over me.

We spent the whole flight playing Texas Hold'em, and it took nearly that long for me to get the winning hands straight in my head again. It was hard to believe I'd forgotten so much of the strategy, and I was grateful for the opportunity to brush up on my skills.

On the plus side, playing so many games kept me from checking the time. That's why it came as a surprise to hear the pilot tell us we were ready to land at a private airstrip just north of Las Vegas.

My stomach cramped with sudden anxiety to know that, in a couple of hours, I'd be playing for a ten-million-dollar jackpot against a ruthless conman. Could I really do this? "I'm not sure I'm ready."

Ramos glanced at me, noting my deer-in-the-headlights expression. "Yes you are. You'll do great."

I took a deep breath and slowly let it out, but it didn't help much. Uncle Joey nodded. "He's right. You're ready."

Uncle Joey had joined the poker game during the last half hour, and I'd easily trounced him. "And we'll be with you the entire time." He thought about Ricky and the information he'd gleaned from Jackie's friend. It cast a new light on the whole deal.

"Why? What did Ricky find out?"

Uncle Joey frowned. "It's a bit of a mystery, but I'm sure with your talents, you can uncover the details when the time comes."

"What details?"

He hadn't wanted to tell me everything since it would only add to my anxiety, but now there was no holding it back. "It sounds like Sonny's involved with a man known as "The Debt Collector." He's a shadowy figure who has financed a lot of the prominent real-estate development along the Las Vegas Strip. He's been at it over the course of several years, but no one really took notice until recently.

"Now it sounds like he's in town to collect on his loans, and Sonny's hotel and casino are on the line. I wish I knew more about him—like why he targeted Sonny in the first place—but Ricky hit a wall. No one wants to talk, and, from what Ricky could gather, his identity and motives are a well-kept secret."

A chill ran down my spine. "That's kind of creepy."

Uncle Joey nodded, thinking this was the first time he'd heard of the man, which was unusual, since he liked to keep informed of the movers and shakers out there. For the first time in his long career, he felt a wave of unease telling him that this might be the one person he needed to avoid.

Unfortunately, playing in Sonny's tournament would shine a light on me, and he almost regretted it. Almost... but if it kept Sonny from winning, it was worth it. Maybe this 'Debt Collector' would take care of Sonny, and he wouldn't have to kill him after all.

I nodded, but refrained from agreeing out loud, a little shocked that there was anyone who could intimidate Uncle Joey. The jet touched down and taxied to the hangar where it came to a stop. The pilot told us we were safe to disembark, and I gathered my things before following Uncle Joey to the exit.

I caught sight of Ricky standing beside a limo, just as the heat hit me square in the face, taking me by surprise. I'd totally forgotten that it would be so hot here. At least I wouldn't be spending any time outdoors, with the tournament starting so soon.

Just thinking about that, coupled with knowing a sinister figure lurked in the shadows, sent my pulse racing. What was I doing here? Could I really pull this off? What if I didn't and Uncle Joey decided to kill Sonny after all?

"Don't worry, Shelby," Ramos said, stepping to my side. "I'll be with you every step of the way. You'll be fine. We'll get through this together."

I sent him a grateful smile. "How did you know I was so worried?"

He smirked. "We've been through enough that I can tell when you're freaked out. You have a nasty habit of chewing on your bottom lip. It's downright disgusting."

A spurt of laughter bubbled out of me. "It is not."

He tipped his head. "Just don't do it while you're playing poker. It's a dead give-away."

"I never do that." At his raised brows, I frowned. "I do? Really?"

His exaggerated nod let me know he was teasing me... mostly.

"I should have brought my sunglasses just for the heck of it. Remember when Carson did that in Orlando?"

"Oh yeah. When you beat him..." He shook his head and let out a big sigh. "It was an unforgettable moment. One of the best moments ever."

"Yeah. It was. Too bad he was such a bad sport about it."

"Don't think about that part. Just remember that feeling, because it's going to happen again." Ramos sent me his sexy smile, and my heart melted a little. He was here by my side.

He cared about me, and he had my back, so nothing was going to go wrong. And... even if it did, we'd get through it.

"Thanks Romeo."

He barked out a laugh and opened the door to the limo. Ricky and Uncle Joey had been talking, and slid in beside us.

"Hey Shelby, Ramos." Ricky nodded at us and turned to Uncle Joey. "Sonny has rooms for everyone at his hotel, so we'll head there. I didn't know how long you wanted to stay, or if you even planned on staying at his hotel overnight, but the rooms are available for as long as you want them."

Uncle Joey nodded. "We'll use them during the tournament, but if we end up staying the night, I'd rather go somewhere else. I'm hoping that after Shelby wins the tournament, we can fly straight back. It will probably be early morning before we get home, but I don't want to spend more time here than we have to."

That sounded good to me, and I couldn't pick up anything about Uncle Joey wanting to kill Sonny, so that eased a lot of the tension in my chest. I glanced out the window to take in the sights of this famous desert town. Soon, we were driving down the Las Vegas Strip, with all the flashing lights and amazing landmark hotels and casinos.

Even this early in the day, the street teemed with people from all over the world. Our driver slowed before turning into the circular drive of the Mojavi Desert Hotel and Casino. Three tall towers included the large hotel, with the casino portion situated on the main level.

"Here we are," Ricky said, opening his door. We had all packed lightly, so it only took a moment to get our bags and hurry inside out of the heat. Ricky led us to the concierge desk and got us checked in. Before we could head to our rooms, a beefy man in a dark suit approached Uncle Joey.

Ramos stepped to Uncle Joey's side in a protective manner, and the man hesitated. "Mr. Manetto. I'm Grant Ellington, Mr. Dixon's personal assistant. I'm here to offer you any assistance that you might require to make sure you have a pleasurable stay with us. May I take you to your suite of rooms? Mr. Dixon has reserved his best suite for you." He glanced at the rest of us. "And your team as well."

"Certainly."

Grant snapped his fingers, and a hotel worker in a smart uniform hurried toward us with a luggage carrier. He took our bags and rolled the carrier toward the elevators. After depositing us on the fifth floor, he led us to the end of the long hallway with a set of dark wooden double-doors. Using Uncle Joey's key card, the attendant briskly opened the doors, holding them as we stepped inside the suite.

Grant followed us inside, pointing out the amenities and the large space which featured a small kitchenette, living room area, entertainment center, and three bedrooms. The main room had floor-to-ceiling windows overlooking the Strip. One master bedroom took up the east end of the floor, with two smaller bedrooms on the west side, each with their own personal bathrooms and closets.

Before he left, Grant sent Uncle Joey a smooth smile. "Mr. Dixon would like to greet you before the tournament begins." He checked his watch. "I'd be happy to escort you to his office."

"Of course. Give me a minute, and I'll be right out." Uncle Joey motioned toward the door, and Grant nodded before stepping into the hall. After the door shut behind him, Uncle Joey turned toward me. "I imagine Sonny wants his entrance fee."

"Yes... I'm sure you're right." I'd picked it up from Grant's mind, but I had to be careful with Ricky standing there, so I kept it vague.

Uncle Joey turned to Ricky. "Did you find out anything else since the last time we spoke?"

He shook his head. "No. But you're the last participant to arrive. Most everyone else came last night or the day before."

Uncle Joey nodded and glanced my way. He needed to change his clothes before the tournament, but he wanted to visit Sonny first. "Shelby... why don't you take the master bedroom?" He motioned toward the room, and I opened my mouth to protest, but he shook his head, cutting me off.

"I insist. While you get ready, the rest of us will pay Sonny a visit. We shouldn't be long." At my nod, he motioned for Ramos and Ricky to follow him out into the hall, leaving me on my own.

I breathed out a sigh after they left and tried to relax. The huge suite enclosed this corner of the building, and I eagerly stepped into the master bedroom to see what wonders it held. A king-size bed, covered in a downy white quilt and several pillows, was centered between matching nightstands on one side of the room.

A large bathroom, with a separate shower, toilet, and bathtub, along with a bathroom vanity holding two sinks beneath a mirror, took up the space opposite the bed. An enormous walk-in closet was located on the other side of the bathroom.

The room was painted a deep turquoise with white casing along the doorframes and decorative crown molding at the ceiling. Luxurious, deeper turquoise carpeting covered the floors, and desert watercolor paintings, in shades of tan, brown, and blue, accented the walls. This room was amazing. I dropped down on the bed, sinking into the soft mattress.

Unable to resist, I put my feet up and laid my head on top of the fluffy pillows. Wow. Maybe it wouldn't be so bad if we stayed here overnight. I closed my eyes for a moment and let the silence wash over me.

Knowing it was time to get ready, I put a quick call through to Chris. "Hey honey. I'm here at the hotel and getting ready to play. How's it going at home?"

"Good. We're here with Lance Hobbs and training Coco... or... I should say he's training us."

"Did Savannah go with you?"

"Yes, she jumped at the chance, but Josh made sure she knew this was his thing. He's doing great, by the way."

I smiled. "He's really good with Coco."

"Yeah. It's fun to watch them."

"Good. Well... I've got to go. I'm a little nervous."

"You'll do great, and we're all rooting for you."

"Thanks honey." Hearing his voice helped calm me down. "The tournament will probably be over around two in the morning, and Uncle Joey wants to head straight back, so I'll be home sometime in the early morning."

Chris let out a breath. "That's good to hear. I'll leave a light on for you. Call me when you can."

"I will." We said our goodbyes and disconnected. Just knowing Chris and my kids would always be there grounded me in my crazy life, and I was so grateful to have them.

Now it was time to get down to business. Placing my bag on the bed, I unzipped it and pulled out my dresses. I'd start out wearing my black dress, and switch to my blue dress for the final round, since it was flashier, with sparkling rhinestones down the sleeves.

I hung the blue dress in the closet and took everything else into the bathroom to freshen up. Feeling a flutter in the pit of my stomach, I tamped it down and splashed water on my face. Pulling out my cosmetics bag, I spent some time on my makeup.

Satisfied, I worked on my hair for a few minutes before slipping on my dress. Next, I added my diamond necklace and earrings.

Hearing low voices in the other room, I finished up, adding red lipstick and making made sure none of it was on my teeth. I examined my reflection in the mirror with a critical eye and nodded. Yeah... I looked pretty good. For the final touch, I spritzed on my favorite perfume. Now I was ready.

I stepped into the main room and found that Uncle Joey and Ramos had both changed into dressier clothing. Uncle Joey wore a dark suit and tie, while Ramos rocked a black dress shirt and slacks. His top button was undone, and the sleeves of his shirt were rolled up.

It surprised me that he didn't wear a jacket so he could carry a gun, but I knew he had other weapons tucked away. Uncle Joey carried a knife as well, and I was sure Ricky had something like that too, although he wasn't here in the room with us.

"How'd it go?" I asked.

Both men turned to greet me, and Uncle Joey nodded appreciatively, happy to have such a beautiful niece. Ramos thought I looked amazing, and distracting enough to fluster the other players at my table. His slow smile sent a shiver of warmth over me, and I couldn't keep the silly grin off my face.

"As expected," Uncle Joey answered. "Sonny was cordial enough, but I'm interested to know what he's planning."

"He was happy enough to take the money," Ramos added. "But he's definitely got something up his sleeve. You should have seen the tournament rules."

Alarm skittered over me. "What rules? He's changing the game's playing rules?"

"No." Uncle Joey shook his head. "Not that. He's added a few of his own tournament rules to the mix that I've never seen before. Besides the 'no cheating' part, he's added that if anyone is late, sick, or otherwise unable to play at the specified time, they forfeit their spot and any claim to the jackpot."

"That seems a little extreme," I agreed. "So how are they running the tournament?"

"There are three rounds in the tournament," Uncle Joey explained, "with twelve tables and ten players at each table. Only one of the ten will advance to the second round. Those twelve winners will be divided into two tables with six players each. The final round is between the winners of those two tables for the ten-million-dollar jackpot."

"What about dinner and breaks?" I asked.

"Dinner will be served after the first round. I think they're having a buffet in another room. There are also regular breaks during the rounds, so at least that's positive. Are you ready? We certainly don't want to be late."

"Yeah... no kidding." With anxiety twisting my stomach into a knot, I picked up my small, clutch purse holding my essentials, which included my key card, phone, lipstick, and tissues.

Ramos stopped me. "Sorry, but the rules state that you can't take that. If you want, I can carry what you need in my pockets."

"Why? They're afraid I'll cheat?"

"Yes."

Frowning, I handed him my things, and they quickly disappeared into his pockets. Taking a deep breath to settle my nerves, I let it out and squared my shoulders. "All right. Let's go."

We took the elevator to the main floor and stepped toward a conference room with a sign near the door that read "First Annual Mojavi Desert Casino Poker Tournament." Grant stood near the door and greeted us warmly before ushering us inside.

We were directed to a desk where a woman took my name and handed me my seat assignment. I counted twelve oblong poker tables spread throughout the room, with chairs for ten players and the dealer chair in the middle of one side. I found my table at the very front of the room with only two empty seats left.

I glanced Ramos's way, and he nodded toward the seat beside the dealer, thinking that was a better spot because I'd be last to play the big blind, and the potential to deplete my chips right away wasn't as high. That seemed the least of my worries, but I sent him a nod and straightened my shoulders.

"We'll be sitting right over there," Ramos said, motioning to the chairs closest to my table. "Don't worry, Shelby. You can do this."

"Thanks." With my head held high, I quickly took the seat Ramos had indicated and glanced at the players surrounding the table. They were all men, which shouldn't have surprised me, and I picked up their sudden interest that I was playing in the tournament.

One of the men wondered if Sonny had placed me at his table as a distraction since he liked beautiful women. Without thinking, I sent him a smile, piquing his interest even further. As the time drew closer to begin, the last player finally slipped into his seat right before the closing call.

He studied each of the players going clockwise around the table, assigning us letters of the alphabet. Because I was last, I became the letter J. Since he was thinking like that, I decided to follow along, knowing this would also help me keep the players straight in my mind.

This player stood out from the rest because he had a razor-sharp focus I'd never encountered before. I zeroed in on his thoughts and noticed that his thinking seemed more organized and less cluttered than most.

Sonny stood nearby, dressed in a black suit and tie with a red shirt. He studied my table with a critical eye, so I focused on his thoughts. He was thinking that Sebastian had better come through for him. As a physicist, with that big brain of his, the probability for him to win was much higher than the rest of us, and he was counting on it.

That's why he'd placed Sebastian at my table for the first round. Eliminating me would send a message to Manetto and everyone there who'd heard the rumors about me and my 'psychic ability.' With Sebastian using his physicist brain and skills, he should have the upper hand.

Sonny didn't quite understand how Sebastian used those skills, but he'd seen him in action, and he was a force to be reckoned with, so it was worth a million or two... as long as he came through. If he didn't, he still had a couple of other players to take me on, but the odds weren't quite as high. Besides them, he had other options as well, so one way or another, he would win the tournament.

Wow... talk about stacking the odds. I studied Sebastian, hoping to figure him out. He must have felt me staring, because he quickly focused his attention on me, thinking about Sonny's warning. According to Sonny, I was his main competition because I was a psychic—whatever the hell that meant—and he planned to keep a close eye on me.

He wondered if my mind worked more like his. Did I model other players' behavior through their styles and tells like he did? It gave him more information and a definite advantage, so maybe that was it? However I did it, he looked forward to the challenge. He'd never met his match yet, and he didn't plan on losing now.

Holy hell! Could my mind-reading skills outweigh his big brain? I wasn't even sure I understood what he meant when he used the term 'modeling other players' behavior,' but I guessed I was about to find out.

Maybe by listening to his observations, I could use his expertise to be an even better poker player? It was worth a shot. Still, I couldn't help the extra layer of unease he brought to the table. By the time this tournament was over, I might not be able to think straight for weeks.

I hardly noticed Sonny giving his welcome speech, instead concentrating on all the observations Sebastian had begun to make about everyone at the table. After the dealer took his seat, Sonny announced that it was time for the games to begin.

The first few games hardly counted, as everyone took the measure of everyone else. I picked up Sebastian's thoughts that poker wasn't about the cards as much as the card players, since the probabilities of card combinations were too high to count.

He calculated that there were about one-hundred-thirty-three million combinations, and I had to admit that was a lot. I eagerly listened to his thoughts and did my best to keep up and learn. I realized I had it easier, because I knew right off the bat when a player was bluffing.

Still, after a while, his observations came pretty close to what I knew, and I could see how his brain created a model for each player that helped him determine how to place his bets.

He couldn't quite figure me out though, thinking that it didn't seem like I ever bluffed, but he couldn't tell for sure. Soon, it became quite clear to him that I really did have a sixth sense about things, and he began to sweat. I was good—no—better than anyone he'd ever played. What was my secret?

He noticed me rub my nose and watched me closely to determine what it meant. Was I finally bluffing? I couldn't help smiling since it only meant that my nose itched. I did chew on my bottom lip once, but as soon as he noticed it, I stopped.

So far, no one at my table had gone broke and left the tournament, but a couple of players' chips were getting low. I'd remained steady, and had begun to gain more chips, but so had Sebastian. After forty-five minutes, our first break was announced, and I sat back with relief.

That was intense, and I could feel the beginnings of a headache coming on. Still, my confidence had grown that I could hold my own against someone who was so mentally gifted.

I stood, needing to visit the restroom and ready for a Diet Coke. Glancing around, it surprised me that the room was so crowded. Where had all these people come from? Ramos came to my side and motioned toward the door.

"You're doing great," he said, tucking my arm into his. "But there's something you need to know."

He led me to the side of the room, away from the crush of people. "Ricky overheard a couple of the workers talking about you. He said it sounded like they had orders to watch you closely, and if Sonny gave the command, they were supposed to hinder your return to the tournament using whatever means necessary."

At my widened eyes, he continued. "That means you can't go anywhere without me."

"But... what if I have to use the restroom? Are you going to come in with me?" I was mostly teasing, but what did I know?

"I'll escort you there and back."

"Okay then, let's go. Hey... we could go to our room instead, if you think that's safer."

"No... it's too risky for now. When we have more time we will."

I nodded, and we stepped toward the restroom. Catching Ramos's arm, I glanced around to make sure we weren't overheard. "So you know that guy sitting at my table with the geeky glasses and wearing a striped, blue shirt?" Ramos nodded. "He's a physicist."

"So?"

"It means he's got mad skills at playing poker. Sonny hired him to beat me."

Ramos's brows rose. "How's that going for him?"

I shrugged. "Not too well, but it's great for me. I'm learning a lot about modeling the other players' behaviors to determine if they have a good hand or not."

His eyes narrowed. "But don't you already know whether they have a good hand?"

"Well... yeah, but... it's still pretty interesting."

He smiled, happy I was enjoying myself. We reached the restroom, and he planted his feet by the door.

Keeping a straight face, I caught his gaze. "Sure you don't want to come in?"

His soft growl and narrowed eyes surprised me, but that didn't stop me from snickering as I hurried inside. It wasn't as crowded as I would have thought, and I returned to his side only a few minutes later.

We started back toward the table, and I took his arm again. "How much time have we got left? I need a Diet Coke." The words had barely left my mouth when a server appeared by my side with a tray of drinks. Diet Coke wasn't one of them, but the server left, promising to come back with one.

Ramos's brows drew together. "Maybe you should just take a bottle of water that hasn't been opened."

"Oh man... really?"

He grinned. "Yes. Really. It's better for you anyway." At my widened eyes, he continued. "I'll get you a Coke on your next break."

I sighed. "Fine."

Ramos escorted me all the way back to my table, and I caught a few stray thoughts that he must be my bodyguard or something, especially after he came back with a cold bottle of water, which he opened before handing it to me.

I inclined my head as regally as I could. "Thank you."

He gave me a slight bow, and I heard *milady* from his mind. It was such a surprise that I nearly burst out laughing. Shaking my head, I took a few sips of water, realizing that it was just what I needed. I bent to set it on the floor, but the man beside me motioned to a cup-holder near my chips, and I thanked him.

The dealers rotated, and a new dealer sat beside me. She waited until everyone was seated before she began the next round, telling us that the big blind had now doubled. That meant that the games would move much faster, and I concentrated even harder to keep everyone's hands straight in my head.

A commotion came from the other end of the room. Everyone glanced up to watch the first losing player stalk from the room. I heard all kinds of swearing coming from his mind, and I knew I should get used to it. As soon as the doors shut behind him, the playing resumed.

The man whom Sebastian had dubbed "C" was the first to lose all his chips at our table, followed closely by "D." A few more players at the other tables followed suit, trimming the competitors down by a third. One more player left our table before the second break was called, and I gladly pushed back my chair.

I'd slipped my shoes off my feet, at some point, and leaned over to put them back on. As I stood, Ramos came to my side, holding a glass filled with sparkling diet soda. "Thanks." I took a few swallows before allowing him to lead me away. "Where are we going?"

"They're giving us half an hour this time, so I'm taking you up to our room."

"That sounds heavenly." I couldn't wait to lie down and put my feet up, even if it was only for a few minutes. "I wish I didn't have to wear these stupid heels and a dress. I think I should get hazard pay."

He chuckled. "You'll have to take it up with Manetto, but since you've already spent fifty grand of it, I don't think you'll get too far."

I sighed. "Maybe not."

Ramos used the key card and opened the door to our rooms. I stepped inside and hurried straight to the couch, kicking off my shoes and propping my feet up on the arm rest. "Where's Uncle Joey?"

"He's with Ricky. I'm not sure, but that guy he told us about... the 'Debt Collector'... might be watching the tournament. At least that's what Ricky overheard. Manetto decided to stay there and observe in case they figured out who he was."

I closed my eyes. "If I wasn't playing in the tournament, I could probably pick him out, but I'm already starting to get a headache."

"You want something for it?"

"Yes. I've got some pain reliever in my make-up bag in the bathroom."

Ramos hurried away, coming back with a couple of pills and another bottle of water since my soda was gone.

"Thanks." I took the pills and swallowed them down, sending him a saucy smile. "I kind of like having you wait on me."

He shook his head. "Don't get used to it."

I relaxed back onto the couch and closed my eyes. Ramos disappeared into his bedroom and emerged several minutes later. "There's about fifteen minutes left."

"Dang. I'd better use the bathroom while I'm here." In the bathroom, I saturated a washcloth with some cool water and held it to the back of my neck. Feeling slightly better, I freshened up my lipstick before joining Ramos.

As we stepped into the hallway, Ramos tensed. I glanced up to see a tall, beefy guy loitering near the elevator. "What's he thinking?" Ramos asked.

I listened closely and picked up that he'd been waiting for us. He didn't like having to face my bodyguard, but he thought he could sneak in a quick punch to my face before Ramos knew what was happening, then he planned to run like hell to the staircase.

I slowed my steps. "He's planning to punch me in the face and hopes to get away before you kill him."

Hot anger poured over Ramos. "When he makes his move, get behind me."

Swallowing, I nodded. The man kept his face averted as we neared him, trying to act like he hadn't noticed us. We came to a stop beside him, and he stepped closer to the doors and turned sideways so he had a better shot at me.

As the doors slid open, he stepped my way and struck out. Anticipating him, I'd already moved, and Ramos used the opening to hit him with a one-two punch in his stomach. As the man doubled over, Ramos sent an upper cut to his jaw, and the guy went down.

The elevator doors began to close, and Ramos stuck his arm inside, forcing them apart. Smiling at me, he inclined his head. "After you."

I chuckled nervously and stepped inside. After a cursory glance at the man, and finding him out cold, Ramos stepped over his legs and joined me.

"How's your hand?" I asked him.

He held it up. "Fine." He thought about how much he enjoyed his job. He loved the advantage my mind-reading skills gave him, and how satisfying it was to hit someone bent on hurting me. "Between the two of us, these guys don't stand a chance."

"Don't get cocky. They might try and sneak up on us."

He shook his head. "But you'll know, right?"

"I should."

The doors opened, and Ramos paused to glance my way. "Anything out there to get us?"

I listened real close, but didn't pick up a threat, and shook my head. Taking Ramos's arm, we stepped into the hotel lobby and through the crowd to the poker room with five minutes to spare. Ramos escorted me to my chair, and I sat down, ready to play. My headache was gone, and I had to admit that seeing Ramos punch that guy had given me a thrill.

I was wide awake and ready to go. I caught sight of Uncle Joey, and my euphoria vanished. Something was wrong, but he shut off his thoughts before I could figure out what it was.

CHAPTER 8

I took my seat at the table and settled in, pushing away my anxiety over Uncle Joey's worries. There wasn't a thing I could do about it now, so I focused on the game. The dealer took his place, but waited for Sonny to give the order to start the next game.

I glanced Sonny's way and found him talking earnestly to a tall man with dark hair and eyes that I'd noticed talking to him a few times before. Sonny was upset about something, and I picked up that the man, Dom, was trying to calm him down, telling Sonny that he had everything under control. Sonny finally nodded, and Dom straightened.

Sonny announced the beginning of the next round and Dom stayed close to his side, thinking he needed to keep Sonny from doing anything stupid. I lost track of him after that, since I had to focus on my game. At least we were down to seven players, so that made it easier for me to keep track of the cards.

After the flop, I had the winning hand, so I doubled the bet. Five of the players called to stay in with the other two folding. The turn revealed a card that wasn't the best, but I still had the winning hand so far, so I doubled the bet again.

Two more players folded, leaving me with Sebastian and players D and B. Sebastian watched me closely for a 'tell' so he could decide whether to stay or fold. If I was bluffing, he'd stay, but I was just too darn good to read, and his frustration rose.

The dealer played the river, giving me two pair aces high. Out of the remaining players, it was the winning hand, but I couldn't seem too eager with Sebastian watching my every twitch. I twisted my lips slightly before returning to my poker face and catching his gaze.

He saw the lip twist and decided I was bluffing. Working hard to keep my expression neutral, I not only called him, but doubled the bet. One of the players dropped out, but both Sebastian and the other man called. They both thought I was bluffing.

I flipped over my cards and waited. With frustration oozing out of them, they both threw their cards down, giving me the pot. With that game, I'd significantly reduced their chips, leaving me with more than enough to outlast everyone else.

Sebastian's nostrils flared, and he wondered if I was cheating. How could I be so consistent? It was like I knew what the cards were before they'd even been played. Was it really due to my psychic abilities? That was hard to believe, but he was losing to me. He never thought I could outwit him, but I was clearly the better player.

I did my best to keep my expression composed, but it was hard not to smile. The time passed quickly, and soon it came down to just me, Sebastian, and player B left at the table. My head was beginning to pound, and I could hardly wait for round one to be over. With Sebastian and B's chips getting low, I hoped it wouldn't take long.

As the dealer shuffled the cards for the next round, the announcer called for another break. A sigh escaped me, and I got to my feet. I spoke to Ramos and we visited the restroom. On my way back to the table, Ramos handed me a bottle of water.

"You've got this," he said, sending me an encouraging smile.

"Thanks." He ushered me to my seat and, after I sat down, he massaged my shoulders. I closed my eyes and couldn't help the sigh that escaped my lips. I picked up his thoughts that this was like a boxing match, and I was the million-dollar-baby. I chuckled.

Finishing up, he patted my shoulder, and I glanced up at him. "Thanks coach."

He leaned close to my ear and whispered. "Knock 'em dead."

Smiling, I took a few swallows of water, refreshed and ready to finish this.

A new dealer sat down, and the back of my neck prickled. He may have been dressed like the other dealers, but something about him was off. Besides being more nervous than he should be, his gaze kept flitting around the room, and I picked up that he hoped no one recognized him from his magic show.

I leaned forward and stared at him until he darted a glance my way. The skin around his eyes tightened slightly, and sweat broke out over his upper lip. Did I know who he was? Sonny had promised him that no one paid any attention to the dealers, so why was I staring?

With nimble fingers, he made a show of opening a fresh deck of cards and shuffled them several times. He deftly dealt them out with a nonchalance he didn't feel.

Why was he so nervous? I listened closely and picked up that, after the next round, he planned to switch the cards with the marked deck in his sock.

Since he'd know what every card was before he dealt it, he could easily make sure that Sebastian ended up with the best hand. With his skills, he'd also make sure to deal good cards to me and the other player, so we'd have good enough hands to bid, but not good enough to win. That way he could guarantee that Sebastian would come out on top, just how Sonny wanted.

What the freak? I had to make sure he never got that deck out of his sock. I played the round, dividing my attention between the dealer and the players. My hand was too good not to bet on, so I kept raising the bid. Both Sebastian and the other player folded, easily reading my aggression, so I didn't win many chips.

With the attention on me and my win, he decided to make his move. I quickly jumped to my feet and glared at him. "This dealer needs to be thrown out. He has a deck of marked cards hidden in his sock."

Everyone froze, staring at me with shock. Finally, both monitors converged on the guy. His mouth dropped open in protest, and he sputtered that I was lying and out to get him. Sonny motioned to Dom, who still stood beside him, to intervene. Dom rushed to my table and ordered the dealer to stand with his hands away from his sides.

Frisking him, Dom reached down to the dealer's socks, trying to decide if he should come up empty-handed so the dealer could stay. He felt the cards in the sock, but brushed over them. "I don't feel anything." He straightened to glare at me. "Are you sure?"

Without pulling my gaze from his, I nodded. "Yes. But since you can't find them, I'll ask my bodyguard to take a closer look. Ramos?"

Ramos stood, but before he made it to my side, Dom held up his hand. "That's not necessary. If you object to the dealer, we'll bring in someone else." He glanced at the dealer and motioned him out of the room.

As the dealer rushed out, Dom spoke in hushed tones to the monitor. Satisfied, he waved another attendant over, telling him to find another dealer. The attendant quickly left the room and came back a moment later with someone new. The monitor gave the new dealer a fresh deck of cards, and he sat down, ready to begin the next round.

I listened closely to this dealer and released a breath, grateful he had nothing up his sleeve. With that disaster averted, I turned my attention back to the game. Another couple of rounds passed and player B finally lost his chips, leaving me and Sebastian to duke it out.

My stack of chips easily doubled his, although he had a fair amount of his own. I won the next two games, and he got a little reckless on the third, but I understood because his cards were great. I folded after the flop, knowing I couldn't beat him, and his confidence returned.

During the next round, Sebastian noticed that I'd begun to chew on my bottom lip. Since I hadn't done that before, it had to be a sign of some sort. I didn't bluff much, but, with the end in sight, and the stakes so high, it made sense that I'd want to end it now. Bluffing would get me there if he fell for it.

He kept a close eye on me and bid me up. My first cards were equal to his, so I called his bet and waited to see what the flop held.

It didn't do either one of us any good, so I called him again. The turn was better for me, but I took my time to consider the bet, hoping to throw him off. I barely chewed on my bottom lip and doubled the bet, waiting to see if he'd call.

Watching my lips, he called to stay in the game, thinking he had a good enough hand to win, even without the river. My hand was better, but, depending on the river, it could still go either way. The dealer turned the final card, and I tried not to respond. It was just the card I needed to win the game, but if Sebastian saw it in my face, I knew he'd fold.

The play went to me to fold or bet, and I had to pretend that I wasn't sure I could win. Sebastian glanced my way, but I kept my gaze down and only slightly moved my lips. I glanced at him one more time before doubling the bet. If he called the bet, he'd have to go all in, and I wasn't sure if I'd fooled him or not.

He studied me, and I swallowed, hoping he'd fall for it. He glanced at his cards and was just about to pass, so I briefly chewed on my bottom lip. He caught the movement and let out a breath. It was just the sign he needed. His eyes brimmed with cold calculation, and he slid all of his chips into the pot.

"All in."

The crowd gasped, so I took a moment to savor the tension. With a tiny smile, I turned my cards over. A jolt of shock came from Sebastian, while the crowd began to clap. Amid the calls of congratulations, I heard Sebastian swearing in his mind. I'd outwitted him. How was it possible? He studied my face, thinking I was an anomaly. A glitch in the law of physics, and he'd never seen anything like it.

Once the shock subsided, he stood in awe and leaned across the table to offer me his hand. I swiftly stood and accepted his handshake. He didn't even think about Sonny being upset with him. More than anything, he wanted to ask me how I'd done it. He wanted to know everything there was to know about my psychic ability, because I'd made a believer out of him.

His questions rattled through his mind, running the gamut from quizzing me about when my abilities started, to asking how they manifested. Did I have a gut feeling, or had I seen it in a vision before it happened?

Broadening his mind with more possibilities, he wondered if I'd used my gift to change my future... or did my ability also help change another's future? How far and wide did my influence spread? To those I loved, or anyone within my vicinity?

I pulled my hand away, hoping to jar him back to the present. He blinked, realizing he'd been holding my hand way too long. "Uh... congratulations. I've never played anyone like you. It's a... phenomenon I never thought I'd see."

I smiled. "Thanks so much. You're a wonderful player yourself. I've learned a lot from you."

His eyes widened. "You have? In what way?"

I stepped away from the table, and he came to my side, curious to know what I had to say. "You're more observant than most. It's almost like you're looking for patterns. I mean... all of us look for other player's 'tells,' but you seem to do it better. Does that make sense?"

He tilted his head to the side and studied me. "It does when you know what I do."

He didn't continue, so I asked. "And what's that?"

"I'm a physicist." He watched me closely to see if giving me that information made his ability clearer.

I widened my eyes. "Okay... but I'm afraid I don't know how that would help you."

His shoulders fell. "That's okay. I'm just someone who's wired to look for probabilities and modeling. I usually do quite well at poker because it gives me a slight advantage."

I lifted my chin. "Oh. So you're like a card shark." I knew that was totally wrong, but I didn't want to give too much away. "Well, it was lovely to meet you. I hope Sonny's not too upset that you lost."

"Oh... he's—" Sebastian froze. "Wait... how did you know about my connection to Sonny?"

Oops, maybe I'd gone too far, but I didn't see the harm, so I shrugged. "Just a feeling. Am I right?"

His brow lifted. "Yes. You are." He shook his head and glanced at his feet before catching my gaze again. "Would you like to share a drink sometime? I'd love to get to know you better."

My jaw dropped, but I turned it into a smile, hoping he hadn't noticed. "Uh... maybe another time?" Ramos came to my side and glared at him.

Sebastian glanced between us and flushed. "Oh. Of course." He rubbed the back of his neck. "Well... good luck. I hope you win the tournament. It will make me feel better."

I chuckled. "Thanks. I'll do my best."

He walked away, catching sight of Sonny and totally unconcerned about the scowl on the man's face. Sonny wasn't out a dime, since he was only going to pay Sebastian if he won, and Sebastian was sure Sonny had made the same deal with other players on the floor. He doubted that they'd have any better luck, especially pitted against me, and he could hardly wait to come back to watch the final match.

I inhaled deeply, buoyed that he had such confidence in me. It would even be nice to talk to him sometime, just to see how his brain worked.

"That must have been the physicist," Ramos said.

"Yes. He was actually pretty nice."

"I could see that." He'd overheard the guy asking me to share a drink with him, and it surprised Ramos that I'd wanted to go.

"I did not." At his raised brows, I conceded that there was some truth to it. "Okay... maybe a little, but only because of his mind. His thought processes were fascinating."

Ramos shook his head, but refrained from rolling his eyes. "So what happened with that dealer?"

I lowered my voice. "He was some sort of a card shark magician, and he was just waiting for the right moment to grab his special deck of cards from his sock. Sonny hired him to make sure Sebastian won, so I had to stop him before he made the switch."

Anger swept over Ramos, along with a raging desire for revenge against Sonny. He'd like to use the man as a punching bag before Manetto plugged him full of holes.

"Uh... I get that, but let's see how the tournament goes first, okay?" He raised a brow, so I continued. "So, what's on the agenda? Is it time for dinner?" I hoped the mention of food would take Ramos's mind off killing Sonny, even if it only worked for a few minutes.

"Oh... yeah." He offered his arm and I took it, noticing that only three tables still had contestants playing at them.

"Are we going to eat at the buffet?"

"Yes. Manetto thought it would be fine, since they can't mess with your food there."

"That makes sense."

We found Uncle Joey talking with Terrence Chatwin just inside the dining room. This was the first time I'd seen Chatwin, and I picked up that he was enjoying himself. Even though his player had lost, he'd loved watching me play, thinking that I was in a league of my own.

As we approached them, Uncle Joey excused himself and came toward us. "Nicely done, Shelby. Even Chatwin was singing your praises. I can't wait to hear about the game, but let's get some food first."

After we loaded our plates, we found an empty table and sat down. Between bites, I told him all about the magician dealer. "Then there was the last guy. Sebastian's a physicist, and Sonny hired him too. Did you know physicists' brains are wired to look at probabilities and modeling behavior?"

Uncle Joey raised his brows, so I told him all about it and how much it interested me. "There's something else you both need to know."

I quickly explained everything I'd heard from Sonny about the tournament, including the other people he had playing for him. "Sonny thought about a few other things he could do, but he wasn't real specific, so, besides the card shark, and Sebastian, I don't know what they are."

Ramos nodded. "It was probably the guy upstairs by our room who tried to attack you."

"Oh yeah." I glanced at Uncle Joey. "Did Ramos tell you about that?"

"Yes he did." Uncle Joey shook his head. "Sonny needs to go." He wished he could take care of it himself, but not after what Ricky had found out.

"What did Ricky find out?"

Uncle Joey's mind shuttered, and he caught my gaze, wishing that, just for once, I'd quit listening to him. "It's not something you need to worry about right now. I'll tell you later."

I nodded, but his worry squelched my appetite. What was so bad that he couldn't tell me now? "But... don't you think not telling me might be worse? What if it ruins my concentration?"

"Shelby..." He shook his head. "If I had something concrete to tell you, I would. For now, I just need you to focus on the tournament and kick Sonny's ass." He hoped that would take care of the problem, so I should trust him to do what he did best and take care of business.

"Oh... okay, you got it."

People had begun to leave, so we finished up our food. After a quick visit to the restroom, we hurried back to the poker tournament. Inside, the room had been rearranged. Instead of twelve poker tables, there were only two, with chairs placed around the tables for the spectators.

Stepping further into the room, I noticed a table with refreshments set up in the back. An attendant approached me with a tall glass of Diet Coke and a lime. I reached for it, but Ramos grabbed it first.

I opened my mouth to protest, but snapped it shut at his arched brow. The server's mouth had dropped open as well, but, instead of protesting, he just asked me if I'd like another one. I picked up that this one was made just for me, so I shook my head. "No... that's okay. I really shouldn't drink the stuff."

After he left, I turned to Ramos. "He's hoping you'll drink it and get sick, because that was just rude."

Ramos chuckled. "I'll bring you one during the next break."

"Promise?"

His eyes narrowed, and he was thinking that I'd better be careful, or he'd stop being so nice.

I laughed. "Hey... I've got to take advantage of it while I can."

He huffed out a breath. "I know. Waiting on you is ruining my reputation. I'm going to have to do something drastic to make up for it."

"Well, look on the bright side. Maybe someone will try to attack me again, and you can beat them up. That should do the trick."

He thought that would only work if it happened while everyone was watching, and I couldn't help grinning. "I'd better find out what table I'm sitting at."

I glanced toward the tables and caught sight of a familiar figure. My eyes widened. The black dress she wore was totally different from her usual blue scrubs, but I'd know her anywhere. She was the only person I'd ever met whose mind I couldn't read.

"Ella?" We stepped toward each other, meeting in the middle of the room.

"Shelby? It is you. I wasn't sure."

"Oh my gosh! What are you doing here?"

"I'm with someone..." She glanced at a wildly handsome man who stood behind her, staring at us with shock. I picked up a wave of protectiveness from him, along with a liberal dose of worry. He thought that if Sonny found out that Ella knew me, they were both in a lot of trouble.

"You're with him?"

"Uh... yeah, Creed. He's playing in the tournament."

"I know..." I glanced from Creed to Dom, who stood beside him, and picked up that Creed wasn't happy about something. "Is he playing for Sonny?"

"Yes... he is. I guess you're playing too? How did you get into this?"

"Uh... I came with my Uncle... uh... Joe Manetto. He's an associate of Sonny's and bought into the game." I lowered my voice. "Are you in trouble? I mean... that guy standing by your friend looks kind of nasty... if you know what I mean. And Sonny is probably worse."

Before she could answer, Sonny spoke into the microphone. "Players, take your places. It's time for round two to begin. If you're not seated within the next two minutes, you will forfeit your spot." He looked straight at me, hoping I'd take my time so he could disqualify me.

"I'd better go. Let's talk after this round, okay?"

"Sure."

I hurried to the tables, picking up from the monitor exactly where I was supposed to sit, which frustrated Sonny. His gaze flicked over my head, and I turned to see Ramos talking to Ella. This infuriated Sonny even more, and he sent a nod to Dom, who strode to Sonny's side.

As they whispered, I watched Ella rushing to Creed's side, her face softening. Other than that, I didn't know how she felt about him, but Creed definitely had feelings for her. Before I could pick up more from Creed's mind, Sonny spoke into the microphone. "Players, take your seats, or you will forfeit your spot."

Sonny's loud voice startled the couple, but they didn't break apart. Ella whispered something to Creed, and he squeezed her hands before leaning down for a quick kiss. He took his place at the table and glanced at Sonny, his face a mask of stone, but his heart filled with rage. Sonny's glare toward Creed was hot enough to burn him alive.

I watched Dom grab Ella's wrist and drag her to a chair. They argued, and I picked up that Dom was asking Ella how she knew me. Ella pulled her wrist out of his grasp and folded her arms so he couldn't drag her out of the room, causing my heart to pound with fury.

What was going on? If Creed was playing for Sonny, why was Sonny so upset? Was Creed playing for Sonny against his will? Whatever was going on, Ella was right in the middle of it. I didn't have time to figure it out now, but if Ella was in trouble, I'd do everything I could to help her out.

The dealers for both tables took their places, along with the game monitors, and Sonny gave the order to begin play. While the dealer shuffled the deck, I put Ella's troubles from my mind, knowing that if I was going to help her, I had to get through the tournament first.

I studied each player at my table, easily picking up that they'd heard rumors about my premonitions. There was also a fair amount of swearing from their thoughts, cursing the fates that they had to play against me.

I tried not to smile, but it did my heart good to know all of these men cowered in fear. One of them was hoping that his sponsor would realize that sitting at my table wasn't his fault. Hearing that little tidbit made me smile, and even bolstered my confidence.

At least there were only five other players at the table this time, making it much easier to keep their cards straight in my head. I decided to use Sebastian's idea of alphabetizing them and settled into my chair for the first game.

As the play progressed, I lost track of time, counting down the players as they left the table in defeat. My head began to ache, but I pushed the pain aside and kept going. More time passed, with only one break, before it finally came down to me and player C. He'd managed to hold his own, but in the last two games, his chips began to dwindle.

After losing for the third time in a row, his concentration fled, and he knew he'd have to do something drastic. He barely had enough chips for another game, and sweat began to roll down his face. The cards came out, and I could hardly believe my luck.

With my head pounding to beat the devil, I knew that, even with a lousy hand, my cards were still better than his. Now was my chance to end the round, so I bid him up, knowing that, if he folded, he didn't have enough chips to play another round. At the river, he went all in and stared at me, hostility smoldering in his dark eyes.

I knew he was about to accuse me of cheating, but I turned my cards over anyway and waited for the explosion.

The dealer realized I'd just won and loudly proclaimed that I was now qualified to play in the final round.

At this, my opponent sputtered and stood. He threw down his cards and swore, his face turning red with anger. He pointed a finger my way and shouted. "You're cheating." He glanced at the dealer. "She should be disqualified. She's been cheating this whole time."

Ramos stepped to the man's side, his face a mask of granite and his tone a quiet snarl. "You need to stop. Right now. Before you regret it."

The man jerked back and dropped his hands to his sides, but he didn't back down. He pointed at the monitor. "You." His upper lip rose in a sneer. "You need to check the cards. And I insist you do a sweep under the table for anything hidden there, like a mirror or extra cards."

The monitor stepped to the man's side. "I've seen no evidence of any cheating going on by the lady or anyone else."

"That doesn't mean anything. I insist you check the cards. Check the cards, damn you!"

Dom stepped to our table and held his hands out in a placating gesture. "Sir. May I remind you that you agreed to the terms of play long before the games began? Let me be clear. If you won't abide by them, you will lose any chance of ever playing in a poker tournament in this casino again. Do I make myself clear?"

Hearing that, the man clamped his lips together, barely holding in another outburst. A security guard came to his side and escorted him out of the room. The man was thinking that his outburst had all been a show for Sonny, and he hoped Sonny was satisfied.

What the freak? My blood boiled, sending a sharp pain twisting into my head. Gasping, I ducked my head and massaged my temples, knowing I needed to calm down, or I was headed for a migraine.

"Shelby?" Ramos's low voice penetrated the pain. "Hang on. I'll get you out of here."

Seconds later, he helped me stand, and I leaned against him. As we left the room, I slammed down my shields and felt a small amount of relief. It wasn't until we got into the elevator that the silence began to soothe me, and I could let go of my control.

"You okay?"

I heaved out a breath. "I will be. I don't know what happened in there. It sort of hit me all at once, but I think I'll be fine after some pain reliever and some peace and quiet." That wasn't quite true, since it felt like a hammer was pounding my brain into tiny little pieces, but I didn't want him to worry.

As the doors opened, his arm tightened around me. Luckily, no one was lurking in the hall, and he led me down to our rooms.

Inside, he took me straight to the bedroom and helped me lie down. I relaxed onto the mattress and closed my eyes with a soft groan. Ramos pulled off my shoes and disappeared, coming back a minute later to lay a cold washcloth on my forehead.

He disappeared again but returned with a glass of water and some pills. I sat up and gulped them down, giving him a shaky smile. "Thanks. That should do the trick. I just need a few minutes of quiet, but I'm worried. Do you think Sonny—"

"I'll take care of it. You just rest."

"But—"

Ramos cupped my cheek with his hand, running his thumb over my lips. "Shhh. We've got time. The other game is still in progress, and I'm sure there will be a break after that. I'll go down and check. You just relax and get some rest. I'll be back in a minute."

I let out a breath and lay back down, closing my eyes against the pain. A bare second later, the door clicked shut behind Ramos, leaving me in a blanket of silence that nearly brought tears to my eyes. The pounding in my head began to subside, and I finally relaxed, hoping I could recover before the next round.

Otherwise, I was in big trouble.

CHAPTER 9

"Shelby?"

My eyes blinked open to find Ramos sitting on the bed beside me, gently nudging my shoulder. "Did I fall asleep?"

He nodded. "Looks like it. How are you feeling?"

"Better. My head's not pounding anymore."

"Do you think you can play?"

My eyes widened. "Of course. How much time do we have?"

"The final round starts in fifteen minutes. You were asleep for half an hour."

"Wow... it must have been just what I needed. I'm going to freshen up and maybe change my dress."

"Need some help?" He was partly serious, but he hoped I'd say no since it would test his resolve to be the good guy I thought he was... and for the record... he wasn't a good guy.

I sent him a grin. "Thanks, but I can manage."

He shrugged. "Okay. But I'll be on the other side of the door if you change your mind."

His lips turned up into that sexy half-grin that always sent my heart racing. I shook my head and hurried into the bathroom. Turning on the hot water, I pulled off my dress before wringing out a hot washcloth. After a quick underarm scrub, I put on some deodorant and touched up my makeup.

Back in the bedroom, I slipped on the royal blue dress I'd packed and found my shoes beside the bed. I could hardly believe that my head wasn't hurting, and I sure hoped it would stay that way. The key would be to remember not to get upset or angry... since high blood pressure must have brought it on. I wasn't sure that was possible, but I'd do my best.

I took a deep breath and blew it out before opening the door. Ramos spoke into his phone, but disconnected after telling Uncle Joey we were coming. "You look great. Ready?"

"Yes."

Peering into the hallway, we found it empty, but Ramos wasn't about to let his guard down. He kept me behind him as the elevator doors swished open. Our luck held to find it empty, and we stepped inside, pushing the button for the lobby.

"So who am I playing against? It's not Ella's boyfriend is it? She told me he was playing for Sonny."

He pursed his lips. "I'm afraid so." He met my gaze. "I know you might be tempted, but you can't let him win." He held up a hand before I could object, knowing I had a big heart and would want to do something. "Don't worry. If he and Ella are in trouble, we'll figure out another way to help."

"Okay."

The elevator doors opened, and Ramos waited for my nod before stepping out. We made our way through the lobby and into the crowded poker room. People parted as Ramos and I entered, like we were big-time celebrities, and I tried not to let it unnerve me.

Anticipation to see who would win the ten-million-dollar jackpot washed over me, and I realized most of the crowd was betting on me to win.

One poker table sat in the center of the room with chairs for the spectators surrounding it. A video camera was positioned above the table, transmitting the game to the big screen on the wall so everyone could see the action.

As I took it all in, a deep voice called my name. "Shelby!"

I turned to find the man who'd accused me of cheating pushing his way through the crowd to my side. How did he get back in? Sonny must have arranged it, since I picked up that the man was up to something. He came closer, but hesitated as Ramos moved to intercept him.

Turning his hopeful glance my way, he hunched his shoulders and lowered his head, glancing up at me with pleading eyes. "My dear lady, I'm so sorry for my terrible behavior earlier. I made a complete ass of myself. It was totally uncalled for, and I apologize. Will you please forgive me?"

He was lying through his teeth, but, before I could call his bluff, I picked up his intent to stab me with the knife he held hidden in his hand. As I stepped back, he lunged at me, but I easily spun out of his way. Acting fast, Ramos stepped between us, blocking the man's assault with his arm.

He grabbed the man's wrist and pivoted inside his reach so the blade pointed outward. With a sharp twist to the man's wrist, the knife fell to the floor. Ramos continued the movement, pushing the man to the floor, face first, and pulling his arm behind his back.

The man screamed out in pain, but Ramos didn't let up until a security guard slapped handcuffs on the attacker's wrists. Amid his loud protests, the security guard hauled him to his feet and escorted him out of the room.

Relieved, I stepped to Ramos's side, and panic clenched my stomach. A stream of red blood dripped from a long cut down his arm, and my breath whooshed out of me.

"You're... you're bleeding. We've got to stop it." I glanced around the room and spotted Ella. I frantically called her over and pointed at Ramos's bleeding arm. Feeling lightheaded and sick to my stomach, I couldn't seem to get any words out.

She glanced at Ramos, but turned her focus back to me. "Shelby, sit down before you faint." She motioned to someone behind me, and Uncle Joey came to my side. "Make her sit down with her head between her legs. I'll take care of Ramos."

Uncle Joey took one look at me and slipped his arm around my waist. He helped me to a chair, and I rested my head on my lap, hoping I wouldn't faint. Uncle Joey sat beside me and rubbed my back. After a few minutes, the black spots fogging my brain cleared from my vision, and I slowly sat up.

"Better?" Uncle Joey asked, handing me a bottle of water. "Here. Drink this. It should help."

I drank most of it down and sat back in my chair. "Where are Ramos and Ella?"

"She took him to the bathroom to clean the wound."

My shoulders relaxed, and I nodded.

"So what was that all about? Was Sonny behind it?"

"Yes." Anger tightened my stomach. "This has turned out to be quite the ordeal. I'll be glad when it's over, but now it looks like I have to play against someone else who's working for Sonny, only... something about his situation is different."

"Ramos told me about him and his girlfriend. What do you think's going on?"

"I'm not sure, but I think he's being coerced into playing." I shrugged. "I'm sure I'll pick up more, but I'd like to help them if we can."

Uncle Joey narrowed his eyes. "Surely you're not thinking of letting him win."

"No... of course not. But we might be able to threaten Sonny somehow. You've got something on him, right? Once the game is over, maybe you could use it to persuade him to leave them alone?"

His brows drew together, but he gave me a reluctant nod. "I'll think about it."

Ramos and Ella came back into the room, and I stood, grateful my head didn't spin. "Thanks. I'll see what I can find out during the game."

I stepped toward them, stopping to examine Ramos's bandaged arm. "How is he?"

"Good," Ella replied. "It wasn't as bad as it looked."

"Thank you Ella. I'm so glad you were here."

"Yeah... me too. That guy who attacked you was so scary. But... you saw right through him and got out of the way. I would have been taken totally by surprise, especially with his apology. I never thought he'd try to hurt you."

"I know... it was definitely a surprise. Listen..." I stepped closer to whisper. "Whatever the outcome, I'm here to help you."

Her eyes widened, and she sighed with relief. "Thank you."

I listened real close to her thoughts, but couldn't pick up a thing, same as before. What made her so different? Before I could say another word, a wall of angry frustration from

Sonny hit me like a ton of bricks. He was going to disqualify me if I didn't sit down within the next thirty seconds.

I turned to glare at him. "Hold your horses. I'm coming."

Sonny's mouth dropped open, and satisfaction washed over me. I sent Ella an apologetic smile and quickly sat at the table, watching Sonny try and get under control.

Tugging at the collar of his shirt, he announced the final round, declaring the game underway. The dealer came forward, taking his place and opening a new deck of cards. After shuffling them, he dealt out our cards and looked to me for the big blind.

Grateful he wasn't another plant for Sonny, I threw out the chips, and Creed followed with the small blind. After I looked at my cards, I doubled the bet. Creed called to stay in the game, and the dealer played the flop. With the cards played so far, my hand was better, so I continued to bet.

Creed took his time, analyzing me and watching for signs of a 'tell.' The game continued through to the river. Since I had the winning hand, I kept betting. He called, and we both showed our cards, with me taking the pot.

The play continued quickly after that. With just two of us at the table, there wasn't a lot of wasted time. I decided to play aggressively, since I didn't want the game to drag out, and I only folded when he had the better hand. I knew it wasn't very sportsmanlike, but I'd had enough of playing poker to last me a lifetime.

My stack of chips steadily grew, and I could feel Creed's mounting frustration. He wasn't getting a single break, and guilt washed over me. I let him win the next game and caught a huff of displeasure from Uncle Joey. I glanced his way and winked, hoping he'd get the message.

After I won the next two games, Uncle Joey settled down, but that wasn't the case for Sonny. Out of the corner of my eye, I caught him gesturing to Dom. After they spoke, Sonny called for a break in the play, and motioned the monitor to his side.

A low murmur filled the room as the monitor came back to our table. She dismissed the dealer and asked us both to stand. The room went quiet while she checked the table where we sat. She slid a pole-like contraption, with a mirror on the end, to check the underside of the table, as well as under our chairs.

Satisfied, she declared the table clean, and we resumed our play. The dealer returned and opened a new deck of cards. Play resumed, and I won the next two rounds. Creed began to sweat, and I picked up the pressure he was under. He'd positioned a couple of cards up his sleeves, but, with so many eyes on the table, he knew he'd get caught if he tried anything.

Sonny expected him to win, and despair washed over him. If he lost, Sonny had threatened to kill Ella. But I was too good to beat. He only hoped he could bargain for Ella's life, even if it meant he'd lose his own. Dom was his only hope. They'd been friends once, and he hoped he wouldn't go through with killing Ella.

Holy hell. This was bad. His worry tightened my stomach, and I wished I could tell him that I was on his side, even though I planned to win. Instead, I just shook my head and vowed that I wouldn't let Sonny kill either one of them.

Creed won the next hand, but that was because the river happened to be just the card he needed. That was his only lucky break, and my stack continued to grow. With his paltry amount of chips, I knew the next round would be the last.

After the river, Creed went all in, hoping I would fold and give him a chance to get back in the game, but I called instead. Creed turned over his cards, revealing two pair, kings over tens. I beat him with a straight, and the tournament was over.

Creed graciously shook my hand before the clapping spectators surrounded me, and I lost sight of him. Ramos came to my side and pulled me into a big hug. Not to be outdone, Uncle Joey did the same. Even Sebastian heartily patted my back, thinking I hadn't let him down.

Once the congratulations were over, Sonny stepped to the podium, working hard to control his disappointment and anger. A staff member brought out a beautiful crystal trophy, featuring three stacks of poker chips in differing colors. The crystal chips balanced on each other with their edges touching, like they were falling from the sky. It was beautiful, and not something I'd expected.

Taking the trophy, Sonny glanced over the crowd and held it up for everyone to see. "The winning prize of this year's Mojavi Casino Poker Tournament goes to Shelby Nichols." He motioned me to the podium, so I joined him there. He handed me the trophy, but kept his hold on it and turned to smile at a photographer.

After several photos, he let me take the trophy and turned to another staff member waiting in the wings. At Sonny's nod, the staffer brought out a big, cardboard money order prop with "ten-million-dollars" written on it.

Someone had filled in my name as the payee, and Sonny presented it to me. I set down the heavy trophy and took hold of the prop, once again posing for the photographer. I picked up Sonny's thoughts that even though he hadn't won, the tournament had still brought in a lot of money, so it wasn't a total loss. But this had ruined his plans to pay off his debt.

With the ceremony over, Sonny smiled and told everyone to please stay and enjoy the rest of the night. As people began to leave, he turned to me with a fake smile plastered on his face. "I don't know how you did it, but I'm never allowing you to play in my casino again."

Before I could form any kind of a retort, Uncle Joey and Ramos came to my side. "What did you just say to her?" Uncle Joey asked.

Sonny pursed his lips. "Nothing. I imagine you want your money. Let's go to my office."

Uncle Joey didn't want to let it go, but I set down the prop and took his arm, shaking my head. He pursed his lips, but stepped behind Sonny, following him down a hall and into a large office.

Sonny took his seat behind the desk, seething with disappointment. He hadn't thought he'd lose, so he had to come up with a creative way to pay Uncle Joey the money. Too bad he couldn't use Jackie against Manetto like he'd first thought, but every avenue leading to her had been a dead end. She'd become untouchable, and Sonny knew, from Manetto's reputation, that Manetto wasn't an enemy he could afford to make.

This whole thing stunk to high heaven, and now he had to give his money away. It went against everything in his nature, and going through with it was killing him. This wasn't supposed to happen. Someone had to pay for this mess, so it might as well be Creed and his girlfriend. Maybe watching them die would make him feel better.

"The money?" Uncle Joey prompted. "Is there a problem?"

"No." Sonny pursed his lips. "But, with such a large sum, I suggest we make a few non-traceable money transfers over several days. That way we can avoid paying taxes."

"I have a better idea." Uncle Joey's dark tone, along with his cold stare, froze Sonny in place. "How about this? If you want to live, I suggest you transfer the whole amount into my off-shore bank account now."

Sonny's breath hitched, and his gaze darted to the door. He'd stupidly sent Dom after Creed, and Grant was running interference with his main financier, so Sonny had no one to watch his back. With the odds against him, he capitulated.

"Fine." He opened his computer and pulled up his offshore bank account. Ten million would shrink his reserves a bit, but he'd find a way to make up for it. "I'm ready. What's your account number?"

Uncle Joey took out his phone. After the transaction, he watched for the transfer to make sure it had gone through. Once the money showed up, he put his phone away and stood. "There's something else you can do for me."

Sonny's eyes nearly popped out of his head. "Are you kidding me?"

Uncle Joey's lips twisted into a sardonic smile. "That last poker player..." He glanced my way with raised brows.

"Creed and his girlfriend, Ella," I said.

"Right... Creed and Ella. They're friends of Shelby's, and I want your guarantee that they won't be harmed."

Sonny's eyes narrowed. "Why would I guarantee that?"

"Because if you don't, I'll shred your reputation. I'll let it be known that you cheated to win your own tournament, and you'll never be able to hold your head up in this town again."

Sonny scoffed. "You have no proof. It would be your word against mine. Why would anyone believe you?"

"Because I have the names of all the people you hired, from the physicist to the magician, and even that last gentleman who tried to stab my niece. I'm certain I could persuade each and every one of them to talk. In fact... I was planning to expose you anyway, but now I'm willing to keep it to myself in return for the safety of Shelby's friends."

Sonny shrugged, thinking that he'd agree and then do as he damn well pleased. "Fine. I'll let them go. But the deal's off if you go back on your word." Sonny could always say that Uncle Joey had broken the deal, and that's why they were dead. After we left, there wasn't a thing we could do about it anyway.

Uncle Joey glanced my way and raised his brow. "What do you say, Shelby?"

"That's not good enough." I caught Sonny's gaze with a glare of my own. "I don't trust you, so we need to see them. Bring them down, and they can leave with us now."

"That's not possible." Sonny wasn't ready to let them out of his grasp. Creed hadn't learned his lesson, and he needed to be punished. If he let Creed walk away, it would send the wrong message.

"We can wait," Uncle Joey said.

Sonny's eyes cleared. That was the perfect solution. Any minute now, Grant would come walking through that door with several men from his security team. Once they arrived, we'd have to leave emptyhanded.

I glanced at Uncle Joey. "He's not listening. I think we need to finish this conversation elsewhere." I motioned with my head to the door.

Uncle Joey nodded with understanding. "Ramos, take him."

Before he knew what hit him, Sonny was on his feet with his arm twisted behind his back, and Ramos's knife pressed against his neck. "Let's go for a walk."

Sonny's surprise gave way to bitter anger. "You can't just take me out of here. I have men everywhere."

"But I think there's another way out." I motioned to a door at the back of the room where Sonny's gaze had flicked. "That door perhaps?"

"No. There's no other way but through the lobby." Sonny pulled against Ramos's hold, desperate and shocked. How did I know that door led down a corridor and directly to the parking lot? The tip of Ramos's knife drew blood from Sonny's neck, and he froze.

"Through there." I stepped toward the door. "It leads to the parking lot. Can Ricky pick us up?"

"Yes," Uncle Joey said, putting the call through to Ricky. "He's already waiting outside in the limo."

I opened the door and led the way down the hallway, with Ramos dragging Sonny along, and Uncle Joey following behind.

We reached the outside door to the parking lot and waited while Uncle Joey told Ricky where we were. Ricky pulled up just a minute later, and we all piled in. Uncle Joey told Ricky to take us to an all-night diner, just off the Strip, and we pulled into the parking lot a few minutes later.

At nearly two in the morning, and after a generous tip, we managed to get the back room to ourselves. At Uncle Joey's insistence, Sonny put a call through to Dom, telling him there was a change of plans and he was letting Creed and Ella go. He also put another call to Grant to come pick him up.

Uncle Joey reminded Sonny that nothing had better happen to them on the way, or he wouldn't be going back to his hotel alive. Sonny groveled just enough to satisfy Uncle Joey, and he sat down at the table.

I listened closely, just to make sure Sonny didn't have any hidden weapons, but he'd come empty-handed. I also picked up that Dom had taken Ella and Creed from her home several hours away, and Sonny planned to tell Dom to drive them only a few miles out of town before kicking them out of the car. It wasn't as good as killing them, but dropping them off in the middle of the desert might do the job.

Grant entered the room first, followed a few minutes later by Dom, with Creed and Ella in tow.

"There," Sonny said. "You can see they are unharmed, and they will be free to go once we are done here." He looked at Dom. "Did you bring their luggage?"

"Yes sir."

"Good." He turned to Manetto. "Are you satisfied? You will agree to our deal?"

Uncle Joey stared at him before leaning toward me. "Anything else I need to know?"

"He basically kidnapped Ella, and they need a car," I whispered.

Nodding, he turned back to Sonny. "On one condition."

"What's that?"

"It seems that you took Ella from her home. I believe it's only fair that she has the ability to return, so she'll need one of your cars."

Sonny's nostrils flared before he sent Manetto a curt nod. "That can be arranged."

"Good. Then we're done here."

Sonny and Grant stood to leave. Sonny boiled inside, but he wasn't about to risk his reputation with Uncle Joey. On the way out, he pulled Dom aside and whispered in his ear, telling him to let Creed and Ella take the Escalade. Dom nodded and watched them leave.

Uncle Joey stood and planted his stern gaze on Ella.

She flushed. "Uh... thanks Mr. Manetto. I don't know what you just did, but I'm in your debt."

His face lit up with a smile. "You're welcome. Glad to help a friend of Shelby's."

He turned his gaze to Creed, and the smile evaporated. "You're lucky you're with her, or you'd probably be dead."

Creed's brows rose at his bluntness. Before he could respond, Uncle Joey continued. "But you're a hell of a poker player, even if you tried to cheat." He sent a nod my way. "Shelby seems to think you're worth saving, so I'll leave it at that."

Creed swallowed. "Thanks... uh... both of you."

Uncle Joey held out his business card to Creed, thinking that it never hurt to cultivate favors. Now that Creed owed him, he intended to collect at some point in the future. "Here's my card. I'd like to keep in touch."

"Of course." Creed took the card, not mistaking Uncle Joey's meaning, and I tried not to roll my eyes.

Before Uncle Joey put his wallet away, I grabbed another business card and wrote my number on the back. Ella stood on the other side of the table, talking to Creed, so I hurried around the table to her side and gave her a quick hug.

She pulled back with a grateful smile. "Thanks for helping us out. I hope it didn't cost your uncle too much."

I laughed. "No... Uncle Joey's still pulling the strings. Don't worry about him."

Ramos joined us, sending Ella a quick nod.

"How's the arm?" she asked.

"Good. It doesn't even hurt anymore. Should I take off the bandage so you can take a look at it?"

"Uh... no, no, you don't need to do that. I mean... leaving the bandage on as long as possible really helps with the healing process, and it keeps all the bad bacteria out, so you should leave it for now. Maybe even until tomorrow. Okay?"

She twisted her hands together, clearly nervous about something. Since I couldn't hear her thoughts, I figured it was because she was standing so close to Ramos. He had that effect on most women.

Ramos's brows rose. He thought Ella was hiding something, so I smacked him. "Stop baiting her. I told you she has healing hands. I'm sure it's doing a lot better than if someone else had treated it."

"You've got that right." He said it sarcastically, and I picked up that his cut was basically healed. Had she really done that? It was something I'd have to ask him later. Right now, Creed and Dom were speaking in hushed tones, and I picked up Dom's surprise that Sonny was letting Creed go. He'd never expected that, but it relieved him, since he hadn't wanted to kill his friend.

"I wonder what they're saying," Ella said.

I cocked my head. "Probably something about letting you take the Escalade? Oh... and Creed wants to get your phones back."

"Huh... and you got that from your premonitions?"

My eyes widened. Oops. "Yeah... mostly."

"Well... it would be nice to get my phone back. They took it last night, and John's probably frantic."

"Who's John?"

Ella dropped her gaze. "Uh... he's my... uh... representative with the hospital board. They want me back in New York." At my raised brows, she continued. "They sent me away after that guy died. You remember him, right?"

I nodded. Ella had refused to assist the doctors in saving a killer, but after he'd killed the young woman Ella felt responsible for, I didn't blame her. "Yeah... Tony Bilotti. I remember how upset you were."

"Right... anyway, it's a long story, but now they want me to come back. Creed had planned to go with me."

Ramos narrowed his eyes. "You sure you can you trust him?"

Ella's expression fell, and she hesitated. Wanting to help her, I spoke up. "I think you can. At least he cares deeply about you... uh... seems to care, I mean."

Her eyes widened. "You think so? I wouldn't mind having some company, you know?"

"Sure. I totally get that."

Uncle Joey cleared his throat, thinking it was time to go, and I smiled at Ella. "Sorry, but we need to go now. Let's keep in touch." I handed her the business card with my name and number on the back. "That's my number. Call me after you get to New York. Okay?"

"Yeah. I will. And... I don't know how to thank you—but if there's ever anything you need, please let me know."

"You bet... just be sure to call me so I'll have your number."

"I will."

Uncle Joey and Ramos had already stepped toward the exit, so I hurried to join them. I slipped my arm through Uncle Joey's and smiled up at him. "Thanks for doing that... for helping them."

He patted my hand. "You're welcome." He was thinking that doing something nice once in a while wasn't so bad, even though it meant letting Sonny off the hook. But that didn't bother him so much, now that he had more information about the Debt Collector. Sonny was on the guy's bad side, and Uncle Joey was happy to stay out of it.

His brief encounter with the man had been enough to set him on edge, and he trusted his gut telling him to leave well enough alone. He'd been a shadowy figure at the tournament, but he'd approached Uncle Joey during a break and introduced himself as Gage Rathmore.

He was tall and imposing, with cold blue eyes and gray at the temples of his black hair. Uncle Joey had met a few people like him before, and he knew instantly that

Rathmore was a predator of the darkest kind. Uncle Joey didn't hold out much hope for Sonny, and he was more than willing to leave Sonny alive.

Hopefully, he'd tempered Rathmore's keen interest in me through his stern warning that I was his niece and under his protection. That had worked this time, but Rathmore's reluctance to back off had raised a red flag, and Uncle Joey realized he could be a problem in the future.

With that in mind, he didn't plan on visiting Las Vegas again for a very long time.

CHAPTER 10

I slid inside the limo, and a cold chill settled over me. I couldn't imagine Uncle Joey being unsettled by anyone, so this Rathmore person must be in a league of his own, and I was more than grateful that Uncle Joey was watching out for me.

Ramos glanced my way, wondering what was wrong. Just a moment earlier, I'd been happy that everything had worked out so well. Now I looked scared and upset.

I sent him a smile and tried to muster some of my previous enthusiasm, but sudden weariness had overtaken me. "I'm exhausted. I guess it's all caught up to me."

Uncle Joey's brows drew together. "I was hoping to fly back home tonight, but if you're—"

"No... no. I think that's a great idea. The sooner we leave this town, the better. And let's not come back for a very long time."

His eyes widened. He'd just been thinking that. Had I been listening to his mind? He shook his head. Was nothing sacred? Did I have to listen to everything?

I grimaced. "Uh... sorry."

"Sorry about what?" Ramos asked.

Uncle Joey sighed. "She knows about Gage Rathmore."

Ramos's lips turned down, and he thought of some pretty bad words to describe the guy. Knowing I'd heard every single one of them, he just shrugged. A spade was a spade, and he wasn't about to apologize.

Uncle Joey shook his head. "I don't know exactly what you picked up, but it's not as bad as you think. I may not know much about him right now, but I will soon enough. In the meantime, I don't want you to give him a second thought. All right?"

I nodded, but I knew that wasn't going to happen. How could it, when everyone else was thinking about what a terrible person he was? Even Ricky had thought his reputation was bad, but actually meeting the guy had made his skin crawl. Sheesh.

Still... it comforted me to know Uncle Joey was handling it, so I tried not to freak out. He was a powerful man who had lots of experience with this sort of thing. We'd be fine.

If only I could get rid of that deep foreboding feeling that turned my stomach into knots, I might believe it.

"I'll call the pilots and tell them we're leaving," Uncle Joey said. "Maybe we can get some sleep on the plane."

It was still dark when we landed.

Before we'd left the hotel, I'd changed back into my comfy clothes, and I managed to sleep for most of the plane ride.

With his pack strapped to the back seat of his motorcycle, Ramos slipped on his helmet and left after a quick wave.

A car waited for us, and Ricky joined Uncle Joey and me for the ride home. They dropped me off first, and I staggered into the house. Chris had left a light on for me, and I tiptoed up the stairs, finding him sound asleep. He stirred as I got into bed, cracking his eyes open and pulling me into his arms.

I breathed out a sigh to be home, safe and sound, and promptly fell asleep.

I woke late the next day, grateful I'd been able to sleep in. Since it was Sunday, Chris had made breakfast, and the smell of bacon woke me up. I threw on some sweats and opened my door to find Coco sitting in the hall, waiting for me.

He jumped to his feet and woofed softly, *you home,* before bumping me with his head. I knelt beside him and stroked his head, telling him I missed him, and was glad to be back. His snuffles sounded like a reprimand that I'd left without him, but that may have just been my imagination.

He woofed *come,* and I followed him down the stairs and into the kitchen. After a round of hugs and greetings from my kids, I was happy to relay the news that I'd won the tournament.

"Cool," Savannah said. "So what did you win?"

Of course I hadn't told my kids about the enormous jackpot, but what about the trophy? Where was it? "I got a really beautiful trophy, but I forgot all about it until just now." I frowned. "I must have left it there. Dang."

Josh scrunched his brow. "A trophy? That's it?" He didn't believe for a moment that there wasn't some type of monetary reward involved. "I thought you were playing for money."

"Well... yeah... of course." I tried to make it sound like I wasn't stupid like he'd insinuated.

"So how much?" he asked, pushing for a response.

This was one of those times I wondered if I should lie; but since I was trying to turn over a new leaf, I decided to tell the truth and hope I didn't live to regret it. "Ten—" I broke off, picking up Chris's warning not to tell them, since it might jade them forever.

Frowning, I continued. "Ten-million-dollars. But you know it's not mine, right? Since I was playing for Uncle Joey?"

"Ten million dollars?" Josh sputtered. "Are you frickin' kidding me? And you won?"

I shrugged. "Yeah."

"But you get to keep some of it, right?"

"Well... yeah... I got a cut... but I might have already spent it."

"What?" Josh couldn't believe the words coming out of my mouth. I'd already spent the money? What would cost that much. At the least, I must have gotten half. That would make it close to five million dollars.

Chris shook his head, wishing I wouldn't have told them. They didn't need to know some things, and this was one of them. Money didn't grow on trees, but, after one night in Las Vegas, I was making it sound like it did.

"Not really. It was hard and I nearly got..." I didn't finish the sentence, since everyone was staring at me.

Chris's eyes widened with alarm. I had just answered his thoughts, but worse, what was I saying? Nearly got what? Killed? What the hell happened?

"What I meant to say is that, sure... ten million is a lot of money, but none of it was meant for me. Uncle Joey's keeping all of it, and the little I might have received I invested into something else."

"What?" Josh asked.

"Uh... well... that's a whole other story. Do you mind if I eat some breakfast first?" I sat at the table and grabbed a couple of pancakes and two strips of bacon. "How did Coco's training go yesterday? Did you have fun?"

With my abrupt change of subject, it took them a minute to switch gears. "Yeah," Savannah said. "It was great. Coco is amazing." They all chimed in about their day, and I took a few bites, happy to hear things had gone so well.

"Lance said we were ready for our first search and rescue," Josh announced.

"Oh wow, that's wonderful."

"Yeah. He said he'd let me know when the next call comes in." His gaze caught mine. "I can probably handle it if you're too busy, especially once I get my driver's license."

"No... I want to come."

He shrugged, thinking that, with my schedule, a call out of the blue probably wouldn't work for me. But, in just a few short months, he'd have enough hours to get his driver's license, and he wouldn't need me, which meant that he'd need a car.

He sighed, knowing the money he'd made from his summer job was hardly enough for a down payment, but I might chip in, especially now that I had all that money. "So what are you doing with that extra money? You never finished."

I swallowed my food but hardly tasted it. How could he think that he didn't need me? He wasn't even sixteen yet, and he was suddenly ready to head out on his own? That couldn't be right.

"Mom?"

"Huh? Oh… sorry. Yeah… the money. Right. Uh… remember the stories I used to tell you about my grandpa and the Lost Taft Mine?" They didn't know what I was talking about, so I quickly told them how I'd gone prospecting with my grandpa a few times.

"He always wanted to find the mine and all that gold. Now it looks like finding the mine could actually happen. A professor found a map to the mine that an old prospector had hidden away, and there's an expedition leaving in the morning. They needed a backer, so Uncle Joey and I are using some of the money we won in the tournament for supplies and stuff."

"Oh… so it's a gold mine?" Josh asked.

"Yeah. And get this… I'm going prospecting with them."

"In the morning?" Savannah asked. "But you just got home."

"Yeah, but I was only gone overnight, and this is just for a couple of days. I've already got everything arranged for you guys, so you don't have to worry about that." Before I could continue, my phone rang. It wasn't a number I knew, but I decided to answer it anyway. "We can go over it later. Okay? I'd better take this."

I stepped out of the kitchen. "Hello?"

"Hi Shelby. This is Ella."

"Ella. How are you? Is everything okay?"

"That's why I'm calling. After we left last night, Dom got a call from Sonny ordering him to kill Creed." I gasped, and she quickly continued. "Don't worry. We got away, but now I'm afraid he might try again. I thought if your Uncle knew what had happened, he might talk to Sonny and straighten this out."

"Holy hell! Sonny is a stupid idiot. Uncle Joey's not going to be happy to hear that. You did the right thing to call me. I'll let Uncle Joey know. I'm sure he'll want to have a word with Sonny."

She let out a sigh. "Thanks so much."

"Of course. I'll call him right now. Let me know if Sonny tries anything. If he knows what's good for him, he won't. I'll be in touch." We disconnected, and I put a call through to Uncle Joey, quickly explaining the situation.

"That bastard," he replied. "I can't believe he went back on his word."

"I know. So what are we going to do?"

"Don't worry. I'll take care of it. I have a contingency plan, and Sonny's going to regret crossing me. We'll talk later." He hung up, and I put my phone away, once again grateful that Uncle Joey was on my side. He may be a bad guy, but he still had a good heart.

I spent the rest of the day with my family, trying to make up for the time I'd been gone, and knowing I'd be gone for a few more days this week as well. By the end of the day, my conscience didn't bother me quite so much to be leaving them again.

I had to make all the travel arrangements with Billie and Ramos, as well as pack the personal items I needed for the trip. At least Ian Smith had sent a list of what I needed to take, so that helped. Uncle Joey had insisted we meet in the parking garage of Thrasher Development at seven-thirty the next morning.

Once the kids were in bed, with Coco in Josh's room, I slipped into the garage with my daypack and loaded it into the trunk. I didn't want to re-live Coco's disappointment that I was leaving him behind again. Not that I hadn't tried. I'd done all I could to convince Uncle Joey that Coco should come, but he'd nixed that idea pretty fast.

I was a little disappointed, but, since it was a strange place with strange people, he might be better off at home.

Plus, the kids would miss him, and I wanted them to have Coco for company while I was away. That was probably silly, but it still made me feel better about leaving.

I slipped into bed that night and snuggled against Chris. It was a relief to tell him the whole story of the tournament.

He could hardly believe that Sonny had used such drastic measures to win. "I'm glad you're okay."

"Yeah... and even better, Uncle Joey's not planning to go back to Las Vegas for a long time."

Chris huffed. "Sounds good to me, and if he ever does, do me a favor and tell him you're not going. Okay?" He didn't like that so many people had witnessed my special talent in action, including Gage Rathmore.

"You know what? I'll do it, but only if you promise me something in return."

"What's that?" His brows dipped together. What did I have up my sleeve?

Since I had no idea, I shrugged. "I'm not sure yet, but it'll be something good."

He chuckled. "Oh yeah? Better than this?" He kissed my neck, then moved his lips down my throat. Before I knew what was happening, he began to massage my legs and then my feet.

I let out a groan. "That wasn't exactly what I had in mind, but... I think you may be onto something."

Soon he had me purring happily in his arms. When his lips finally met mine, I was ready for much more. "Oh baby, oh baby."

I pulled into Thrasher, a few minutes late, and caught sight of a brand-new black Jeep Wrangler waiting in front of the elevators. Ramos stood at the back loading it up, but the person standing beside him surprised me. What was Uncle Joey doing wearing a flannel shirt and khaki pants with hiking boots?

I quickly parked my car and hurried over. "Are you coming too?"

Uncle Joey sent me a smile. "I decided I couldn't let you guys have all the fun. Besides, I got this beauty yesterday, and I wanted to try her out." He patted the Jeep like it was a puppy. "It's a Jeep Wrangler 4xe."

"Oh. Cool."

Since it was obvious I had no clue how awesome it was, he continued. "It's a hybrid and fully loaded, perfect for off-roading."

My brows rose. "So we're going off-roading?"

Uncle Joey sighed. "Not necessarily, but we can if we need to. Be prepared, I always say."

I'd never heard him say that, but this was a whole new side of Uncle Joey that I'd never seen before, so what did I know? "Okay. Nice."

Ramos came to my side, thinking he'd better rescue me. "Do you have your pack?"

"Oh yeah. In my trunk." We stepped back to my car and I popped it open. Ramos grabbed my pack, while I picked up my hat and jacket, and followed him to the back of the Jeep next to Uncle Joey. Ramos fit my pack next to theirs with plenty of room to spare.

"There's a lot of room back here," I said, trying to make up for my earlier response. "It's really nice."

Uncle Joey nodded. "Yeah, the drive up should be pretty smooth, and you won't even feel the bumpy, dirt roads."

Another car pulled up, and Billie waved at us. She parked next to my car and hurried to my side. I picked up her surprise to see Uncle Joey since she hadn't known he was coming.

"You want to put your stuff in the back?" I asked her. "We can all drive up together."

I picked up a spike of displeasure from Uncle Joey. He didn't want her in his car asking questions all the way up the mountain. I shouldn't have invited her.

Oops. I glanced at Billie. She'd easily read the look of disapproval on Uncle Joey's face. It was almost enough of a challenge to make her agree. Too bad she couldn't take me up on my offer.

Billie folded her arms, but managed a friendly smile. "Actually, I was thinking of driving up myself. Michael's only giving me a couple of days for the story, so I'll probably need to come back tomorrow night."

Everyone relaxed, and I nodded. "That makes sense."

"Yeah... so I'll just follow you up." She was hoping that I'd drive up with her, but she didn't want to ask since Manetto was glaring at her.

"Why don't I drive up with you?"

She perked up. "That would be great."

After making sure I had everything I needed for the ride up, I jumped in Billie's car, and we followed the Jeep out of the parking garage.

"Did you know Manetto was coming?" she asked.

"No. I'm just as surprised as you are. But I think it had something to do with his new car. I'm pretty sure he got it yesterday, just for this little trip."

She shook her head. "How would it be to have that much money?"

"I know, right?"

"So, how was your weekend? Drew told me you were headed to Las Vegas to play in a poker tournament. How did that go?"

I told her what I could about the tournament, leaving out most of the good stuff. When she heard that I won, she gasped in surprise. "You won all that money? You're a millionaire?"

I shook my head, hating to have to explain. "No. I won the tournament, but Uncle Joey got the money. He had to pay a huge fee to enter, and he hired me to play for him."

She sent me a shocked glance. What the hell? Manetto was my uncle?

Crap! "Uh... sometimes I call him my uncle because he's like an uncle... but you know he's not my uncle, right?"

She let out a breath. "Oh... sure." Noticing my distress, she quickly continued. "It's okay, Shelby. I've known for quite a while that you're in real deep with him. I don't need to know the particulars if it puts you in danger, but I'll always be willing to help you out if you need it."

She thought that working for a mob boss was more dangerous than I wanted to admit, but I seemed to be doing okay for now. "He's not such a bad sort, is he? At least not with you. And Ramos... well... he's kind of scary, but somehow, you've managed to tame them both." She shook her head, wondering how I'd done it. Now that would be quite the story.

She grinned at me. "Someday, promise you'll tell me the whole story, okay? Even if I have to wait until we're both old and gray."

My brows rose, and I let out a sigh. "Sure. Someday, I'd be happy to."

Delighted, she chuckled. "So did he give you anything for winning the tournament?" She was thinking I should have gotten a couple million at the least. In that respect, maybe working for a mob boss wasn't so bad.

"I sort of asked him to back these guys instead of paying me. Now I'm thinking that was a stupid thing to do." That wasn't exactly the truth, but it sounded a lot better than squandering my own money.

She silently agreed, but tried to be positive for my sake. "Oh... well. It might not be so bad, especially if you find the mine with all that gold." She thought taking the sure bet would have been a lot smarter, but she didn't know if I could actually bargain with Manetto anyway. "So... since it's your investment, you'd at least get a cut of the mine, right?"

"Yes. At least I did that right."

"Good for you." She felt kind of bad that the odds of actually finding the gold mine were so low, but she didn't want to burst my bubble, especially if it was a dream I'd had for years. Hopefully, I wouldn't be too depressed if we failed.

"So, how was your weekend?" I asked, wanting to change the subject.

We spent the rest of the drive in pleasant conversation, and Billie steered away from asking too many questions about Uncle Joey, which I appreciated.

After passing through the last little town, we headed up a narrow highway into the mountain range. We followed Uncle Joey onto the turn off for Stewart's cabin. It was a dirt road, and the jeep left a trail of dust in its wake, so we ended up following at a distance to keep from choking.

Three miles down the dirt road, we came to another turn-off which continued another quarter mile until we came to an old cabin, set in a meadow, surrounded by a group of aspen trees. A Land Rover was parked in front, so that meant Stewart and Ian must already be there.

The cabin was bigger than I'd imagined, although not as big as a house. It was large and square, with a pitched roof and a rock chimney on an outside wall. It looked sturdy enough, but patches of shingles were falling off the roof, and the wooden beams above the porch sagged a bit.

At our arrival, the front door opened, and Stewart stepped out. He wasn't surprised to see Uncle Joey, so that was good. Eager to get started, he hurried down the steps to greet us and gestured toward the cabin. "Come on in and let's get organized."

The small living room got even smaller with all of us crowded inside. Most of the dust had been cleared away, but there was still a musty smell to it. "I got the place cleaned up a bit and brought in a couch and some chairs. Why don't you all have a seat?"

A wooden chair, along with a rocking chair, took up the space beside the couch. Billie took the rocking chair, Uncle Joey took a wooden chair, which left Ramos and me to sit on the couch behind a worn coffee table.

Ian entered from the kitchen, wiping his hands on a dish towel. He was thinking that Manetto's last minute decision to join us had thrown a wrench in the works, but luckily, he'd managed to get all the extra equipment he'd need. "Hello everyone, it's good to see you. We've been working on all the preparations, and we're just about ready to go."

"Good. Let's take a look at your plans. I'd like to see where you want to start," Uncle Joey said.

Stewart unfolded a large map and laid it on the coffee table. He outlined his efforts so far, and pointed out where he'd like to go next. "We've been using this as a base camp all summer, so that's where we'll be." He pointed to an area outlined in red. It was close to the ravine he'd thought about the last time we'd been together, and I knew that was the place he wanted to look first.

"It's about four or five miles from here, which puts it in the range we're focusing on. I'm almost certain the mine will be in this vicinity, so we'll start there."

He pointed to the surrounding area, leaving out the ravine. He wanted to check that out without the rest of us.

"If we leave soon, we can get camp set up before dark, and begin our search first thing in the morning."

Stewart straightened and began folding the map. "Ian has backpacks for all of you, along with the supplies we need, but we'll have to divide them up to carry between us. Why don't you bring your things in and we'll get started divvying them up."

Being a novice to backpacking, I had no idea what we had to take with us. Besides the tents, Ian had bought sleeping bags and inflatable pads to go under them. He'd also purchased the special sleeping hammock that Ramos had asked for.

After loading up my backpack, Ramos offered to carry the tent I would share with Billie. Ian took the tent meant for Uncle Joey, which I thought was smart of him, and Stewart took the one he and Ian planned to share.

Besides our snacks, the food we took was dehydrated, so it wasn't as heavy. Still, along with my personal items, my pack had to weigh at least forty pounds. Ramos said it was closer to thirty-five, but I didn't believe him, especially after climbing to the crest of the first hill.

Ian had offered us some special trekking poles, which I happily accepted. Still, I was huffing and out of breath in no time. Luckily, my hiking shoes were broken in, but my hips and legs were already aching from the weight.

There wasn't much of a trail, but, since Stewart and Ian had gone that way all summer long, at least they knew where we were going. The rest of us followed behind them in single file, and I did my best to keep up, not wanting to slow everyone down.

As we continued to climb higher into the mountain range, pine trees and quaking aspen groves surrounded us. The aspen leaves had changed to a beautiful golden-yellow color, and they drifted to the ground like feathers. The fresh scent of pine and dirt, along with the sounds of birds and squirrels undercut the silence. The sound of the wind whistling through the trees, fought the noise of my heavy footsteps and harsh breathing.

When Stewart had told us our campsite was only four or five miles from the cabin, he'd failed to mention that most of those miles were uphill. I did my best to keep up, but I had to rest more often than the others, and I soon lagged behind.

Even Uncle Joey kept up better than I did, and it was starting to get on my nerves. I thought I was in better shape than this. Billie practically sprinted up the next hill, and I could barely keep one foot in front of the other.

After nearly three hours, I found it hard to take another step. Stewart kept saying it wasn't much further, but I was beginning to doubt that he knew what he was talking about. Needing another break, I sat down on a rock. If they were in such a hurry, they could just set up camp without me.

They'd all disappeared over the ridge, leaving me behind, but I just couldn't go any further. Finally, my breathing and heart rate slowed, and I listened to the quiet. Wind rushed through the tops of the trees, making them sway and creak. A breeze came from behind, playing with my hair.

Somewhere, a bird called, cutting into the silence. The wind picked up again, only this time it seemed colder. I realized I was damp with sweat, so that explained it. Still, I couldn't help the shiver that ran down my arms.

I rose to my feet and staggered. My muscles protested, and I stifled a groan. I'd been sitting there too long, and now I was stiff and cold. Not liking the idea of getting lost, I knew I'd have to hurry to catch up. After taking a few agonizing steps up the mountain, a shadow fell across me. I sucked in a breath and glanced up to find Ramos coming my way.

"You came back."

He smiled. "Of course. Here. Give me your pack."

"Where's yours?"

"Our camp's just over the ridge. We're not far."

"Hallelujah." I shrugged out of my backpack, and Ramos caught it. Without the heavy weight, I could finally breathe again. Ramos slung it over his shoulders, like it was nothing, and motioned me forward. I picked my way up the hillside, trying not to groan too loud, since I didn't want Ramos to think I was a wimp.

We finally topped the ridge and looked over a small meadow. Ian and Stewart were working on their tent, and Billie was helping Uncle Joey set up another one. Joining them, Ramos relinquished my pack and picked up another small bag. "Want to help me?"

"Sure. What are we doing?"

"This is the tent for you and Billie. I thought you could help me set it up." He was thinking that he'd carried it all the way up here for me, so helping was the least I could do.

"Oh... of course. What do you need me to do?"

"Let's put it over there." He pointed to an area not far from the spot where Billie and Uncle Joey worked. It was a relatively flat area, and Ramos pulled the tent and poles from the bag. After unfolding the tent, we began fitting the poles together.

I noticed that all three tents were identical and looked like they were brand new, probably bought with our investment money. All the tent poles were on the outside, with two main poles crisscrossing over the top, and two others on the sides to strengthen them.

It took me longer than Ramos to get the poles into the eyelets, and Ramos ended up doing most of the work to set it up. He didn't complain, so I tried not to feel too bad.

After staking the corners, we unzipped the doorway, and I peeked inside.

"Hey. That looks pretty roomy." It surprised me that such a small tent seemed so big.

Ramos was thinking that, for two women, it was plenty of room, but wouldn't I rather sleep in the hammock with him? He pictured lying next to me, holding me close with my back against his stomach. It would be nice and cozy, and he could keep me warm and safe. With his protection, I wouldn't have to worry about spiders or bears.

I jerked my head around to stare at him. "Hey... not fair. You're just trying to scare me into it."

He shrugged. "Your choice."

I rolled my eyes. "Nice try. But it's not going to happen."

"Oh come on... you're not even a little tempted?" With his big, muscled arms folded together, and his lips twisted into that trademark smile of his, my insides turned to mush. I could certainly imagine how nice it would be to snuggle up with him and feel safe. His big body beside mine would certainly keep me warm... no... hot... so hot.

I shook my head. What was I thinking? "Heaven help me." Oops... did I just say that out loud? "I mean... no... not even a little." Hearing his soft chuckle, I hurried past him and pounced on my heavy backpack. With more enthusiasm than it warranted, I focused all my attention on brushing off the dirt.

As soon as Ramos stepped away from the door of my tent, I pushed my pack inside and got busy untying my sleeping bag. Billie joined me, and we managed to blow up our air pads and lay out our sleeping bags.

It had taken most of the afternoon to get to this spot and set up camp, probably because of me, and the sun hung low in the sky. With the chill in the air, I found my hoodie and slipped it on.

"That's a good idea," Billie said, finding her jacket. "I'm starving. What kinds of dinners do you think they brought to eat?" She was worried about the dehydrated food. "Do you think they'll be any good?"

"I have no idea. To be honest, I've never gone backpacking like this before. Have you?"

Her brows drew together. "I thought you said you went prospecting with your grandpa."

"Well, yeah. I did. But we just came up here and hiked around for the day."

She scratched her chin. "Oh. Well, I've gone backpacking, but only a couple of times. To be honest, I didn't like it much. This hasn't been too bad, but I'm going to miss using a real bathroom."

"I hear ya. Let's ask what we're supposed to do about that, and see if we can get something to eat."

We joined the others and found that Ian had everything under control. He and Stewart had set up a latrine at the beginning of the summer, and they showed us where it was. They also had a bear canister they'd left up here for storing food, and we all got busy putting the packets and snacks inside.

Before we'd left the cabin, Ian had given each of us a water purifier bottle so we didn't have to carry water with us. He showed us to a small stream, further away, for washing up and we replenished our water supply.

With all of that taken care of, Ian set up a small camp stove and heated up some water for our dinners. After the water was hot, each of us chose a meal and found a place to sit and eat. Our conversation turned to the mine and the area Stewart wanted to look first. He pointed eastward toward a rocky ridge. "I think it's got to be in that area. There are a lot of places with crevices that could lead into a mine."

"So is the gold in a cave or a mine?" I asked.

He shook his head. "I'm not really sure, but I think it started out as a cave before they began to mine it. What I do know is that the entrance is near a rocky ridge." He was also thinking there was a rock formation in the shape of a man that was on the south side of the area. If he could find that, he'd know which ridge to search.

With our dinner consumed, Ian showed us how to fold up the remains of the pouch, then passed around a garbage bag for disposal. Being a newbie to backpacking, I hadn't realized that everything we'd carried in would also have to be carried out.

I took a seat on a log beside Uncle Joey, who'd been enjoying the silence of the setting. I picked up that he was glad he'd come, and was thinking that this was a nice break. Now that he could see how vast the mountain range was, he didn't hold out much hope of finding any gold, but he could understand the draw of getting away from everything for a day or two.

"It is peaceful here," I agreed. "And quiet."

Ramos had stowed his backpack in Uncle Joey's tent, and now he disappeared inside. He came out a moment later, wearing a sweatshirt and carrying the bag holding his hammock. Opening it up, he pulled out the hammock and began to tie it between two trees. Since he'd helped me set up my tent, helping him was only fair, so I hurried to his side.

"I have to admit that this looks comfortable."

"Yeah. I thought it would be nice." He finished tying the knots and sent me a challenging smile. "You want to be the first to try it out?"

When he put it like that, how could I resist? "Sure."

He held it for me while I sat down. Before I got settled, he scrunched in beside me. With his heavier weight, I slid on top of him, and sprawled across his lap. I tried to push away and just made it worse. With our weight unevenly balanced, we tilted back a little too far, and the hammock flipped us out onto the ground.

Lucky for me, I fell on top of Ramos, but my elbow jabbed him in the stomach. He let out an 'oof' and grabbed my upper arms while I fought to get off of him. Somehow, I ended up straddling him, which alarmed me even more. He hissed, and I struggled even harder.

"Hold still," he groaned. I stopped struggling, and he rolled to his side, pushing me off of him. I heard loud cursing coming from his mind, but it was drowned out by Billie and Uncle Joey's laughter. Ian and Stewart soon joined them.

Mortified, I scrambled to my feet and glanced down at Ramos, who looked like he was dying. "Are you okay?" I crouched down to touch his arm, and he held a hand up in surrender.

"Just give me a second." He clenched his jaw like he was in pain, but his mind was shuttered, so I didn't know what was wrong. My gaze wandered a little lower, and my eyes widened. Holy hell. I thought I'd elbowed him in the stomach!

"Shelby." His low growl did something to my stomach, and I jerked my gaze back to his.

"Uh... sorry about that." Before I could stop, a laugh burst out of me. I covered my mouth with both hands, and laughed even harder. Ramos sat up, and I could see murder in his eyes. Worried, I got to my feet and backed away.

Unfortunately, I tripped over a limb and lost my balance, tipping backwards onto my butt. Ramos slowly stood over me, and my eyes wandered downward again. Holy hell. Oops. Why did I keep doing that?

He caught me looking, and I jumped to my feet, beating a hasty retreat to my tent. By then, everyone had calmed down, and I got busy brushing the dirt from my pants like nothing was wrong.

Billie came to my side, still giggling a little. "That was hilarious. You should have seen it. I wish I had caught that on video so I could see it again and again."

I shook my head. Thank goodness she hadn't. It was already bad enough as it was. The light was beginning to fade, with only a little time left before it got full dark. "Do you have a flashlight on you?"

"No," she answered. "It's in the tent. Didn't you bring one?"

"Yeah... I just thought... I'll get mine, and we can visit the latrine together." I crawled into the tent and found my flashlight. Pointedly ignoring Ramos, I took Billie's arm, and we left to take care of business.

When we came back, it was almost full dark, and Stewart and Ian were stowing all the supplies for the night. Ramos had his hammock all set up with his sleeping bag inside and netting over the top. Heaving a sigh, I had to admit that it looked pretty cozy.

Billie told everyone goodnight and slipped inside our tent, leaving Ramos and Uncle Joey waiting for me. Uncle Joey motioned me to follow him until we were out of earshot of the others. "Well? Anything we need to know before we retire for the night?"

"Just one thing. Stewart was thinking about a journal entry where Jeremiah mentioned a rock formation in the shape of a man, sitting beside the ridge where the mine is located. So we should watch for that. I still think he wants to keep us away from finding the mine before he does, so we need to keep a close eye on where he goes tomorrow."

"That's good to know. Thanks Shelby. I'm going to bed. Let's hope we can all get a good sleep tonight." Uncle Joey ambled back to his tent and crawled inside, thinking that the hike had tired him out more than he liked to admit. At least he had the tent to himself, and he hoped the air pad and sleeping bag were comfortable.

"He's amazing. Does he work out?"

Ramos nodded. "He has a personal trainer."

"Oh." I chuckled and shook my head. "Of course he does." I glanced up at the dark sky, and my breath caught. "Wow. Look at all those stars." Through the trees, the view was amazing. Wanting to see more, I stepped away from our campsite, closer to the hill.

Ramos followed behind, and we climbed all the way up to the top of the ridge. From here, our view was unobstructed, and the whole sky was a mess of stars. We watched them in silence for a minute or two, and I found my neck had started to stiffen.

"Want to sit down?" he asked me.

"We might as well. I don't think my pants can get any dirtier."

He cleared a spot with his foot, and we both sat on the hard ground. Ramos inched closer to me and leaned back on his hands. I held the back of my neck, to relieve some of the tension, and kept my gaze on the sky, hoping to see a shooting star.

"Why don't you lean your head against me for a minute?"

I wasn't sure that was a good idea, but the temptation was too much, so I scooted closer and leaned against him, letting my head rest on his shoulder. I stifled a groan and let out a sigh. "That's better."

He rested his cheek on the top of my head, and I caught his familiar scent. Relaxing against him, I felt the peace and silence of the moment wrap around us like a warm blanket.

Two shooting stars blazed across the sky, one right after the other.

My breath caught. "Did you see that?"

"Yeah. This view is amazing. I can see why people might like to go camping." He was thinking it wasn't so bad, but maybe that was because I was here with him.

A cool breeze blew across me, and I shivered. He wrapped his arm around me and tugged me close. "Better?"

I nodded, knowing I shouldn't be sitting here like this, but not quite ready to leave. "Have you ever been camping?"

"Sure. I've been camping, but not backpacking like this."

I chuckled. "I haven't either. This is a whole new kind of camping. I've never been so far away from everything. It's crazy how quiet it is."

"Yeah, and you don't see stars like that in the city. I can even make out the Milky Way. Can you see it?"

"You're right. We're lucky the moon's not up yet."

Ramos nodded and rested his cheek against the top of my head.

It was so tempting to turn around in his arms and lose myself in him. He smelled so good, and he was... I caught my breath and pulled away. "Uh... I'd better go."

"Stay," Ramos said. "Just for another minute or two." The longing in his voice caught at my heart, and I hesitated. Knowing I wasn't convinced, he continued. "Nothing's going to happen. Even if you wanted to kiss me, I wouldn't fall for it."

His teasing tone brought a smile to my lips. "Okay. But only until the next shooting star." I relaxed against his shoulder and he tightened his arm around me.

His cheek rested on my head again, and I felt his smile as he spoke. "I don't know if I can sit here that long... but whatever."

My lips quirked up, and we sat in silence for a few more minutes. I soaked in this rare moment between us, knowing it couldn't last, but enjoying it just the same.

A sudden rustling noise came from behind us, and my heart jumped. I let out a little yelp and scrambled to my feet. "Did you hear that?"

Ramos chuckled. "I'm sure it's nothing to worry about."

"Ha, ha. What if it's a bear? Are there really bears up here? I mean... there must be with that bear canister they have back at camp, right?" I backed up and nearly tripped on a rock.

Ramos jumped to his feet and caught my arm. "I'm sure it's not a bear. If anything, it's a cat... a big cat."

Even though he was teasing me, I didn't like it. "That's not helping."

Ramos switched on his flashlight and we started down the hill. I stumbled, and he wrapped his arm around my waist, holding me tightly so I wouldn't fall. After making it back to our camp in one piece, we stopped in front of my tent, and he dropped his arm.

"You sure you don't want to sleep in the hammock with me?"

I chuckled. "Uh... not with our track record. But thanks anyway."

I crouched next to the zipper on my tent and tugged at it. After a few yanks, it still didn't budge. Ramos let out a deep sigh, and knelt beside me, thinking that I couldn't seem to manage without him, no matter how hard I tried.

It must mean that I really wanted him tonight, even though I didn't want to admit it, and this was my way of keeping him close for as long as possible.

"I think the zipper's just stuck," I whispered.

He snorted and held the bottom of the zipper with one hand and tugged up with the other. It opened right up.

Damn, how did he do that?

"Goodnight Shelby."

"Night." I quickly stepped inside and pulled the zipper back down. He disappeared from view, and I sat down to slip off my hiking shoes. Leaving them by the entrance, I crawled onto my sleeping bag. It was too dark to see if Billie was asleep, so I took off my hoodie and pants in the darkness before climbing inside my bag.

Using my hoodie for a pillow, I nestled in deep and tried to get comfortable. The air pad wasn't as soft as a mattress, but it was lots better than the hard ground. Giving in to the exhaustion of the day, I turned on my side and promptly fell asleep.

CHAPTER 11

Sounds outside the tent woke me, and I sat up, surprised that I'd slept so well. I stretched, feeling the pain of every stiff muscle in my body.

A groan sounded beside me, and Billie pushed her sleeping bag away from her face. "Is it morning?"

"Yeah." I checked my watch. "It's just after seven." The cold morning air sent me back under the covers.

"Ugh." Billie sat up and pushed her hair away from her eyes. She searched for her pants and began to get dressed.

After she left the tent, I braved the cold and did the same. Donning a fresh shirt, I slapped on some deodorant and slipped my hoodie back on. My shoes and a double pair of socks came last. Before leaving, I found a comb to run through my hair and pulled it into a ponytail. Finally ready, I could hardly wait to get out of the tent where I could stand up straight.

Emerging into the brisk air, I joined the others near Ian and Stewart's tent. The sun peeked over the Eastern mountain ridge and began to warm the air. We spoke quietly while eating our breakfast bars. Most of us had slept well, and I picked up that Uncle Joey was enjoying the solitude. If he could stop thinking about all the work he had to do at home, he could relax and enjoy it more.

After washing up at the stream, we drank our fill of purified water and refilled our bottles. Ian handed out bags of trail mix, granola bars, and dried fruit to take with us. He also passed out headlamps and told us to bring our flashlights. I put everything in my small backpack along with the first-aid kit, sunscreen, and other essentials that I'd brought.

Before we left, I glanced at Stewart, knowing it was time to put my plan into action. "Before we go, can I look at the map again?"

Stewart frowned, but shrugged and reached into his inner jacket pocket. As he did, I noticed a small, worn book tucked behind it. Was that Jeremiah's journal? He opened the map, and we all crowded around him to see it better. He turned so the map was oriented in the same direction as our position and pointed to the east.

"That's where the ridges are with the crevices I spoke about yesterday. That's where we'll go first."

Just as I thought, the place he was more interested in was further away. He began to close up the map, but I stopped him. "Wait. What's this area right here?" I pointed at the ravine he'd wanted to keep secret.

His brows rose, and he swallowed. "It's a little further than I think we need to go." He wondered if I'd overheard his conversation with Ian, since that was the only reason I'd be interested in that place.

"I think we should go there first. I don't know what it is, but I have a feeling that's where we need to start."

"A feeling?" Ian asked. "What are you talking about?"

"Shelby's a psychic," Billie said. "She gets premonitions about things. If she says we need to start there, then I agree with her."

This was the first time Stewart and Ian had heard about my psychic abilities, and they stared at me in shock.

I shrugged. "It's true, but you know what would really help me out?"

Neither of them spoke, so I continued, "Jeramiah's journal. Old things like that usually have a latent energy about them that can help me pick up more information. Did you happen to bring it along?"

Stewart's mouth worked before any sound came out. He didn't want to show me, but since I was staring right at it, he didn't have much of a choice. "Yes. I did. It's right here." He stuck his hand inside his inner jacket pocket and pulled out the journal. "Do you need to touch it or something?"

"That would help."

Resigned, he handed it over. The leather-bound book was small, more like an old address book of some kind. The brown leather was stained and worn, with yellowed pages inside. I held it in my hands for a few seconds before opening it up. "Where's the map?"

Stewart huffed. "On the last couple of pages, but be careful, they're fragile."

I turned to the map and studied it to find any resemblance to the actual map Stewart had just showed us. I couldn't make out a thing. The writing on the other side of the page was hard to read, but I caught a couple of words in a sentence about rocks.

A slight breeze, carrying the subtle scent of mint, caressed my cheek, and my eyes widened. Had anyone else smelled it? I glanced at the faces surrounding me, but none of them seemed to notice. A breeze coming from the direction of the mountain ridge carried the scent again, only this time it was stronger and hit me straight in the face. "I think you're right. We need to head that way." I nodded toward the mountain ridge.

Stewart pursed his lips, thinking that I'd looked surprised for a minute, like I'd really gotten something, but it could all be an act. Since that was the same direction he'd already told us to go, he thought it likely. He reached his hand out for the book, but I shook my head. "Can I keep it a little longer?"

He let out a sigh, so I continued. "I'll keep it safe. I promise."

"Fine."

"Thanks." I tucked it into a pocket on my backpack and zipped it shut.

With his lips pressed together, Stewart took the lead, and Ian followed behind him. Billie came next, and I followed her, with Uncle Joey and Ramos bringing up the rear.

Ramos wondered if I was really getting something from the journal. Now that he knew I sometimes heard dead people, he wouldn't rule it out unless I said so. I slowed my step until both he and Uncle Joey were within earshot. "It's true, I'm getting something."

They both nodded, and we continued on our journey. The smell of sage and mint came and went, but it never let up, sending a thrill of excitement through me. Maybe Stewart had it right after all? We kept to the trail Stewart set and continued deeper into the mountains.

An hour later, we were at the base of a ridge. We split up, staying within earshot, to look for crevices or spaces that we could explore. Stewart and Ian both looked for a rock formation that looked like a man, and Uncle Joey and Ramos did the same.

I glanced at Billie. "Do you see a rock that looks like a man sitting down?"

Her brows crinkled. "No. Why?"

I shrugged. "I don't know for sure, but I think it might be a sign to tell us where to go."

Both Stewart and Ian were close enough to hear me, and they froze. How did I know that? Maybe I really was psychic? If that was the case, maybe I could actually find it. But where would that leave them? They'd have to share it with us, and they didn't want to do that. Still, it was a catch-twenty-two, since they might not find it at all without me.

Then it hit me. I'd lost the scent of mint. Did that mean we'd gone too far? I turned in a circle and sniffed the air, catching a fleeting scent as I faced north. "I think we should go in that direction."

Stewart's brows rose. That was the direction for the gulch he'd wanted to explore. Resigned, he nodded, and we all headed that way. We came upon some thick vegetation and tried to find a path through, but it was too dense, so we ended up turning back the way we'd come to go around.

After we'd circled back, we headed north again. Trudging up a narrow path, we finally came to an opening that led down into a small ravine.

Stewart froze. "This is it." His pulse raced. This had to be the place. He glanced at the rocks to the right, hoping to see something that resembled a man's body, but nothing stood out to him. Still, it wasn't enough to stop him from continuing down the rise into the gulley.

I sniffed the air, hoping to catch the smell of mint, but couldn't find it. Maybe it would come back at the bottom of the ravine?

The way down was rocky and steep, so it was slow going. It leveled out closer to the bottom, and we found ourselves surrounded by a meadow of grasses with a small stream running through it. Following the stream, we found that it continued much further than we thought, leading into a narrow canyon.

"Do we keep going?" Ian asked.

Stewart's brow furrowed. "I don't know. Let's look around here first."

We spent another hour exploring both sides of the gulch. Ian and Stewart took one side, and the rest of us took the other. A few fissures opened up, and we eagerly followed them as far as we could go, but they dead-ended, and we had to turn back.

Twenty minutes later, a shout came from across the ravine, and we hurried in that direction. Another fissure opened up on that side, and Stewart stood at the top of several rocks, but couldn't seem to go any further. Ian was nowhere to be found.

"Ian's down there, but I can't see him, and he hasn't responded." Stewart shouted, pointing to a place we couldn't see.

"Is he hurt?" Ramos asked.

"I don't know."

I picked up from Stewart that Ian had gone around a boulder and disappeared. He hadn't responded to any of his shouts, so Stewart had stayed put and called to us. From where he stood, it was too steep to head down without risk of causing a landslide.

"I'll come up." Ramos began to climb over the boulders.

"Wait. I'm in a bad spot, and there's no way down from here. Go over that way." Stewart pointed to the other side of the crevice, and Ramos followed his directions. Soon, he'd made it to the top and started down. "Be careful. Those rocks are loose."

A few minutes later, we heard Ramos's shout. "I found him."

"Is he okay?" Stewart asked.

Several tense seconds passed before Ramos responded. "Yeah, but you might want to come down here. Go around the way I did."

Stewart picked his way back down the boulders. Before he could reach the bottom, Uncle Joey had already started up, taking Ramos's path. I followed right behind him, and Billie came behind me. The boulders were big, but they weren't insurmountable. It was getting down the other side that was the tricky part.

I worried about Uncle Joey, but he didn't have any trouble. I mostly scooted on my butt to make it down and Billie followed my example. Stewart wasn't far behind, but he was cursing in his mind that we were all beating him to it.

"What's down there?" he shouted, unable to wait any longer.

I reached the bottom and hurried around the boulder behind Uncle Joey. In front of us was a small opening leading into a cave. Ramos stood at the opening, but Ian had already gone inside.

Stewart caught up to us, and his breath hitched. He rushed to Ramos's side. "Is Ian in there?"

"Yes. When I got here, he'd just come back out, and he was putting on his headlamp. I guess he didn't want to wait for the rest of us."

Stewart stepped into the cave after Ian, but stopped short. "It's pitch black in there." He riffled through his back pack until finding his headlamp. Flipping it on, he headed inside. Following his example, the rest of us found our headlamps.

Uncle Joey turned to me. "Do you think it's in there?"

I sniffed the air for mint, but couldn't smell a thing. "I'm not sure. I'm not getting anything." A sudden fear that a bear might be deep inside the cave caught at my chest. "What about bears? Could one be in there?"

Ramos glanced at me, his brows arched in surprise. "You want to wait?"

I nodded. "Maybe for a few minutes. Just to make sure."

"Really?" Billie asked, surprised. "But this looks like the place he described. I can't just stand here. Come on. Let's go in." She was thinking that, with Ian and Stewart already inside, they'd be the first to be attacked anyway.

She had a point. "Okay. But let's stick together."

Ramos took the lead with Billie right behind him. I went next, and Uncle Joey took up the rear. There was no sign of Ian or Stewart, and, after thirty feet, we found out why. The cave took a sharp turn to the right and blocked out all the light from the entrance.

Shinning my headlamp on both sides of the cave, I found nothing but hard rock that seemed to soak up the light. Rocks and boulders littered the ground and made it difficult to advance. The smell of dark earth and musty air was nothing like the mint I'd smelled earlier.

After stepping over and skirting around several more boulders, we continued deeper into the cave, and I started to get nervous. The walls closed in on us a few times, and we had to duck under large boulders before we were able to continue. How far were we going to go?

A few minutes later, Ramos stopped. "There's a branch up ahead that goes in a different direction. I think they may have gone right. Should we keep going?"

Uncle Joey nodded. "Yes. But if we don't catch up to them soon, let's turn back."

We continued on, going much further than I liked, especially after ducking under several more rocks and boulders. Uncle Joey was just about to call a halt when we heard voices up ahead. Following them, we found Ian and Stewart examining the cave walls.

Ian glanced at us and shook his head, harsh disappointment rolling off him. "This is as deep as it goes."

"I thought this was it." Stewart ran his hands over the walls, searching for a vein of gold. "But I don't see anything."

The rest of us turned to examine the walls for signs of gold, but found nothing.

"Let's go back," Stewart said. "Maybe we missed something." He couldn't go around us in the tight space, so we all turned around and began the trek back to the entrance in single file.

With everyone searching the cave walls for any sign of gold, we worked steadily forward. Uncle Joey was in the lead, and he came to the previous fork in the path. He stopped, making sure we were all together, before he took the path on the left.

"What's the hold up?" Stewart called.

"There's a fork on the path. I just wanted to make sure we went the right way."

"This doesn't seem right," I said. "Shouldn't it be further down?"

"This was the only fork I remember." Uncle Joey glanced back at Ramos. "What do you think? Should we go right or left?"

Ramos wasn't sure, but he nodded anyway. "I think that's it. So go left."

Uncle Joey nodded and continued down the path. We climbed over several boulders and I tried to remember if any of them seemed familiar, but I was completely turned around. Before we'd gone too far, Stewart asked if we could see any light from the entrance. It was pitch dark ahead, and Uncle Joey stopped. "No. Nothing. Should we be there by now?"

Alarm tightened my stomach. Wouldn't it be ironic if, with all our combined expertise, and my super power, we all got lost in this stupid cave?

Uncle Joey was thinking that we'd been so focused on exploring for gold that we'd forgotten to take precautions. We should have marked the walls, or at least laid a rope along the way to guide us back.

"Hold up." Stewart called. "I'm not far from the first fork in the path, so let's think about this."

We turned around. Billie was in front of me now, but I couldn't see anyone else. Ramos was still on the other side of the rocks, but at least I could make out the light from his headlamp.

"Too bad we don't have a way to mark our path," Uncle Joey said.

"We could drop trail mix on the ground every few steps," I suggested. "Would that work?"

Uncle Joey nodded. "Yes. But not the raisins. I don't think we'd be able to see them."

"That's true. I'll use mine first. When I run out, we'll use someone else's."

"Okay." Uncle Joey raised his head so the others could hear him. "I say we keep going, everyone okay with that?"

At their affirmative replies, Uncle Joey turned back around, and I began dropping the brightly colored candy about every ten steps. The pathway narrowed, and another big boulder blocked our way. Had we come to this one before and climbed around it?

Uncle Joey wondered the same thing, but he kept going and climbed over it. I followed him, but slipped and nearly fell. "I don't remember this being so hard."

At the top, I turned to slide down on my stomach, reaching for footholds as I went. Near the bottom, Uncle Joey steadied me, and I landed next to him. My headlamp glistened off the walls of a ten foot cavern. The open space carried the sound of dripping water, but I couldn't see another way out.

"I don't think this is the right way," I said.

Uncle Joey stepped further into the space, his attention caught on something in the corner.

"What is it?" I asked.

"I'm not sure."

I followed Uncle Joey to a jumble of rocks, where something white reflected the light of our lamps. As we got closer, the rocks turned into shoes, and the white stones became bones. I gasped and took a step back.

By then, everyone else had joined us in the cavern. Stewart hurried to Uncle Joey's side and froze, shocked at what lay in front of him. He knelt beside the bones and found a rock pick hammer and a small shovel. "It must be a lost prospector."

Stewart began to search what was left of the skeleton's clothing. Ian watched him for a moment, before turning his attention to the cavern walls, convinced there had to be gold in here somewhere.

Uncle Joey was thinking that the poor fool had been lost in here, and, if we weren't careful, it could happen to us.

Stewart sat back, holding an old tin in his hand. He opened it to find a few coins and some chewing tobacco. "There's no identification on him, but if this is any indication, I'd say he was here in the early nineteen hundreds; that would mean he's been here for a hundred years." He glanced at Ian. "Did you find anything?"

Ian shook his head. "No. There's no sign of gold in here. That miner must have gotten lost."

"Let's see if we can get out of here," Stewart said. "We can always come back another day if we want to."

He said that for Ian's sake, thinking that it might be worth exploring without the rest of us. To find a miner was a sign that this cave had possibilities, and we might be on the right track. In fact, those remains could even belong to Jeremiah Taft.

I didn't think so. Not once had I smelled the minty scent from before. If that had come from Jeremiah, then this wasn't the place.

Once again, Uncle Joey took the lead, with me behind him and everyone following. We made it over the boulder without too much trouble and followed the trail mix all the way back to the junction. How long it took to get there surprised me. My perception of distance was thoroughly skewed in this place, and panic began to rise in my chest.

"So which direction do we go now?" I was so turned around, that I wasn't sure what way to go.

From behind us, Stewart shouted. "Go left at the junction."

We turned in that direction, and I ran out of trail mix. Billie got out her bag and took over, dropping the mix every ten feet or so. Before we knew it, she'd run out as well, and Uncle Joey called a halt.

"Did we miss another fork in the path?" I asked, worried that we'd taken the wrong turn again. "It didn't seem like we'd gone this far from the entrance."

Uncle Joey shook his head. "I didn't see any other turnoffs, but it's hard to tell. I could have missed it." He glanced back at Ramos. "Does any of this look familiar to you?"

Ramos shook his head. "It all looks the same to me."

"That's what I was afraid of." Uncle Joey opened his pack and pulled out another packet of trail mix. "We'd better keep dropping these, just in case."

I took it from him. "I'll do it."

After taking a quick water break, we started off again, sweeping the sides of the cave with our headlamps to make sure we didn't miss anything. Climbing over boulders and rocks, everything seemed the same. In fact, we could be going in circles for all I knew. Would we ever get out of here?

The path in front of Uncle Joey stopped in a mound of rocks, and he swore. "What the hell?"

He glanced to the left and let out a breath. "Wait... it's this way." A small opening to the left beckoned him, and we squeezed between several boulders to try this new direction. After we climbed over several more rocks, a faint light suddenly penetrated the darkness, and my heart raced.

"There it is," I shouted. "The entrance is just ahead."

The last hundred feet or so seemed to stretch out forever until we finally stepped out into the light of day. My knees nearly buckled under me, and I wanted to kiss the earth. Instead, I sat down on a boulder and pulled off my headlamp. With a huge sigh, I turned my face toward the sun and closed my eyes.

Ramos sat beside me. "Feels good, doesn't it?"

"Yes. I'll never go in another cave again."

Everyone sat down. Billie heaved out a shaky breath and turned to Stewart. "So what do you think? Is that the right cave?"

He shrugged. "I don't know. It's the closest we've come to an actual mine, and with that skeleton... it could be. There might be another path in there that would lead us to the gold, but I don't know."

"Do you think you'll come back?"

He held back his excitement and tried to look circumspect. "I'll have to think about it."

"What do you think, Shelby?" She turned my way. "What do your premonitions tell you?"

I shook my head. "I don't think the gold is in there."

Ian's head jerked toward me, and disbelief filled his face. "Why do you say that?"

I shrugged. "It's just a feeling, but I think going back inside is a waste of time."

Ian wondered if I was just saying that so I could come back without him. It's what he'd do, so he wasn't going to give up. He'd just make sure he was better prepared. He and Stewart could come back in the next couple of days and leave us to fend for ourselves.

I sighed. If he wanted to go back in there it was fine with me. Suddenly famished, I rummaged through my backpack for a granola bar and drank most of my water. Everyone else did the same. About ten minutes later, we were ready to leave.

I checked my watch, surprised at how late it was. "It's almost three. I didn't think we'd been in there that long. We'd better head back." I glanced at Billie. "Were you still thinking of leaving today?"

She shook her head. "It's too late now. I'll probably head back in the morning though." She was thinking that finding the skeleton would give her something to write about, but she wasn't sure it was enough, especially when we didn't know who it was.

"There was a story about several men who left to search for the mine and never made it back," I told her. "Maybe one of them got lost in there."

Billie nodded. "What if that was Jeremiah? Maybe he busted an ankle or something and couldn't get out?"

"It's possible," I agreed, not wanting to sound too sure of myself. "But I don't think so. No... I think the Taft mine is somewhere else."

Stewart couldn't believe how sure I was acting, and it made him doubt me. "We'll see. I might want to come back sometime. I don't think it would hurt to check it out, as long as we bring the right equipment. Taking a metal detector would help. But for now, let's head back to camp." He got to his feet and started up the rocks, Ian close behind him.

Billie and I went next, followed by Uncle Joey, with Ramos bringing up the rear. Leaving the gorge behind, we trekked up the steep side of the gully. It was slow-going and, by the time we got out of the ravine, and onto the ridge, I was sweating. The heat of the day shocked me, and I took off my hoodie to tie it around my waist.

Stewart plotted our direction with his compass, and we started off, keeping to the edge of the mountain ridge and following it a lot further than I thought we'd gone. Finally, he checked his compass again and changed our route to a western direction.

To be honest, everything looked different going back, so I didn't know where we were. As the others continued ahead, I needed to stop for a potty break. I'd put it off as long as I could, but I couldn't wait another minute. Luckily, Ramos said he'd wait for me, and I hurried off into a grove of trees.

I went further than was probably necessary, but I wanted to make sure I had my privacy. After taking care of business, I began the trek back. I got to the spot where I'd left Ramos, but couldn't see him anywhere. My heart skipped a beat. Had I gone the wrong way?

I glanced over my shoulder to the stand of pine trees and backtracked. In the grove, I looked for anything familiar, but it all looked the same. I hadn't noticed the slant of the sun before, but figured I should try to head west again.

Several hundred yards later, there was still no Ramos in sight. This time, real panic set in. What was I supposed to do now? I stopped, turning in a full circle to get my bearings, but nothing stood out. I was truly and completely lost.

"Ramos." I shouted. "Where are you?"

Straining my ears for a response, I heard nothing but the wind. Dread tightened my stomach. How could this be happening? I hadn't gone that far. Before I could yell again, the subtle scent of mint hit my nose. I sniffed, finding it coming from my right.

I didn't know if it was Jeremiah helping me, but I was willing to see where it led. The fact that the scent came from a direction I wouldn't have gone worried me. But I was so turned around that I didn't trust my instincts anymore.

I called Ramos's name a few more times, but when no response came, I stepped cautiously forward, heading deeper into the dense stand of pine trees. Had I been here before? Was this the first grove of trees I'd walked to? Losing the minty scent, I stopped. Heaving a breath, I turned until picking it up again.

With my heart in my throat, I continued forward, telling myself that, soon, there would be a break in the trees, and I'd see Ramos. Just a few more steps and I'd find him. I followed the scent, going further and further without coming to anything I recognized.

Certain I had gone too far, I turned around and headed in what I hoped was a more westerly direction. It felt like the right way to go, but what did I know? After walking for a while, with nothing but growing dread, I stopped again. This was all wrong. I'd gone too far.

The scent wavered for a moment and then completely disappeared. Fear churned in my stomach, and I turned, sniffing for the mint that had led me so far. Taking a few steps forward, I picked it up again and nearly groaned with relief.

I followed the scent until I came to a clearing, and hope sprang up inside me. This was it. I hurried the last few steps out of the trees, but stopped short, finding no rocky ridge and no Ramos.

Despair nearly overwhelmed me. Now what? Inside the clearing, a huge tree rose up, higher than all the others. The roots were jumbled and twisted around the base, but the intense scent of mint drew me close. My gaze rose to the top of the tree, and I knew that if I could just climb even halfway up, I'd be able to see for miles.

I stepped forward, studying the tree for a place to start my climb, and my foot slipped into a hole. Before I knew what was happening, the earth crumbled beneath both of my feet, and I slid into a narrow opening that swallowed me whole.

Dirt rained down on my head as I continued to fall. I scrambled to grab anything to stop my forward motion, but I was going too fast. I managed to turn to my stomach and grab a protruding root. It slowed my descent, but broke under my weight.

Plunging into the darkness, my feet lost contact with the earth, and I fell with nothing beneath me but air.

CHAPTER 12

I landed on my backpack, and the impact sent the air whooshing out of me. Still on an incline, I slid several more feet before coming to a stop. I couldn't catch my breath, and panic tightened my chest.

Wheezing, I finally managed to suck in some air. As it filled my lungs, tears filled my eyes. What had just happened? Shocked and dazed, I lay unmoving on the hard ground.

Through a sheen of tears, I became aware of a shaft of light that angled down through the opening above me. The distance of the hole sent terror down my spine. How had I fallen so far? The final drop from the ledge had only been about nine or ten feet, but including the fall to the ledge, the nine foot drop, and the slide down, I was a long way from the surface.

After catching my breath, I tried moving. Slowly at first, I managed to move my arms and legs, grateful they still worked with little pain. I pushed into a sitting position without too much trouble, but the back of my head began to pound, and I tasted blood.

Touching my mouth, I found my lower lip swelling, and blood seeping down my chin. My cheek hurt as well, and my fingers came away bloody from an abrasion.

I felt the back of my head, wincing at the pain from a large bump, but at least it wasn't bleeding like my face. A chill swept over me, and I glanced at my surroundings. Where was I? In the dim light, I couldn't see far, but the dark spread out before me like I was in a deep pit of some kind.

Unable to see anything in front of me, the spreading darkness sent shards of fear into my heart. Panicked, I wanted nothing more than to get out of there. Pushing to my feet, a spasm of pain radiated from my ankle, and I plopped back down. Worried it was sprained or worse, I carefully rotated my foot. It didn't hurt too badly, and relief poured over me. It wasn't broken, so I could probably put some weight on it.

I glanced up to the hole I'd fallen through and fear pulsed through me, draining me of strength. The distance looked too far to climb out. The sides of the narrow shaft were filled with dirt and rocks that might give me something to hang onto, but getting above the ledge would be a problem.

Still, I had to try. I managed to get to my feet before a wave of dizziness washed over me. I sat back down and gently rested my pounding head on my knees until the dizziness passed. As much as I wanted to get out of this hole, I needed to give myself some time to quit shaking first.

Leaning back against the tumble of rocks, I tugged off my backpack and pulled out my flashlight. Flicking it on, I could see an opening to the right of me that continued several feet into the darkness. Was this a mine? Was that why the scent of mint had brought me here?

Nothing beyond the light into the hole seemed threatening, so I took stock of my injuries. I lifted my shirt to find cuts and bruises all along my stomach and arms. My head pounded and I ached everywhere. Grateful for my first-aid kit, I pulled it out and got busy.

I cleaned my lip and cheek with a wet alcohol wipe, hissing from the sting, and applied antiseptic. After untying my sweatshirt from around my waist, I did the same with the small abrasions all over my arms and stomach, getting them as clean as possible. Luckily, my kit also contained some aspirin, and I swallowed a couple, grateful I still had water in my bottle.

A sudden chill washed over me, so I slipped my hoodie back on, grateful I still had it. As the sleeves brushed over my skin, I felt the sting of the abrasions on my arms and sucked in a groan. Waiting for the pain to subside, I sat still, resting until my strength returned.

Glancing up at the small opening, I knew I had to get out of here while there was still enough light to see. No one would ever find me down here. Putting my things back into my backpack, I eased it onto my shoulders and winced. Taking a breath, I pushed the pain away, and began to crawl up the rockslide, careful to take my time and find solid footing with each step.

I made it about two feet before the rocks gave way and I slipped back down. Breathing heavily, I picked another spot, closer to the side of the shaft and tried again. This time, I got a little closer to the drop off point before I slid back down. Growing weary, with my ankle throbbing, I knew I couldn't keep this up.

I had one more attempt left in me. This time, I mustered all the strength I had left and began to climb over the boulders, taking my time to secure my footing with each step. Without falling, I made it to just below the small ledge, but could go no further. It was straight up, and too high above me to reach without a rope.

Desperate, I dug my fingers into the dirt to carve out an indentation big enough for a handhold. I couldn't make much of a dent, so I grabbed a nearby rock to gouge out the dirt. Some of it came loose, but the dirt was still too hard to give me a handhold.

My legs began to tremble from exhaustion. I couldn't stay on my perch any longer. I'd just have to try again later. Slowly inching my way back down the slide, the rocks beneath my feet suddenly gave way. I yelped, and slid all the way to the bottom on my stomach, hitting my chin several times.

Coming to a stop, I lay in a heap and groaned in pain. Touching my chin, I found that it was tender and bleeding. I pushed to a sitting position and pulled off my backpack, taking out my kit to bandage it up. Using my last sterile alcohol wipe, I ripped it open and held it against the cut, wincing at the searing pain.

As I wiped the cut, drops of blood continued to soak into my sweatshirt. Desperate, I found a gauze packet in my kit and ripped the package open. With shaking fingers, I held it against my chin to stop the bleeding.

Swallowing, I closed my eyes and took a few calming breaths, hoping I could finish bandaging my chin without passing out. Several seconds later, I felt composed enough to open a couple of bandaids, and taped them across the gauze to hold it in place.

With that done, I sat in a blank stupor, shocked at my predicament. How had this happened? What was I going to do now?

Tears gathered in my eyes, but I willed them away, and studied the darkness in front of me. Maybe there was another way out? Taking hold of my flashlight, I flipped it on and rose to my feet, careful not to move my head too quickly.

Limping toward the dark hole, I shined my light inside, and the scent of mint wafted across my nose. My light hit the walls of a small cavern, and a vein of gold shimmered beneath it. My heart hammered. With shortened breaths, I stepped closer. What in the world? Was this the mine? My foot hit something hard, and I glanced down, shining my flashlight so I could make it out.

The sight of an old leather boot shocked me, and I gasped, nearly dropping my flashlight. The boot lay on its side, attached to fraying clothing and the white bones of a dead man. Raising my light higher, I let it rest on the empty face of a skeleton. My shoulders and neck tensed with fear.

The sudden scent of mint permeated the space, and clarification hit me. "Jeremiah? What happened to you?"

Gathering my courage, I knelt beside him, finding that his bony fingers still held nuggets of gold. "Why didn't you leave?" Maybe he'd been injured? There didn't seem to be any breaks in his arms or legs, but I wasn't about to touch him to find out.

Straightening, I continued forward, traveling deeper into the darkness. Could this lead to the original entrance? The cavern narrowed, turning into a tunnel of sorts, and continued on for at least a hundred feet, maybe more. It began to slant upward, and my heart soared.

I hobbled forward along the tunnel for several more feet. My elation rose until I found my way blocked by huge boulders and fallen stones. This must have been the reason Jeremiah couldn't get out. The mine had collapsed, leaving him a prisoner inside. Damn.

Turning around, I shambled back, this time shining my light along the walls. Deep veins of gold cut through the rocks, covering the entire area. So much gold it took my breath away. I shook my head. I'd found the mine, but now I was stuck down here with Jeremiah's skeleton. How ironic was that?

Reaching the spot where I'd fallen in, I glanced back up. The light above me had dimmed slightly. Soon, there would be no light at all. In the deepening silence, the enormity of my situation washed over me. How was I ever going to get out of here? They had to know I was missing by now, but how would they find me in this hole? Would I end up like Jeremiah?

Not wanting to go there, I took stock of my food supplies. I had one breakfast bar along with a few pieces of dried fruit to see me through. My water bottle was half empty, but, if I could find some water down here, I could purify it, so that was positive.

But what if there was no water? How long would I last down here? I shivered, knowing there was nothing I could do about it right now except wait and do my best to stay alive. I could try and climb out again, but I didn't think I'd be successful, no matter how hard I tried.

If there was another way out, I had to believe that Jeremiah would have found it. But... maybe this sinkhole wasn't the only one? I shone my light around the area again. Closer to the rock slide where I sat, I noticed several tree roots with darkness behind them. Had this rock slide covered that part of the mine? Could something be back there?

I limped forward. The dirt and rocks surrounded a small opening, but it looked big enough to crawl through. I ducked down and shined my light to the other side. It looked like another tunnel. Should I risk it?

Crouching onto my hands and knees, I left my backpack behind and managed to wiggle through the small opening. I came out into a small tunnel carved through with layers of earth and rocks. The top was high enough for me to stand, so I examined the walls, finding more golden veins.

Stepping further in, I could see that the tunnel continued a few more feet before opening into a small, solid rock cavern. Shining my light on the cavern walls, surprise filled me to find carved figures on all sides.

With growing wonder, I stepped closer to examine the petroglyphs, noting that several figures wore feathers atop their heads, and held spears, or bows and arrows, in their hands. They faced other figures who had distinctly pointed hats on their heads. These figures held shields and upraised swords in their hands.

As I followed the petroglyphs that circled the cavern, I tried to make sense of the story behind them. In the silence, a barely audible, low tone registered in my mind. It came and went, sounding like the beat of a heart. A slight breeze blew across my face, smelling of wild grasses and smoke and sending goosebumps along my arms and down my neck.

The beats grew louder, and the carvings seemed to come alive. As I followed the curve of the cavern, the petroglyphs showed the feathered figures defeating the helmeted men. The last image showed a chieftain, his head outlined in a spray of feathers, and standing with his arms outspread and raised high above his head.

Just below the figure on the ground sat a configuration of flat rocks in the shape of a box. The flat rock on top of the box had been pushed aside, leaving the contents exposed. What was in there? From the extent of petroglyphs in the room, it had to be important.

Drawn forward by an insatiable curiosity, I stepped close enough to peer inside. At first it appeared empty, but as I studied the contents, I made out bits of bones, along with several golden nuggets. Was this someone's body? I glanced above the box, looking closer at the chief depicted in the glyph. The warm scent of wild grass and smoke filled my senses. Panicking, I gasped and coughed.

The beating tone became louder, growing in volume until it pierced my head with pain. Wanting it to stop, I pushed at the flat rock and tried to shove it back into place. It was heavier than I'd thought, but after a few tries, it finally moved. As soon as it covered the opening, the pounding stopped, leaving me panting.

As I stood unmoving in the weighty silence, another soft breeze wafted past me. This time it smelled of green meadows and dark earth, and the scent of smoke was gone. I swallowed, hoping that meant I'd done the right thing.

More than ready to leave this place, I stepped away, slowly retreating toward the tunnel that brought me here. Whatever this place was, it seemed sacred, and I felt like an intruder.

I slipped quietly down the tunnel and found the small hole I'd come through. After crawling to the other side, I retreated to the rock slide, where I'd fallen in, and sat down, trying to catch my breath. What had just happened?

From what I could remember about the legends of this place, it seemed like the Native American tribes had made a deal with the settlers. But those men with the helmets were much further back in history. Could they have been Spanish Conquistadors? Could the discovery of this gold mine really have happened that long ago?

If this spot was sacred, like it seemed, maybe that was one of the reasons no one had ever exploited it. Maybe that's why the gold was still here after all these years. If this place wasn't meant to be found, maybe that's why those who did never made it home again.

Even as I thought it, I knew I was playing into superstition, but after what I'd just witnessed, it totally made sense. Now that I'd seen it, did that mean I would die here too? I had replaced the burial stone, like the beating seemed to want me to, so maybe that would count for something.

The soft light coming from the hole above me began to dim, and I knew it wouldn't last much longer. With no other way out, it was time to accept the fact that I was stuck here until someone came to rescue me. And that depended on one thing.

My dog.

I closed my eyes and tried to think. My head pounded, and my body ached. I couldn't remember if I'd told Uncle Joey or Ramos that Coco was a search-and-rescue dog. Even if I had, would they remember that Coco was an option and call Chris?

But wouldn't they call Chris anyway? With darkness closing in, I just hoped that Ramos and Uncle Joey wouldn't waste time looking for me tonight. They needed to get back to someplace with cell phone reception and call Chris. If Chris brought Josh and Coco up here, I had a chance.

With so many worries, and absolutely nothing I could do about them, I let out a resigned breath, feeling tears prickle at the backs of my eyes. This was bad. I could easily die here. Despair threatened to overwhelm me, but I shook my head and fought against it. I may be stuck here for a while, but that didn't mean I wouldn't make it out. I wasn't going to give up hope that quickly.

Swallowing back my tears, I switched off my flashlight, knowing I needed to conserve the batteries. Pulling the hood of my sweatshirt over my head, I found a dry place and huddled against the wall, pulling my knees against my chest and under my sweatshirt. Using my backpack as a pillow, I rested my head and closed my eyes. With my stomach a ball of nerves, and my head pounding, I tried to relax and conserve my energy.

It was going to be a long night.

I jerked awake, my leg cramping up in the cold. Opening my eyes, I couldn't see a thing, but that didn't stop me from jumping up and stretching my leg out. I moaned in agony and massaged the muscle until the cramp went away.

I'd left my flashlight next to me, and now I flipped it on, needing some light to keep from freaking out. My heart rate slowed, and I carefully did some stretches to warm up. My watch read two o'clock in the morning, and I swore out loud a few times just to help me feel better.

That calmed me down a bit, and I limped around the small space, swinging my arms to get my circulation moving. I wasn't sure what the temperature was, but I was freezing. Remembering my headlamp, I pulled it out of my pack, turned it on, and slipped it over my head. That way I could conserve my flashlight batteries without giving up my light.

The headlamp wasn't as bright as my flashlight, but it was better than nothing. Needing to keep moving, I stepped through the tunnel and back into the space where Jeremiah's bones lay.

Standing near his bones didn't bother me as much as before. I even felt a slight kinship with him, until I remembered that he'd brought me here with his minty scent. Of course, I'd wanted to find the mine, and he'd led me right to it, so I couldn't be too mad at him.

I examined the area around him and found a leather pouch filled with golden nuggets. He must have been ready to leave when the tunnel collapsed. I couldn't imagine a worse fate than lying there waiting to die. Studying him more closely, I noticed that his skull sat at an unnatural angle.

I crouched down closer and examined his skull. With a shock, I realized there was a big hole in the side of his head. Had he shot himself? I scanned the area again and found the gun nestled beside him in his decayed clothing. Well... I guess he hadn't waited after all.

Not wanting to dwell on that, I decided to explore the tunnel at the cave-in. This time, I noticed that several rocks had been removed from the pile. He must have tried to dig his way out. Near the top of the pile, a rock sat at the outside edge. It didn't look too big for me to move, and removing it might create an opening wide enough for me to crawl through.

After jostling the rock back and forth a few times, it started to come loose. I pulled a little harder, and several of the rocks around it shifted. With a gasp, I released my hold and took a step back, realizing that the whole thing could come down on top of me.

The rock beside it slipped, sending one rock to the ground. Another rock fell, then another, and another. I backed away as fast as I could and turned to run. As the rocks crashed behind me, I ducked back into the cavern with Jeremiah's remains.

Hurrying toward my own rock slide, the sound of falling stones behind me abated, and I sagged in relief. A cloud of dust surged toward me, and I quickly turned my back. Once the dust had settled, I decided to head back to see the damage.

A small hope burned in my heart that the rocks may have shifted enough to leave an opening I could get though. Stepping cautiously into the tunnel, I found the way completely blocked. If anything, it was worse than before. Damn. Of all the bad luck. Or was it the curse?

Shaking my head, I let out a sigh and headed back to the cavern. At least the excitement had warmed me up. I glanced once more at Jeremiah, searching for a blanket or something to keep me warm. Just a few minutes ago, I didn't even want to touch him, but now it didn't seem so bad.

The clothing I did touch basically fell apart, so I knew that was a wasted effort. With a sigh, I turned back to peer up at the sky from the hole I'd fallen through. Amazingly, I could see a few stars in the blackness.

Just seeing those stars helped me settle down, and I stepped back to my corner to huddle against my back pack. Turning off my headlamp, I curled into a tight ball and closed my eyes, determined to rest, even if I couldn't sleep. Soon, it would be morning, and Chris would bring Coco to find me.

I repeated that mantra several times before drifting into a fitful sleep.

Faint light penetrated my prison, sending hope into my heart. Finally. I'd never spent such a long night in my life. After checking my watch every few minutes, I didn't think the night would ever end.

At six in the morning, I knew it was too early for anyone to find me. Still, it would happen today. I just had to believe it. My empty stomach growled, so I got out my breakfast bar and began to eat. I hadn't planned on eating the whole thing, but it was gone before I could stop. I hadn't seen any sign of water in the cave, so I only drank a few swallows and saved the rest.

Now that I had some light, I used it to examine the rocks around me. Those from the slide just seemed like regular old rocks, so I looked over some that were further away. I came across a beauty, and held it up toward the light.

From prospecting with my grandpa, I knew most gold was found in white quartz. This piece of white quartz held several veins of golden color and was the size of my fist. I found several more stones of equal quality, but none of them were as pretty as this one.

My grandpa would have had a heart attack to see what I'd found. It would have been a dream come true. He'd told me about all the good things he'd do with the money, and all the people he'd help. That was the main reason he thought he'd find the mine, since he'd use the gold for good.

If he could see me now, he'd probably be shaking his head and thinking that, even though I'd found the gold, it wasn't worth risking my life. But how was I supposed to know this would happen? Prospecting wasn't supposed to be life-threatening.

I glanced at poor Jeremiah and changed my mind. Maybe it was after all. I stepped beside him and examined the ground, finding several broken, golden rocks along the ground where Jeremiah sat. The amount of gold in the cavern astounded me.

Uncle Joey had told me earlier that just one ounce of good-quality gold was worth eighteen hundred dollars. Judging on the amount of gold I could see, this mine was easily worth millions. But was taking it a good idea? Based on what had happened to Jeremiah, and now me, I wasn't so sure. Maybe it really was cursed.

As crazy as that sounded, I also had to consider the other cavern with the petroglyphs. That was probably a huge find, but it somehow seemed like a bad idea to disturb that place. I certainly didn't want to go back in there.

Still, seeing this amount of gold all in one place was enough to make me dizzy. I let out a breath. None of this would matter if Coco didn't find me. In the end, I'd rather live than die in here with a bunch of gold.

An hour passed, then two. Growing impatient, I wondered if I should try to climb out again. But how was being outside any different than staying in here? If I got out, I'd be no closer to finding our camp than I was in here. I should have just hugged a tree and yelled for Ramos. Why didn't I do that?

Two more hours passed, and I tried not to panic. I needed to give them time. I might even have to wait until tomorrow, but I could do that. I knew they were looking for me, and just knowing that helped calm me down. They'd find me. They had to.

I spent the next three hours singing some of my favorite songs. After that, I began to pray. I'd been praying in my mind a lot already, but maybe I wasn't praying hard enough?

At five o'clock, true despair set in. Why hadn't they found me yet? Coco was amazing. He knew my scent better than any dog on the planet. He should be able to follow my trail, so what was going on? Maybe Ramos and Uncle Joey hadn't called Chris until after they'd searched for me themselves. Maybe Coco wasn't even here yet.

I shook my head. It was okay. I was still alive and basically uninjured. There was plenty of time for them to find me.

My mouth had gone dry three hours ago, after I ate the last of my fruit. I knew I needed to drink some water, but what would I do once it was gone? Giving in, I took a couple of sips. It hardly helped at all. Maybe I should just drink the rest? I wasn't sure making it last would help me more than drinking it all at once.

With that in mind, I raised it to my lips, ready to finish it off. Before I took the second swallow, the water ran out. Really? I tipped it upside down, hoping for another drop or two, but nothing came out.

Frustrated and ready to cry, I took a deep breath and calmed down. This wasn't the end. I could last another night, and I was nowhere near dying. Besides that, there was still time for them to find me before it got dark.

As the next couple of hours passed, my hope began to wane.

Watching the dim light above me turn into darkness sent fear into my heart. I tried to shake it off. Facing another night in this dark, damp place was hard to swallow, but I could do it. Since they hadn't found me by now, they'd probably call off the search until morning.

But that was okay. Looking for me in the dark was dangerous for everyone, and I'd be fine. I scrunched my eyes together and took a deep breath, not about to cry. It was okay, another night wouldn't kill me.

Somehow, I managed to curl up and drift to sleep. I felt myself falling and jerked awake. Complete darkness surrounded me, and, for a fleeting moment, I wondered if I'd gone blind. I reached up and flipped on my headlamp, letting out a breath of relief.

As I straightened from my huddled position, my muscles screamed. My neck hurt, and spasms ran across my back. I struggled to my feet and did a few stretches to loosen up. That helped, and I took a couple of steps toward the cavern to continue the process.

Sudden weakness came over me, leaving me panting for breath. Surprised that I could barely shuffle along, I stopped to rest. My headlamp dimmed, and I staggered back to my spot just before it went out. I felt for my backpack and sat down, taking off my head lamp and stuffing it inside. I still had my flashlight, but I wasn't about to turn it on now.

Tempted to glance at my watch for the time, I debated if I should. What if it was only nine or ten? In the end, I looked anyway, finding it was just after midnight. But hey, that was better than ten, right? That meant only six hours until daylight.

I dozed off and on after that. Dreams of falling kept jarring me awake, but, after a while, I was too tired and cold to care. Right before six in the morning, I couldn't take it any longer and climbed to my feet. I moved to a place below the slide, where the light could hit me in the face, and counted the seconds as it grew lighter.

Somewhere around one thousand and ninety-nine, I stopped counting. A new day had dawned, and I'd done it. I'd made it through the night, and today was the day they'd find me.

After an hour, I grew tired of facing the rocks and moved back so I could lean against them. Another hour passed, and I stood to stretch. Even though I ached everywhere, the bump on the back of my head had gone down, and my ankle was only a little stiff.

I spent the next few minutes rearranging my hair, combing through it with my fingers. I even managed to braid it, and used the elastic band to hold it together. Today, my lip didn't seem quite as swollen, and the rest of my cuts and bruises were on the mend, so at least I wouldn't look too bad when they got here.

Morning slowly gave way to afternoon. I still had hope that they'd make it, but I needed to be prepared in case they didn't. One more night wouldn't kill me. I knew a person could go for three days without water, and I'd had a few swallows yesterday, so I could last another day or two, right?

I sat in my spot, feeling weaker than I liked to admit. I'd need all the energy I could get to climb out, once they got here, so resting was a good idea. I closed my eyes and listened to all the sounds I could hear above me. I picked up the chirping of a few birds, but nothing more seemed to penetrate this deep hole.

As the hours slipped by, I couldn't bear to look at my watch, and I drifted into a light sleep.

CHAPTER 13

I woke with a start, hearing a sound I hadn't heard for days. My heart began to pound. I rose unsteadily to my feet and looked up at the hole. A louder bark sounded, closer than the last one, and tears filled my eyes.

"Coco." My voice cracked. Clearing my throat, I tried again. "Coco." I leaned against the rocks, looking up at the circle of blue sky.

Coco's head came into view, and he barked and whined like he was in pain.

"Coco! You made it! I'm down here." I yelled as loud as I could, but my voice sounded weak and breathless.

"Mom? Mom! Are you down there?"

"Josh! Yes. I'm here."

"Shelby?" Chris called.

"I'm down here." I fought to hold back my tears.

"Are you okay?"

"Yes."

Chris's head came into view, but I couldn't make out his face. "We're going to get you out. Just hang on."

I heard Josh yelling in the background. "She's alive. She's down in a hole. We need the ropes."

I couldn't hold back my sobs, even though my eyes were mostly dry. Chris stepped too close to the edge, and a few rocks came loose. "Shelby! Look out."

I got out of the way in time, but several more rocks slid down after the first. Once the dust cleared, Chris called to me. "Shelby? Shelby! Are you okay?"

"Yes. I'm okay. They missed."

"Hang on. We're trying to figure this out."

"Just send me a rope. I can climb out with a little help."

"The ground is unstable up here, and we don't want to cause a cave-in, so we're taking it slow." Chris disappeared, but Josh took his place. From here, it looked like he was lying down on his stomach, and with his lighter weight, he could stay there and talk to me without causing a landslide.

"Mom? You okay?"

"Yeah."

"We've got a rope, and we're attaching it to a rock climbing harness. If we send it down, can you put it on?"

"Yes. Send it down."

"Okay. We're getting it ready."

"Could you send some water down with it?"

"You got it!" He disappeared, and I heard him yell. "She wants water."

I waited, hearing other voices, along with Coco's frantic barking. I'd never heard anything so wonderful in all my life.

"Okay," Josh called, leaning over the edge. "I'm sending it down now." His gloved hands lowered the harness and length of rope. "It's too dark to see you from here, so I'm going slow. Tell me when you get it."

"I will." I watched it descend, but it got stuck on the ledge. "Josh. It's stuck. Pull it back up and lower it more to your left."

"Okay." He pulled it back up and inched to his left, dislodging a few clods of dirt, but nothing more. He lowered it again. This time, it crossed over the side of the ledge and kept coming down, finally landing on the slope of rocks in front of me.

I scrambled over the rocks to the harness and grabbed it, then carefully stepped back to solid ground. Josh continued to lower the rope, giving me plenty of slack. "Okay," I called. "That's good."

"Let me know when you're ready."

"I will." The water bottle was clipped to the harness, and I pulled it off. It took me a couple of tries before I could get the stupid cap off. Holding it to my lips, I took several slow swallows and groaned. Nothing had ever tasted so good. I tried to pace myself, but it wasn't long before I'd drunk the whole thing. Now I understood what it really felt like to be dying of thirst.

Ready to get out of there, I slipped on my backpack and studied the harness. There were two leg loops and a waist loop, so I slipped my legs in, one at a time, and pulled the loops up to my thighs. Pulling the waist loop around me, I fastened it tightly around my middle and double-looped the belt.

"Dad wants to know if you're doing okay," Josh called.

"Yes... I'm just about ready."

I took one last look around the mine, making sure I didn't leave anything behind. "Okay. I'm going to start climbing up the rock slide. If you'll keep the rope taut, it will keep me steady and help me climb. There's a place where I can't get up any higher, so you're going to have to pull me past that. I'll let you know when I get there."

"Hang on." Josh disappeared, and I heard him talking to someone, then he came back. "Okay. We're ready when you are."

"I'm starting to climb now." The rope went taut, and it began to pull me up the slide, causing me to lose my footing. "Slow down. It's too fast."

Josh called over his shoulder. "You're going too fast for her. Just keep the tension on the line until I say so."

The tension eased and I let out a breath. Several rocks had already slid out from under me, but at least I hadn't gone tumbling back down on my face. I took my time, carefully picking my way up to the nine foot drop beneath the ledge. Getting over the ledge would be the tricky part.

"Hold," I called, and Josh repeated my call to whoever was manning the line. The tension held steady and I examined the rope. It was centered on the rock ledge, and I worried that pulling me up would cut through the rope. "Josh. I'm below a ledge and I can't go any further. Is the rope sturdy enough to pull me up?"

"Mom... it's the best. It will do the job."

I let out a shaky breath. "Okay. Then I need you to pull me up, but do it slowly."

"Okay. Just tell me to stop if you get in trouble."

"I will."

He spoke over his shoulder, before turning back to me. "He's ready."

"Okay, go ahead."

Josh gave a thumb's up, and the rope tightened. It began to lift me up, and I leaned back so my head wouldn't hit the ledge. As the rope pulled me closer, I grabbed the ledge with my hands and pushed away so I could clear it.

"Stop!"

Josh repeated my command, and the pulling stopped.

Now that I was waist-high above the ledge, I clambered on top of it, managing to get to my knees. Balancing against the rocks in front of me, I slowly rose to my feet. A wave of dizziness washed over me, but, after making it this far, elation filled my heart.

I studied the loose dirt and rocks above me. It was still a long way up, but after the first few feet, it slanted to more of an incline, so it shouldn't be too hard. I leaned forward, getting ready to climb.

Without warning, the ledge underneath me gave way. I dropped several inches before the rope picked up the slack. Sounds of crashing rock brought several shouts from above.

"Mom? You okay?"

"Shelby!" Chris called. "Shelby?"

"I'm fine," I called, hanging in mid-air. My heart pounded in my chest. I was so done with this. "Just pull me up. Get me out of here."

The line went taut, and I grabbed the rope as it lifted me higher. Coming to the incline, I released the rope to keep my hands and face from scraping against the rocks. I managed to push away with my hands and feet to protect my body from the worst of it.

At last, Josh's face came into view. He helped me up as I crawled over the edge, and I collapsed on the ground. I couldn't seem to move and just lay there for a moment, relief and gratitude washing over me.

Josh knelt beside me, and Chris ran to my side. Between the two of them, they took my arms and helped me up, walking me away from the edge of the hole. As I got my feet under me, both of them wrapped their arms around me. I sank my face against Chris's chest and bawled.

A furry body joined us, barking and head butting me. I pulled away from Chris and Josh and knelt down to give Coco a hug. "Thanks for finding me, buddy."

He whined and began to lick my face, woofing, *you hurt, I help.*

"You did help me. It's okay. I'm fine now."

After giving Coco another pat, I was pulled to my feet. Chris was done sharing me with the dog, and he pushed my backpack off my shoulders so he could wrap his arms around me in a tight hug. I caught his thoughts of gratitude that they'd found me, along with his worry, fear, and deep relief.

I gave in to my tears and sobbed against his chest. I was really out of that hole, and I'd never take my life for granted again. No amount of gold or money or any worldly possession I had was greater than this moment.

Chris held me until my sobs subsided, murmuring that I was okay now, and telling me over and over that everything was all right. Finally calming down, I pulled away to wipe my face with my sleeve.

Others in the group approached, and Chris gently let me go, keeping one arm around me for support. I glanced at the group of rescuers, finding familiar faces I hadn't been sure I'd ever see again.

"You look like you got beat up," Billie said, rushing over to give me a quick hug. "I'm so glad you're okay, but I think you need some medical attention."

"Not until I hug her." Uncle Joey stepped to my side and wrapped his arms around me. "You scared us to death."

Ramos crowded in beside him and nearly shoved Uncle Joey out of the way. He gave me a gentle hug, thinking that he'd never been so scared in his life. It was like I'd vanished into thin air, and there was nothing he could do about it. "I'm glad you're okay."

Before I could respond, he let me go, and Dimples immediately took his place. "Shelby... what are we going do with you? You can't keep doing things like this to us." His hug was a little too tight, and I worked hard to keep from wincing.

"Give the lady some space." Dante Mitchell, my firearms instructor, stepped into view. Noticing my surprise, he grinned. "When Harris said you were missing, I thought I'd come help. There are a few others up here as well, but they're with another group." He glanced at Chris. "Did anyone radio them?"

"Yes. I did." Dimples said. "They're all meeting us at base camp."

"Good." Dante studied my face. "I've been trained in first aid, so let me take a look at you." He glanced over his shoulder. "Let's get Shelby some more water. And bring me that first aid kit." He turned back to me, not liking the cuts and bruises on my face and the blood on my sweatshirt. "Come sit down over here."

Taking my arm, he led me to a rock in the sun. Grateful he was taking charge, I sat down and closed my eyes, soaking in the warmth. I'd been so cold that I wasn't sure I'd ever get warm again. Chris handed me a bottle of water, and I took a long drink. "Thanks."

Chris knelt beside me. "Here. Let's get that harness off of you."

I stood and let him undo the belt. He helped me slip it off, and I sank back down.

Dante looked into my eyes. "Did you hit your head?"

"Yeah. But it's feeling better."

"Did it knock you out?"

"No." I showed him the bump on the back of my head, and he touched it with gentle fingers. Nodding, he thought it wasn't too bad. In fact, it was a stroke of luck that it wasn't worse after falling so far.

He asked me a bunch of questions before taking the bandage off my chin. "You might need some stitches in that." He put another bandage on it and looked me over. "Are you hurt anywhere else?"

I let out a huff. "Does everywhere count?" I tried to smile, but it tugged at the cut on my swollen lip. "I twisted my ankle, but I can walk on it. I think my hiking boot saved it from being worse."

He glanced at my feet, taking note of my ankle-high boots. "Which one?"

"My right."

He knelt down to check my ankle, pulling up the pant leg to see if there was any bruising. "It looks okay, so I'm not going to mess with it. Your boot's better than a splint right now."

I nodded and finished off the rest of my water. "This water is amazing. I'm feeling better already."

"Good. When was the last time you had any?"

"I had a few swallows yesterday, and maybe half my water bottle the day before... I think. It's a little fuzzy."

He nodded, thinking I was dangerously dehydrated. Walking three miles back to camp might be more than I could manage.

I didn't want to argue, but how else was I supposed to get there? "I can make it back to camp. I'll be fine."

His brows rose in confusion. Why did I say that? "Don't worry, Shelby. We'll get you back."

Oops. I nodded. "Oh... of course. That's not what I meant... I'm just a little weak, but I can manage." I'd do my best, but I knew I'd need a lot of help to make it all the way back to camp. From there to the cabin might have to wait until tomorrow.

Dante picked up on my distress and lowered his voice. "Your uncle wants to bring in a helicopter to take you to the hospital. I think it's a good idea."

I straightened and glanced at Uncle Joey. As much as I might want to do that, it was a lot to ask when I wasn't hurt that bad. Besides, I didn't want to leave Chris, Josh, or Coco behind. "I don't need that."

"You sure?" He thought that was a mistake. Even as healthy as I was, I'd been through a lot, and he thought it might be too much for me to walk out of here.

I sighed. "I think so. I just need a walking stick of some kind. I can make it."

He shrugged. "All right. Then let's go."

I felt his urgency to get back to camp while there was still daylight left. While he'd been helping me, the others had put away all their gear. Dante joined them, and Chris came to my side. He put his arm around me for support and helped me to my feet. "Manetto wants to send for a helicopter."

"I know, but I'm okay." I leaned against Chris. "As long as I can lean on you, I think I'll make it."

He wasn't so sure about that, but there wasn't a place for a chopper to land in this rugged terrain anyway, so he didn't argue.

Josh came to my side, slipping my backpack over his shoulders. "I've got your backpack. Is there anything else you need?"

"No." I shook my head. "Thanks Josh." He nodded and put his arm around me. With Chris on one side, and Josh on the other, we started off. "Wait."

They stopped, and I turned around, needing one more look at the spot where I'd fallen. The big tree was still there, beckoning me forward, just like it had a few days ago. The sinkhole where I'd fallen was barely visible from here. It was tempting to mark it, but with what? I could always stack a few rocks in front of it, like a cairn or something. But would they stay that way?

"Josh, did you bring a GPS tracker?"

"Yeah." He wondered why I asked, since I should know it was general procedure for search and rescue teams. "Don't worry Mom, we'll make it back. I know where we are."

"Let's go Shelby," Chris said, urging me forward. His eyes held worry and concern, along with bone-deep weariness. He'd gone through hell these last few days, and my heart softened with love and a little guilt at what I'd put him through.

I opened my mouth to tell him about the gold, but found that I couldn't speak of it. I just wasn't ready to tell anyone what was down there—and I wasn't sure if I'd ever want to. Right now, the only thing that mattered was making it out alive and being here with the people I loved.

Swallowing, I nodded, and turned my back on the most amazing discovery of a lifetime.

Walking between Chris and Josh, I kept up with them for a while, but my energy soon flagged. I had to keep stopping more and more often to catch my breath. Uncle Joey came back to check on me a few times. He even offered to spell Chris and Josh off, but neither of them wanted to let go of me.

Since they were practically carrying me along, I asked them to stop for a minute. They found a boulder just the right size to sit on, and I sank down on top of it. Coco stayed by my side, while Chris and Josh went ahead to talk to the others.

"You want some more water?" Ramos asked, coming to check on me. I shook my head, and his brows drew together. "How about a granola bar or something? When was the last time you ate?"

"I don't know." I leaned over and braced my arms on my knees and closed my eyes. "But I'm not hungry. Let's just keep going."

"Hold on." Ramos crouched down beside me. "You need to eat something." It shocked him that no one had thought to give me something to eat. What was the matter with them? He handed me a granola bar full of chocolate, thinking that I wouldn't be able to resist it. "Eat that."

I fumbled with the wrapper, so he opened it with one quick twist of his fingers. "Here."

I mumbled my thanks and took a small bite, knowing that he wouldn't let me go anywhere until I'd eaten some of it. Up ahead, Chris spoke with Uncle Joey and Dimples. Dante joined them, and he nodded his agreement. I picked up Uncle Joey's plan to radio for a helicopter.

It wouldn't be here for about an hour, but by then we'd be out of this rocky area, and a suitable spot for them to land was just beyond that. I didn't have the energy to argue, and it surprised me. What had happened to my unstoppable attitude? Now that I'd been found, all I wanted to do was sleep.

Wanting to prove that I could manage, I tried to jump to my feet, but staggered instead. My head spun, and I sat back down. Ramos grabbed my arm to steady me, and worry tightened his eyes.

"I'm sorry," I said, meeting his gaze. "I'm sorry I kept walking instead of hugging a tree. I should have known better." Tears slipped down my face.

"Shhh," Ramos said, crouching beside me and wiping a tear from my cheek. "It's okay. Don't give it a second thought. You're exhausted. Let us take care of you. Okay?" I frowned and he continued. "Please?"

With reluctance, I nodded. "Okay, but this is embarrassing."

He chuckled, and I managed a small smile. He helped me up, wrapping an arm around my waist, and we joined the others. From then on, I got passed from person to person and lost count of who helped me keep one foot in front of the other.

An hour later, we made it back to base camp before the helicopter landed. The other group had arrived long before us, but they'd waited to see me before heading back to the cabin. Besides Bates, Williams, and Clue from the police department, a couple of people from Chris's law firm were also there.

More of our friends, along with a few search-and-rescue team members, had volunteered to come up in the morning, but Dimples had radioed the command center with the local sheriff's department that I'd been found, so they didn't need to come.

Each of them greeted me enthusiastically, and I couldn't hold back the tears. Bates even gave me a warm hug, although he was thinking I looked terrible. Since I knew he was right, it didn't even bother me, mostly because I was too tired to care.

By the time the helicopter landed, I was more than willing to climb on board. I picked up that everyone else was glad I was leaving too, since I was slowing them down and they were ready to go home. Uncle Joey had decided that he and Chris would accompany me, but that was all the helicopter could hold.

"But what about Josh and Coco?" I asked. Several voices chimed in, telling me that they'd be happy to take them home, but Uncle Joey shushed them all.

"Ramos will take care of them. He'll see that they get home safely."

That shut everyone up. Uncle Joey was thinking that, although everyone there was capable, he didn't trust any of them like he did Ramos. Hearing that almost undid me, and I swallowed back more tears.

After a quick wave to Josh, and a grateful nod to Ramos, I climbed inside the chopper beside Chris. The pilot shut the door, and Chris and I fastened our seatbelts. Uncle Joey sat in front, with Chris and me in the back. Once everyone was secure, with headphones and seatbelts on, the pilot took off.

My stomach did a little flip-flop, and I nearly lost my granola bar. I grabbed Chris's hand and swallowed. Soon, we were high above the trees and headed home. I relaxed against Chris and let out a breath, grateful to just sit and do nothing. I couldn't wait to get home and take a hot bath and sleep in my own bed.

About an hour later, the chopper came to rest on the helipad at the hospital. The sun had just set by then, and a team of medical personnel waited for me. I was a little embarrassed by all the fuss, but the fact that I'd been lost for a few days in the mountains qualified me for the special treatment. Or maybe it was Uncle Joey's influence? It was hard to know.

Soon they had me situated in the emergency room and were taking my vitals and starting an IV. After evaluating my condition, it was determined that I'd stay for a few hours with a special IV drip and get a few stitches in my chin before they sent me home.

Chris left to call Savannah and my mom to tell them we were at the hospital, and when we'd be home. While he was gone, Uncle Joey stayed by my side. He wanted to make sure I was all right, but I picked up how bone-tired he was, and my heart swelled with gratitude.

"Thanks Uncle Joey. I'm so sorry I got lost." I studied his face, noticing the few days' growth of beard and the tired set of his jaw.

He shook his head. "Me too. But you're okay now, and everything's going to be all right."

Tears filled my eyes, and I raised my arms for a hug. He held me close for several long seconds. Before pulling away, he kissed my forehead. Giving me a tremulous smile, he patted my arm. "I'll call you tomorrow."

Chris came back just as Uncle Joey was leaving, and they spoke in hushed tones for several minutes. It was something about me, but I was just too tired to listen. Chris came to my side and pulled a chair close. He took my hand and raised it to his lips.

He studied my face, and his eyes filled with tears, but he blinked them away and managed a lopsided smile. I opened my mouth to apologize, but he shushed me. "Honey.... don't apologize. It wasn't your fault. We found you, and it all worked out."

I swallowed around the lump in my throat. "I was so scared. But I knew you'd come. That's what got me through it. You and Josh... and Coco."

He nodded. "Josh and Coco were amazing. I've never been so grateful for a dog in my life."

I smiled in spite of my tears. "So what happened? When did Uncle Joey call you?"

Chris took a deep breath and composed himself. His eyes cleared, and he began. "From what I heard, I guess Ramos waited for you longer than he should have before he sounded the alarm. By the time he alerted everyone, you were nowhere to be found."

He couldn't understand how I'd gotten so far away without hearing them shouting for me, or why I didn't start yelling myself. Knowing I'd heard that, he quickly continued. "At least Stewart had the presence of mind to take the coordinates of the last place you'd been seen with his GPS tracker. It still makes me mad that you didn't all have them."

His frustration grew, but he tried to tamp it down for my sake. "By the time they called off the search that night, it was dark, and they still had to hike back to camp. They decided to wait until morning to hike out and call for help. I got the call around eight-thirty the next day, so they must have left the campsite before dawn."

He was thinking that he'd been with a client when Uncle Joey's call came through. When Elise told him Manetto was on the phone with an urgent message, Chris had felt a moment of utter terror. He'd known immediately that something bad had happened to me.

Finding out I was only lost, and not dead, helped. Then, knowing he had a search-and-rescue dog at his beck and call saved him from total panic. "I knew if anyone could find you, it would be Coco."

Tears welled up in my eyes again. Seeing them, Chris squeezed my hand tightly. "I canceled everything at the office and left. On my way home, I pulled Josh out of school, and we threw our gear together. I called Savannah at her school and talked to her. I'm afraid she isn't happy with me because I wouldn't let her come, but I didn't want to worry about her, too."

I nodded. "So she's at my mom's house?"

"Not right now… actually I think your mom stayed at our house with her, but I'm not sure. I just know that they're at our house now." He was thinking that they could hardly wait to see me… and there might be a surprise—

Glancing my way, he cleared his throat. "Anyway, Josh and I didn't get to the cabin until noon yesterday. Manetto and Billie were waiting for us. While Manetto took us back to the campsite, Billie drove to the local sheriff's department to set up a command center and wait for Harris and the others who were on their way to join the search."

He shook his head. "It surprised me how many came. And more were planning on coming tomorrow if we hadn't found you."

I could only nod, afraid that, if I tried to speak, I'd just start crying again.

"They all got to camp this morning, and we split up into two groups. Stewart and Ian led the other group toward the area where you'd found a cave. I guess he thought you might have gone in that direction."

"But what happened yesterday? You said you got to the cabin at noon."

"Yes we did, and Manetto led us to the campsite, but when we arrived, Ramos, Stewart, and Ian were gone. They were out looking for you. It was after three by then, and we had to wait for them to get back before we knew where to start searching." He rubbed his hand through his hair and huffed out a breath. He'd been so frustrated that they'd had to wait.

"When they came back empty-handed, Ramos offered to go back out with us, while Stewart, Ian, and Manetto stayed at the camp. I think Manetto wanted to come, but he was beat." Chris thought Uncle Joey was in great shape for a guy his age, but losing me up there had taken a toll on him.

"Anyway, we tried so hard to find you yesterday and last night, but Coco couldn't track your scent." He shook his head. "It turned out that we'd started looking in the wrong spot."

"What? How come?"

"Stewart wrote down the wrong numbers. I honestly don't know if he did it on purpose, or if he was too rattled, or what. By the time we figured it out, it was too dark to continue the search. I'm so sorry we didn't find you yesterday."

I shook my head. "No... don't be... it's fine."

Chris sat back in his chair and closed his eyes. "It was rough. Josh and I both knew that our chances of finding you alive were getting slimmer with each passing hour. Coco didn't want to stop either, but we couldn't risk it in the dark. Anyway, this morning, we made it back to the correct starting point, and Coco picked up your scent pretty quick."

He shook his head. "You don't know this, but you went a long way before you fell into that hole, probably a good three or four miles. It wasn't in a straight line either, and it wasn't anywhere near where you should have been."

I sighed. "I'm not surprised. I got turned around and then I panicked. I should have stopped walking long before I fell down the hole. I'm so sorry I put you through that. All of you."

"Hey... I know. It's okay. You're safe now."

I nodded and tried not to cry, but my eyes filled with tears anyway. Seeing them, Chris came to the edge of the bed and sat beside me. He pulled me into a warm hug, rubbing my back in comforting motions. I rested my head on his shoulder and let him soothe me. I took several deep breaths, and the tears subsided.

Chris pulled away, and I rested my head back on the pillow. "So now it's your turn. How did you end up in that hole?"

"That's the weird thing, I—" The beeper went off on my IV machine. "Does that mean I'm done?"

Chris glanced at the bag and nodded. "I hope so. I'll find a nurse."

He came back a few minutes later with a nurse, who checked everything out and told me I was good to go home. While she took out the IV, Chris left to call Uncle Joey. He'd given Chris strict instructions to call when I was discharged so he could send a car for us.

It took another half-hour to finish up the paperwork. The nurse put me in a wheelchair and wheeled me out to the patient pick-up zone. I wasn't sure what to expect, so it caught me off-guard to have a black limo pull up. The nurse was surprised too, and she wondered if I was a celebrity or something.

I held back a smile and thanked her while Chris helped me inside. I sat back in sleek luxury, feeling horribly dirty and unkempt. I'd purposely avoided looking in a mirror, afraid of what I would see, but now I wished I had. I might have been able to do something about my appearance before I got home. Oh well.

It was full dark when we pulled in front of our house, but lights blazed from all the windows. Chris helped me out, and the front door flew open. Savannah rushed out the door and threw her arms around me.

"I knew Coco would find you!" She hugged me tight, and I held her close, struggling to keep from crying.

She pulled away and raised her arm in a sweeping gesture. "Do you like it?"

I took a closer look at my house, and my breath caught. The driveway, garage, sidewalk, and the whole front of the house was covered in red, pink, and purple hearts.

"Oh my gosh." I held my hand to my mouth, and unexpected tears splashed down my cheeks.

"After Dad called with the news, a ton of people came over and did this." She was thinking that a lot of people loved me, and it had helped make up for how scared she'd been.

I sniffed, and cleared my throat to get my tears under control. "Whose idea was it?"

She shrugged, thinking it was Holly, but she didn't know for sure. "I don't know. Look, there's Grandma. She's been waiting for you too."

We hurried to the house, and the hug from my mother was one of the best hugs I'd ever gotten. No one loved me the same as she did. As she held me tight, she poured her strength and love right into my heart, and it was then that I knew I'd be okay.

Josh and Coco came home around midnight, tired and worn-out. Even though I'd been in bed asleep, I heard the commotion and got up to see them. We spoke for a few minutes, and I gave them both lots of hugs before Chris ordered me back to bed. I fell asleep quickly and didn't wake up again until eight the next morning.

I wasn't sure what day it was and got up to find Chris in the kitchen making breakfast. "What day is it?"

"Friday."

"Did the kids go to school?"

"No. I let them stay home, but they're still asleep."

Just then, Coco came rushing in through the doggy door, woofing *you home, you home.* I knelt down to rub his head and kiss his nose. He was so happy to see me that I almost started crying again. What was wrong with me?

After giving him another rub, I stood up and glanced Chris's way. "So, are you taking the day off too?"

"Yes. I got all my court cases and appointments rescheduled for next week."

I swallowed. "Thanks honey."

He came to my side and pulled me into his arms. "I'm just glad you're okay. You never finished telling me your story. How did you fall into that hole anyway?"

I shook my head. "I was looking up at that big tree. I thought maybe if I climbed up high enough, I could see which way to go. The next thing I knew, the ground gave way, and I was sliding down into the pit. At least it went down at an angle until I hit the ledge, or I might not have survived."

Chris nodded. "Yeah, you were lucky."

"I tried climbing out, but it was too steep. It was awful. Knowing I was stuck down there in the dark was the worst. If you hadn't found me..." I shivered.

Chris pulled me against him and held me tight. My stomach made a gurgling noise, and he chuckled before leading me to the kitchen table. "I've got some eggs and toast ready, do you want some?"

I grinned, but winced as it pulled on my cut lip. "Yes. That would be great."

For some reason, I couldn't talk about all the gold I'd found, or Jeremiah's remains and the cavern with the petroglyphs. I wasn't sure why, but every time I thought about sharing, the words got stuck in my throat.

Maybe I didn't want Chris to be burdened with that knowledge. Or maybe it wasn't the right time. Since I didn't feel bad about keeping it a secret, maybe it was just as well.

I spent the rest of the weekend with my family, taking it easy. It wasn't hard since everyone wanted to take care of me, and, with all my cuts and bruises, not to mention the aches and pains, I had to admit that I enjoyed being pampered. It was also great to talk to so many of my family members and friends who'd been worried about me.

Uncle Joey even told me to take a few days off before coming into the office. Still, by the time Monday morning came along, I was ready to get back to my normal life. If I had known what the day held in store for me, I might have stayed in bed.

CHAPTER 14

I arrived at the precinct at nine that morning with two dozen donuts. Besides Dimples, Bates, Williams and Clue, I wanted to thank everyone else for all the well wishes. Most of them had called me, even Chief Winder, and their concern had filled me with warmth.

After the donuts disappeared, Dimples motioned me over to his desk. "You ready to get back to work?" He wasn't sure I'd want to yet, but he could still use my help.

Since he was right, I asked him a question instead. "How's the case going? Did you make any progress?"

"Yes and no," he began. "I tracked Jinx down, but I haven't spoken with him yet. That's where I could use your help. Want to go with me?"

"Maybe."

Dimples sent me his biggest smile, knowing how much I loved watching his dimples move around in his cheeks. Working with me was the best, and he was grateful I'd come in today. He couldn't always solve the cases he worked on alone, but, together, we were unstoppable, and he was lucky I was his partner.

Wow. He was certainly loading it on. Why was that? Under all of those positive thoughts, I caught a tendril of unease, and I knew there was something he kept from me that I wouldn't like. Hmm... that didn't sound good.

I raised my right brow. "Where would we be going, exactly?"

"Uh... we're going to corner Jinx at work. It should be a piece of cake."

Now I knew something was up. "And where is that?"

His shoulders slumped. "He's a maintenance worker for the sewage treatment plant."

My eyes widened. I'd driven by that plant before, and the smell was bad, even from the street. "Seriously? Maybe we should wait until he goes home for the day."

"I'd like to do that, but it's better to catch him at work."

"But it stinks there."

His lips turned down. "I know, but it's not that bad."

I wrinkled my nose. "Speak for yourself. Can't you send a couple of cops to pick him up and bring him down here?"

Dimples sighed. "I would, but it's a lot less problematic to talk to him at work. He can't avoid us if we show up, and, more importantly, I think it's better not to draw attention to him in case word gets back to his gang."

Now it was my turn to sigh. How could I argue with that? "Fine. Let's get this over with."

Dimples smiled again, giving me another look at his cheeks to soften the blow. I just rolled my eyes and followed him out to his car.

On the drive over, Dimples filled me in on the case. "Jinx isn't his real name of course. It's Joel Bardsley, and I found him through his ties to the vigilante group. They've got a big following on social media, and Jinx is one of the biggest hotheads of the group. He's not someone you'd want to meet on a dark street."

"Well... as long as he doesn't jinx us... right?"

Dimples rolled his eyes and snorted. "I think catching him at work means he'll be less volatile."

"Volatile?" I snickered. "That's not a word you use much. But you might have a point. Although I'd say catching him at work means it's going to be more... malodorous, or putrid, or even foul. Yes... foul's a good word to describe where we're going."

He shook his head. "Say whatever you want. But at least we'll be able to talk to him."

"True, true."

We exited the freeway and began the drive down a long stretch of road on the edge of the city. About a block away, the first fumes of the sewage plant reached my nose. "Crap. You can already smell it."

"Yup," Dimples said. "A lot of crap going on around here."

"Ha ha."

Dimples pulled into the parking lot, trying his best not to react to the smell.

Didn't he know he couldn't fool me? "If I'd known we were coming here, I would have put a few drops of essential oils in a handkerchief to hold over my nose."

A muscle in his jaw ticked, but he kept his mouth shut. He was thinking that I could complain all I wanted, but catching a killer should be worth a little inconvenience, right?

He had me there.

Inside the plant, Dimples pulled out his badge and introduced us to the receptionist. "We just need a word with one of your employees, Joel Bardsley. We'd rather he didn't know we were coming, so if you'll just point us in the right direction, we'll be happy to find him."

The young woman shrugged and typed his name into her computer. "It looks like he works in the pretreatment processing area." She stood, pointing toward a double door on the far side of the wall. "Go through there and all the way to the end of the hallway. Another set of double doors will take you to the pretreatment area."

"Thanks." Dimples and I followed her directions through the doors and down the long hallway. We didn't see many people, but those we did see were wearing white coveralls with white helmets and protective glasses. Some even wore gloves.

It made me just a little nervous, especially when we pushed through the double doors and stepped inside a large, open area that housed huge pipes and three big storage tanks. Raw sewage came through the pipes and was processed through a series of filters before entering the tanks.

The smell was bad, but not nearly as bad as I'd expected. Two workers monitored the drainage pipes and filtering process to make sure nothing got past the filters to clog the pumps. Noticing us, one of the workers approached.

"What can I do for you?" he asked, pitching his voice loud enough to carry over the machinery.

"We're looking for Joel Bardsley." Dimples showed the man his badge. "We just need to ask him a few questions."

The man nodded, thinking that Joel had finally gone too far with his vigilante justice agenda, and it didn't surprise him. "I'll send him over." He headed to the third set of workers and pointed toward us. I couldn't hear him, but I easily picked up that he was telling Joel that we wanted to talk to him.

Joel froze, staring at us with half-lidded eyes, and easily determined that we were cops. He contemplated running, but he didn't want to look guilty in front of his coworkers, so at least Dimples had that part right. A slow walk later, he came to stand beside us.

"You wanted to see me?"

"Yes." Dimples motioned to the double doors. "Let's talk out there."

Dimples and I led the way. I didn't like turning my back on Joel, especially since he was thinking that he could shove between us and run if it came down to it. But he held back, thinking that he wouldn't do anything so stupid, since he needed to know why we were there first.

The double doors shut behind us, and we turned to face him. Dimples introduced us before he began. "We're here because we'd like to ask you a few questions about Troy Hudson's murder. He was a friend of yours, right?"

Alarm rushed over Joel, causing his heart rate to spike, but he covered it with a shrug. "I knew him, sure, but we weren't close, and I have no idea who might have killed him."

"No?" Dimples continued. "We heard he owed you a big debt, and he was in the process of paying you off when he was killed. What can you tell us about that?"

He shrugged. "Don't know what you mean. He didn't owe me nothin'. Whoever told you that was full of crap. Maybe they're the ones with something to hide. Like I already told you, we weren't close, and I don't know what you're talking about. If that's all, I've got to get back to work." He stepped back toward the double doors.

"Jinx. We're not done with you." I used my authoritarian mom voice, hoping to put some fear into him.

Hearing his street name sent his heart racing, but he covered his panic and turned back with a sneer. "Oh I think you are. Unless you're here to arrest me, I don't have to talk to you."

"It would go better for you if you did," I continued. "I don't think you meant to kill Troy. And, if you help us out, we might be able to cut a deal with the D.A.'s office. Maybe even get the charges dropped from murder to manslaughter."

Jinx scoffed. "Whatever happened to Troy... it had nothing to do with me." He was thinking that this was all Troy's fault, and we weren't going to pin this on him. Troy was the idiot who thought his debt was repaid. He was even more stupid to threaten Jinx with exposure if he didn't say they were even. An idiot like him didn't deserve to live.

"We know Troy threatened to expose you and your group if you didn't cut him loose. I think that's why you killed him. How did Redman take it? I don't imagine he was too happy about it."

Jinx sucked in a breath, finally realizing he might be in deeper trouble than he'd thought. There was no way I could know any of that, unless someone had been there and seen him kill Troy. But that didn't make sense. He could have sworn they were alone. Something fishy was going on here.

Knowing he'd killed Troy, I decided to capitalize on his thoughts. "When Redman finds out we have a witness to your murder of Troy Hudson, I don't think your life will be worth much, do you?"

Jinx panicked. We had a witness? He couldn't risk going to jail, and if Redman found out, he'd kill him for being so sloppy. His only option was to find out who our witness was and kill him. The only way to do that, was to run.

Turning, he ran back through the double doors and into the treatment center. We took off after him, chasing him past the first two treatment tanks. He reached the third and climbed up a ladder to run along a steel walkway above the churning tank of sewage water. On the other side of the building, he could slip out of the exit and disappear.

Dimples surged up the ladder right behind Jinx, but I stayed back, not about to risk falling into an open sewage tank. Just above the tank, Dimples tackled Jinx on the narrow walkway. Jinx fought back, elbowing Dimples in the stomach. Dimples lost his hold, and Jinx rose to his feet. Before Jinx could turn to run, Dimples took a swing at him, catching Jinx in the jaw.

The force of Dimples's punch sent Jinx colliding into the railing. Jinx's upper body began to tip over the edge, and his face contorted with fear. At the last moment, Dimples grabbed Jinx's coveralls, but Jinx was too heavy, and they both toppled over the handrail and fell into the smelly tank.

I may have screamed, since the supervisor quickly pushed an alarm which stopped the rotation device inside the tank. Several workers quickly ran to the tank, managing to pull Dimples and Jinx out without too much trouble.

They hustled the men to the back corner and immediately sprayed them down with a hose mounted on the tiled wall. Several more workers rushed in, shouting that they needed to be taken to the decontamination unit right away, and I lost sight of them.

The smell was so much worse now, causing me to gag. Poor Dimples. I tried to breathe through my mouth so I wouldn't throw up, but I knew I had to get out of there. I turned and nearly collided with a worker who'd come to get me. "Detective? If you'll come with me, please?"

I managed a nod and rushed out of the room, holding my hand over my nose and breathing through my mouth. In the hall, I glanced his way. "Is my partner going to be okay? Are there harmful chemicals in that vat or is it just... you know... poop?"

"He'll be fine. We have protocols in place for something like this." He was thinking that they'd never had to use them before today, but at least they had procedures to follow. It should be enough to keep my partner's exposure to the harmful bacteria at a minimum.

Eww... my stomach roiled, and I clenched my teeth to keep the nausea away.

The worker led me to a break room with a comfortable couch along one side of the wall. It didn't smell bad in here, and the windows looked out over a nice lawn area with shade trees and flowers.

"Please have a seat. We'll have your partner back to you in no time."

"Okay... thanks. Uh... the guy with him needs to come with us as well. We're arresting him, so don't let him go."

The man's brows rose, but he nodded and left. I turned my gaze out the window and took a couple of deep breaths to get under control. Still... just thinking about Dimples falling into a vat full of raw sewage sent shudders through me.

Luckily, I only had to wait about half an hour before the door opened, and Dimples stepped inside. He wore white coveralls with slippers on his feet. His face was drawn, and he carried a large, plastic bag containing his clothes, along with a smaller bag holding his phone, wallet, and gun. With his hair poking up in all directions, and his skin a little pink, he looked like he'd been through a car wash.

"Are you okay?"

"Yes." Totally humiliated, he didn't want to talk about it. "I'm fine. I've got Jinx. Let's go."

"Okay."

I followed Dimples into the hall where another worker stood beside Jinx, who was wearing handcuffs and a smirk. Dimples took Jinx's arm and led him out of the building. After stuffing Jinx in the backseat, Dimples opened the trunk and threw his dirty clothing inside, but kept the bag with his personal items with him.

He came back around and got in the car. I settled down in the passenger seat and wrinkled my nose. Even though they'd both been detoxed, the smell was still pretty bad. "Did they spray you guys with something?"

"Yes." Dimples glanced my way. "And I'd appreciate it if you didn't tell anyone at the precinct what happened."

I raised a brow. "Uh... but... don't we need to put it in a report or something?"

A low growl escaped from his throat, and I picked up his humiliation that he'd fallen in a tank of shit. The guys would never let him forget it. If I valued our partnership at all, I would keep it to myself.

"Oh... right. Sure. Of course. I won't tell a soul, but how are you going to explain your nice, white coveralls?"

He had another set of clothes in his locker. He'd change as soon as we got there.

"But what about him?" I motioned toward Jinx.

"You can put him in a room. Just wait for me there."

"Okay." I didn't want to point out that plenty of officers would know something was up with the way Jinx was dressed... and the way he smelled was bound to draw attention. Even if Dimples changed his clothes, someone would probably see him in his white coveralls. "I won't say a word, but if someone figures it out, don't blame me."

Dimples responded by flattening his lips, and giving me a terse nod. After parking at the station, we parted ways, and I managed to get Jinx into an interrogation room. Several minutes later, Dimples joined us.

After taking one look at Jinx, Dimples motioned me out into the hall. Even though he'd changed, he hadn't planned on needing shoes, so he didn't have any. He'd managed to find a pair in a lost-and-found crate, close to his size, so that worked.

He'd turned in his gun for a replacement, but kept his wallet and badge, even though they were both a little soggy. Still, he couldn't seem to get the smell out of his nose, and it was killing him.

"Feeling any better?"

"Don't mention it... literally. Don't."

I swallowed down a chuckle. "I'll try. But you have to admit—" He lifted his index finger to threaten me, and my eyes widened. "Okay. You got it, partner."

He shook his head and pursed his lips, thinking that, of all the horrible things he'd been through, this was probably the worst. "Let's get back to Jinx. What did you pick up? We don't really have a witness, so what was that all about?" Dimples worried that we could even hold this guy since we didn't have any solid evidence against him.

"I know, but he thought that the only way we could possibly know he'd killed Troy was because we had a witness, so I went with it." I explained everything Jinx had been thinking about Troy, his debt, and that Troy had threatened to expose Jinx and the whole vigilante group.

"Wait... so Troy actually threatened to expose them?"

I shrugged. "I guess. Jinx was thinking he'd have to kill the witness, or Redman would kill him first."

Dimples rubbed his chin. "We might be able to work with that."

"How?"

"We make him a deal. If we can get him to turn on Redman, we could put a stop to their whole operation. Let me give Grizzo a call. He's been working with vice, and I think they've been watching The Punishers. It would be a real accomplishment for us if we could take them down."

I hadn't seen Grizzo for a while, and I didn't want to see him now. Not long ago, he'd found out about my ties to Uncle Joey, but he hadn't pursued it because I'd handed the ringleaders of a drug operation to him on a silver platter. Seeing me, he was sure to remember all that, and I'd be on his radar again.

Dimples put the call through to Grizzo, and the man came right up. He hadn't expected to see me, but, after we explained what we had, he forgot all about my ties to organized crime.

"Do you know what this means?" His eyes widened. "We've been trying to get Redman off the streets for months. He's the biggest gun runner in the city. Do you think this guy you've got will cooperate?"

Dimples nodded. "If he thinks we've got him dead to rights on the murder charge, he might, especially if we convince him we have a witness."

Grizzo could hardly believe his luck. "Let's see what we can do. Why don't you and Shelby go talk to him, and I'll watch from the observation room. When he's ready to make a deal, I'll come in."

I followed Dimples into the interrogation room and picked up pretty fast that Jinx had decided he wasn't talking to us without a lawyer. That might be bad, but, since I'd pick up everything from his mind, he didn't need to say a word. I just didn't like having Grizzo watching me, but there was nothing for it now.

Dimples picked up right where I'd left off at the sewage treatment plant, telling Jinx that we had an eye witness who put him at the scene of the crime. "You're going down for murder in the first degree, and that doesn't even count the body in the crematorium."

Jinx flinched. If we'd found out about Ryan Cox, he was done for. Redman would never trust him again, no matter what he said or did.

"We know it was Ryan Cox, so you might as well stop pretending." At his gasp, I leaned forward. "But today's your lucky day. Detective Harris has a deal for you. It's a way out, where you don't end up dead. I'd consider it if I were you."

Jinx focused on me, his eyes big and his mind blown. "This makes no sense. How could you know?"

I sat back in my chair. "Like I said, we have a witness. You're going down no matter what. In fact, it might be just what Redman wanted." I shrugged. "It almost seems like he set you up to take the fall."

Jinx's brows drew together. How could that be? Would Redman really do that? His lips twisted with the answer. If Redman had known, or even suspected, that Jinx had taken a few jobs of his own, it was a definite possibility. In fact, it was the only thing that made sense. Redman must have set him up because he wanted the competition eliminated.

"It makes sense, doesn't it?" I continued. "So the question remains; do you want to take Redman down? You know you can. He's the bigger fish we're after, and now's your only chance to do it. So do you want the deal or not?"

"Fine. I'll take the deal. What do you want to know?"

His eagerness took Dimples by surprise. Wow... I really was a miracle worker. Dimples shrugged, trying to keep a straight face so Jinx wouldn't know how excited he was. "We need something on Redman."

Jinx's face turned gray. Double-crossing Redman was a big risk, but what choice did he have? At least this way, he might get out of this alive, and he'd get revenge on the lying bastard.

"I might have something I can offer you, but you have to make it worth my while." He was thinking about the shipment of guns that was coming in today. If he gave us the place and time, Redman would go down for sure.

"Is it about a gun shipment happening today? That would certainly do the trick."

Jinx blinked. "How... how did you know?"

I shrugged. "That's not for me to say. But if you give us the place and time, I'm sure we could cut you a deal." I turned to the mirror. "Right, Grizzo?"

A few seconds later, the door flew open, and Grizzo stepped in. He was thinking that I'd blown this case wide open. If he could catch Redman red-handed during a gun deal, it would be huge.

He glanced at Jinx and introduced himself. "I'm a specialist with the vice squad, and I'm here to make you a deal."

Jinx and Grizzo bargained for several long moments before Jinx finally agreed to a lesser sentence in return for his cooperation. "But you'd better hurry." Jinx glanced at the clock. "The deal's going down in an hour."

Both Dimples and Grizzo swore in their minds, thinking it wasn't enough time. Jinx told them where the exchange was taking place, and Grizzo left to mobilize a swat team.

Dimples motioned me out of the room, and Jinx protested. "Hey. What about me?"

"If this all works out, you'll get your deal." Dimples told an officer to process Jinx's arrest, and we hurried to Grizzo's office.

Grizzo was on the phone, but Dimples spoke as soon as he hung up. "Shelby and I will head over there now to see what we're up against. I'll radio what we see, and you can get into place. We'll let you know when the guns arrive, and then we can storm the warehouse."

"Sounds good." Grizzo nodded. "Go."

As we left Grizzo's office, Dimples caught my gaze. "I know I'm asking a lot after everything you've been through, but I'd like you to come, just in case you can pick up anything." He raised a hand to cut off my protest. "But you can stay in the car when it all goes down. You won't be in any danger, I promise. Will that work?"

How could I turn him down when he looked at me with those big, brown, puppy-dog eyes? "All right, I can do that." Since I was his partner, I should be going with him, but just the thought of being involved in a shoot-out was enough to give me heartburn.

We stopped at his desk on the way out. He pulled out a handgun, checked the chamber, and grabbed a clip of bullets, stuffing them into his jacket pocket. He didn't want to leave me defenseless, even if I was just staying in the car.

"That's for me?"

"Yes. Don't argue."

My brows rose. Did he just say that out loud? Of course, he knew how I felt about guns, especially considering that I'd avoided going to the gun range for weeks. But I was better now. Geez.

We climbed into his car and pulled out of the parking lot. As we drove along, a terrible smell wafted through the entire car, and I wrinkled my nose. "Are your clothes still in the trunk?"

"Damn." Dimples shook his head. He'd been hoping they were salvageable, but now he knew that was out of the question. The smell got worse, even with the air conditioning on high. He finally pulled into a store parking lot and followed a side alley to the back to find a dumpster.

Taking the bag from his trunk, he threw it in the dumpster and got back in the car. As we continued, the smell subsided, but didn't completely disappear. Since he'd thrown out his bag of clothes, did that mean it was him? It wasn't too bad, so I swallowed and pressed my lips together, deciding not to say anything.

We drove to a part of town that had seen better days. A few small businesses fronted the street, alongside a collection of others that had been abandoned. The building we needed was part of an old car dealership, with a service center in the back corner where the exchange would take place.

Dimples pulled to the curb on a side street that gave us a partial view of the service center. A metal, roll-up garage door fronted the street, and we watched it closely. Dimples radioed in our position and told everyone to stay clear until we had a visual on the shipment.

While we waited, Dimples handed me the gun and clip. "You should load that, just in case you need it."

I frowned, but did as he asked, making sure I had the safety on before setting it on the floor by my feet. I also rolled down my window for some fresh air. Now that we were here, my stomach clenched with nerves. Even though the smell wasn't too bad at the moment, I didn't want to risk throwing up.

"This is happening so quickly. Will Grizzo have enough back-up to go in?"

"Yes. There are usually enough police officers to come in at a moment's notice on something like this, even if the SWAT team is unavailable. We'll be fine."

Just minutes later, a black SUV pulled up to the garage door. A man jumped out and rolled up the metal door to the service center. While he waited for the SUV to drive inside, he glanced up and down the street. After the car drove in, he took another cautious glance before stepping inside and pulling the metal door back down.

With my window rolled down, I had picked up the man's thoughts about the guns in the back of the SUV, and that Redman better have the money ready, since he didn't want to stay any longer than necessary. I also picked up his eagerness for a job coming up, but I lost the rest when the door closed. "It's them. He was thinking about the guns in the SUV."

Dimples spoke into his radio. "It's a go. The guns have arrived. All units close in."

Several police cars pulled up, and Dimples left me in the car to join the other officers. As they took up their positions in front of the service center, I recognized Dante Mitchell as part of the SWAT team. He must have volunteered to help. With hand signals, they coordinated the attack. Counting down, one of the team members pulled the garage door open, and they charged inside.

The yelling and shooting started, sending shivers down my spine. I automatically grabbed the gun by my feet and held it carefully, just in case. More gunfire sounded, but I couldn't tell what was going on from here.

On the side of the building, close to my position, a man toppled out of a window. He struggled to his feet and took off at a run. I grabbed the radio. "A man just left the building. I'm in pursuit."

I jumped out of the car, just as he rounded the corner and came toward me. Pointing my gun at him, I yelled. "Stop right there! Get your hands in the air."

He skidded to a stop, but, instead of raising his hands, he turned and ran back the way he'd come. Shocked, I swore and ran after him. He dodged around a couple of parked cars and then headed toward an empty parking lot. I followed him, not sure what I was doing. I didn't want to shoot him, but I didn't want him to get away, either.

At the end of the parking lot, he ran around a corner, and I lost sight of him. I slowed before stepping around the corner and found him at the end of an alley. He tried to climb up the tall, brick wall that blocked his way, but he wasn't having any luck.

This time, I remembered to flip off the safety and raised my gun in his direction. "Get your hands in the air and turn around."

He whipped around, and his face slackened in surprise. Dipping his hand into his pocket, he pulled out a gun and took a shot at me.

Luckily, I knew he was going to shoot before he did, and I managed to duck behind a steel container. He fired a couple more shots and began to stalk toward me. Knowing I was a sitting duck, I popped up, pointing the barrel in his direction. I squeezed off a shot, but, since I'd scrunched my eyes shut, it didn't come close to hitting him.

Keeping my eyes open this time, I fired a couple more shots, but my aim didn't get any better, and time was running out.

He took another shot at me, and I ducked down. With his footsteps coming closer, I began to panic. I took another shot at him and managed to slip around the corner, just as a bullet from his gun hit the ground where I'd been.

Apparently, I couldn't hit the side of a barn, so running back to the car seemed like my best option. Hearing the man's footsteps approaching, I took off running. As I ran across the parking lot, I realized I had no cover out here in the open, so I picked up the pace.

A figure in black came running toward me, and I recognized Dante. From his mind, I picked up his horror that the man had come out of the alley and was raising his gun to shoot me in the back. With a startled breath, I dropped to the ground and rolled to the side, leaving Dante with a clear line of fire.

The guns went off, one right after the other. I cringed, but felt no pain and waited for another shot. Hearing nothing, I cautiously raised my head. Dante sprinted toward me, and I breathed a sigh of relief. Glancing back toward the other guy, I found him crumpled and unmoving on the ground.

"Are you okay?" Dante reached my side and knelt down, letting his gaze rove over me for any signs of blood.

"Yeah, I'm okay. Are you all right?"

"Me? Yes. Of course." He couldn't understand why I was asking him that. He had a rifle, and that guy was aiming for me, not him. "How did you know?"

"I saw you with the rifle earlier... when you went into the garage."

His brow creased. What was I talking about? "No... I mean him." He pointed toward the gang member.

"Oh... you mean... how did I know to duck?" At his raised brow, I continued. "Uh... my premonitions. Plus, you looked scared. I mean... not that you ever look scared... but maybe concerned? You know...for me?"

He let out a breath and nodded. "Right." He thought I was pretty far away from him, so he didn't think I could see his face that well. But... whatever.

"Stay here." He walked to the body and examined the man. He was dead all right. And he'd shot him right between the eyes. Letting out a sigh, he shook his head. He was going to get an earful after that shot. He'd tried to stay on the sidelines, but now that he'd participated in this operation, he'd probably be assigned to go on more.

He'd rather be known as a great firearm instructor than a decorated, special-ops sniper from the past. He glanced my way and shook his head. When he'd heard they were slapping this op together, and that I was involved, he'd known he couldn't sit it out.

He knew I wasn't ready for this, and he'd come partly to watch out for me. It was a good thing he had. What was I thinking to go after that guy?

As he rejoined me, he helped me to my feet. "So what happened? Over the radio, I heard you say you were following a guy, so I decided to see if you needed some help. I'm glad I made it."

"Yeah, me too. Thanks for coming."

He nodded and stared at me expectantly, so I quickly explained that the guy had jumped out a window to escape, and that I'd followed him into the dead-end alley where he took a shot at me. "I shot at him too, but we both missed." I shrugged. "I guess I need more practice."

"That's a good idea, especially if you're going to be chasing bad guys." He thought I should know better, but there was just something in me that didn't listen to reason. His gaze narrowed, and his right brow rose, reminding me of how Ramos sometimes looked at me when I was in trouble.

Oops. Oh well... what else was new? "Yeah... I get that. But I didn't want him to get away, you know?"

Unfortunately, he knew what I meant all too well, but it still didn't cancel out the risks. I definitely needed more training.

Not wanting to get chewed out, even if it was just in his mind, I changed the subject. "Uh... did you get a donut this morning? I brought donuts to the precinct to thank everyone for helping me... you know... when I got lost."

"No... I didn't get one." He feigned disappointment, even though he was thinking that he didn't eat donuts anymore. At my frown, he chuckled. "But it's okay. You can bring me a donut the next time you come to the shooting range... which should be sometime this week."

I shook my head. "Not if you don't eat them anymore."

He froze. "What?"

Oops. "I think you told me once that you don't eat donuts because they're bad for you. You like to eat all that natural-foods, healthy stuff. Right?"

He couldn't remember ever telling me that, but he must have, since I knew. "Well... sure, but I'd eat one if you brought it. I'm not that much of a stickler."

"Oh... good to know." I hoped that meant he wasn't as straight-laced as he seemed, since I could use a little leeway now and then. "Anyways... I'll see about coming to the shooting range."

"That's a good idea." Before I could turn away, he stopped me. "Just out of curiosity, did you close your eyes when you shot at him?"

"Uh... maybe the first shot, but not after that."

He sighed. "Try and come in this week, okay? Especially if you're going to be working with vice on things like this. That was close." He was thinking that, for someone who was supposed to stay out of the way, it boggled his mind that I could still get into a shootout with a gun runner. If anyone needed the training, it was me.

"Yeah... I guess you have a point."

"Good."

Several people came rushing toward us, with Dimples leading the pack. "Shelby. What happened? Are you okay?"

"Yeah... I'm fine. Did you get Redman?"

Dimples looked past me to the body on the ground. "If that's him, we did."

"It is." Dante glanced my way, wishing he could tell the detective that I hadn't put my life in danger to do it. Now he might have to have a serious talk with him about my safety. "Thanks to Shelby. She stopped him from getting away."

Dimples widened his eyes. "Did you—"

"That's Redman?" I shook my head. "Now I don't feel so bad that he's dead. And... no, I didn't shoot him. I tried, but I missed." At his raised brows, I shrugged. "I may need more practice at the shooting range."

More officers joined us, and one of them took charge of the scene. I headed back to the garage with Dimples and Dante, waiting as far from the dead bodies as I could, while they spoke to Grizzo.

I picked up that, along with arresting everyone who wasn't dead, they'd found several crates full of guns. Grizzo shook his head, thinking we'd hit the jackpot.

He glanced my way. How did I do it? What he wouldn't give to have me on his team. He'd have to talk to the chief about it. Maybe they could work something out? But what if I objected? He hadn't been the nicest person to work with, but he could change. He could be nicer.

On impulse, Grizzo stepped to my side and flashed a smile. "I don't know how to thank you Shelby. We wouldn't have made the bust without you."

"Without me and Detective Harris, you mean. It was mostly him."

"Is that right?"

Dimples had followed him over and quickly spoke up. "Yeah. Shelby and I make a good team, don't you think?"

Grizzo snorted, knowing he'd just been put in his place. Raising his nose in the air, he sniffed and shook his head. "Man... what's that smell?" His right brow arched. Stepping closer to Dimples, he recoiled. "Whew. I heard you had a run-in with a shit tank. It must be true. You stink."

Dimples caught my gaze, and I shrugged. "It wasn't me."

A few of the others joined in, teasing Dimples with well-placed barbs. He shook his head. "Come on, Shelby. Let's get out of here."

"If it's too stinky in the car, I can take you," someone yelled.

A few others laughed and joked some more, but I waved them off and followed Dimples to his car. Since my window was still open, I left it that way to help with the smell. Then I cranked up the air conditioning.

"Do I really stink?"

"Uh... yeah. You do. But just a little. And it's not too bad. Maybe it's coming from your wallet, or your phone?"

He swore under his breath, wondering how the officers had found out. It couldn't have been just the smell. Someone must have seen him in the locker room, or Jinx might have said something. "I think I'll take the rest of the day off."

"Yeah... me too." I grinned at him, and he managed to smile back. "Hey... at least we solved the case, right?"

"Yes... yes we did."

CHAPTER 15

The next morning began with a phone call from Billie. We hadn't spoken much since camping together, and she wanted to meet for lunch. "I've got my article written for the paper about our prospecting experience, and I thought I'd pass it by you before it goes to print."

My heart sank. "Is that because I'm in it?"

"I may have mentioned you, but that's because you got lost, and it was already in the news. But don't worry, it's not bad."

"Okay, but... you'll change it if it's too personal, right?"

"Of course."

We agreed to meet downtown, near her office, and disconnected.

Since it was early, I still had plenty of time to take Coco on a walk before I had to get ready. With the kids in school, we'd become best buds, and, after he'd rescued me, we had a special bond.

While we were out, I got another phone call from Uncle Joey. After a quick greeting, he got down to business. "I'd like you to come in today. Stewart and Ian are stopping by, and I'd like to know what they're up to."

"Sounds good to me. Would around one this afternoon work?"

"I'll set it up."

"Great. See you then."

Billie waved to me as I walked into the restaurant, excitement glowing on her face. We hugged each other, and the hostess led us to our table. A server came by with menus and asked for our drink orders. After taking a moment to decide what food entrees we wanted, Billie focused her attention on me.

"I'm so glad to see you're looking better." Billie was surprised that my lip and cheek weren't swollen, and the cut on my chin was barely noticeable. "I can't imagine how horrifying that must have been."

"Yeah... it was pretty bad. I'm just grateful Coco found me."

"He's an amazing dog. Did they tell you how hard Coco worked on the first day he got there?" She shook her head. "It was too bad they started in the wrong place, because that dog tried so hard to find your scent that his nose was bleeding. Poor thing."

My heart lurched. "No... they didn't tell me. That's awful." Remorse caught in my throat for what I'd put my dog through. "You know I didn't mean to get lost, right?"

Her breath caught. "Oh... of course not. I didn't mean to make you feel bad, but I just wanted you to know how much your dog must love you... along with everyone else. A lot of people came, and even those who couldn't come were praying for you."

She'd been terrified herself, and she'd never seen Drew so upset. Witnessing Chris and Josh's frantic worry had nearly broken her heart. Even the gruff mob boss had shed a tear when Chris and Josh arrived with Coco at the cabin. It was a close thing, and it had scared them all.

She thanked God there had been a happy ending. Otherwise, my dog would probably still be up there looking for me... and probably a certain hitman, too. He'd tried not to show it, but she couldn't mistake the feelings he had for me.

He'd insisted on taking the rope to pull me out, and no one dared defy him. She'd watched him strain to slow down when it was clear that he'd wanted to pull me out of there as fast as possible. She also hadn't missed the look of longing on his face when I'd emerged, and fallen into Chris's and Josh's arms. He'd swallowed and wiped at his eyes when he thought no one was looking.

It puzzled her. We weren't lovers, but we were more than friends. The depth to our relationship was something she'd never seen between two people who weren't together. She'd call it devotion and a healthy respect for one another, which somehow worked, but she knew it cost him, and she hoped I didn't take it for granted.

Well hell. Tears stung my eyes, and I blinked, hoping I could control all the emotions that threatened to overwhelm me. "You're... you're making me cry."

"Oh... I'm sorry." She patted my hand. "I'm a terrible friend. I didn't mean to upset you. It must have been a terrifying experience, but it all turned out okay, and you're here. That's what matters the most, right?"

I nodded. She had no idea how her thoughts had affected me, and I wasn't sure I was grateful I'd heard them or not. I knew everyone had worried about me, but seeing it from her point of view made it even harder.

I wiped my eyes and sent her a smile. "It's just so fresh that it's hard to talk about right now. I know I've been given a second chance, and I'm really grateful for that."

"I understand. And when you're ready to tell me what you went through, I'd love to listen."

"Thanks Billie. I'll keep that in mind."

Always thinking about the next great angle, her thoughts raced toward how my experience could become one of those 'drama in real life' stories, and how she could write it for me. Maybe in a week or two, she'd ask me if I was ready to share.

I managed to keep from sighing too loudly, but honestly, what could I expect? She was a reporter, and one of the best. Beyond that, she was also my friend, so I'd have to cut her some slack.

The server came back with our drinks and took our food orders before leaving again. I smiled at Billie, ready to move on. "So what did you want to tell me about your article? Were you impressed with Stewart and Ian?"

She shook her head. "Not after we got lost in that cave. I thought they'd be better prepared with ropes and things like that. It doesn't make a lot of sense when you think about it. I mean, they were prospecting for a gold mine. Wouldn't that mean you needed mining things?"

I nodded. "Well... yeah I see what you mean. But they did supply all of us with headlamps and our camping supplies and equipment. Did something happen after I got lost?"

"No. It was just a feeling I got. They were upset that you got lost, but I think it was more because that meant putting off their exploration of that cave. I heard them talking about going back with metal detectors. I think finding that dead miner made it look like the right place. Do you think it was?"

"I don't know." That was a total lie, but I wasn't ready to share my secret with anyone.

She was thinking that, without seeing any gold, it didn't seem like it. But maybe we'd taken a wrong turn and the gold was there, but just in a different place? If that cave did turn out to be the mine, it would change her whole story.

Wanting to be helpful, I asked, "what have you got so far?"

She shrugged. "I'm making it into a special-interest story with a cautionary twist. I'm starting out with telling a little history about the legend of the lost mine, and then I'm telling about how vast that mountain range is and ending with the inherent danger of getting lost." She didn't say *like you*, but of course, I heard it.

"But if that cave turns out to be the mine," she continued. "I'm leaving the story a little open-ended, so I can revisit it. Do you know if Stewart and Ian are still up there?"

She'd kept the question casual, but the eagerness behind it made me realize that this was the main reason for our lunch. She wanted to know if they'd found any gold and if this was the real deal.

Before I could respond, the server came back with our lunches. After taking a few bites of my chef salad, I answered her question. "I just found out this morning that they're back for a few days. I'm actually meeting with them at Uncle Joey's office right after we get done with lunch."

"Oh yeah?" Her eyes widened. She wanted to come with me in the worst way. "Uh... I guess I can't come, but will you let me know if it's something big?" I didn't respond right away, and she continued. "Not that you need to tell me the whole story, but you know I can keep a secret, right? I certainly wouldn't mention it until you gave me the go ahead."

I shrugged. "I'll see what I can do, but don't hold your breath. I don't think the cave we were in is the lost mine."

Her expression fell. "Is that because of your premonitions?"

I hesitated, not sure how to answer that. "You know... I can't really say for sure. They could find some gold in there, so I guess we'll have to wait and see. I'd be more interested in who the lost miner was. Are you including him in your article?"

"No. Stewart warned me not to, so I can't."

"That's too bad. But maybe it's a good idea. Who knows how many people would head up there to try and find the gold themselves, right?"

"Exactly. That's why I'm including the stories of all the lost miners, and our own experience of you getting lost. The mountains can be unforgiving, even if you're prepared, and people need to know that."

"It sounds like a great story. You're leaving Uncle Joey and Ramos out of it though... right?"

"Oh... yes. Of course." She'd had to do that since leaving out their participation was in the non-disclosure agreement that she'd signed. "I mean, I mention that we have a few people with us, but I don't give out their names."

I nodded. "Well, if I find out anything interesting in my meeting with them, I'll let you know."

"I appreciate it."

"So how's Dimples doing? Does he still stink?"

"Oh my gosh!" She chuckled. "It was bad. He showered when he got home, and I made him shower again before we went to bed. We had to get rid of everything, even his wallet and his badge case. His phone was waterproof, so that was good, and it still works, but we had to clean it, and his badge, and all his plastic cards about a hundred times.

"Drew wasn't real specific about what happened, so you have to tell me the whole story. And don't you dare leave anything out."

I was happy to oblige, and it was easy to laugh about it today. "I hope the other officers don't give him too much of a hard time."

She shrugged. "They will for a while, but it will fade, and something new will come along."

"Isn't that the truth?"

We spoke about other things while we finished our meal, and we soon parted ways.

I drove to Thrasher, excited to see Uncle Joey and Ramos after all we'd been through. Of course, my main objective was to hear what Stewart and Ian had to say for themselves, but that didn't stop me from hoping for a motorcycle ride later. After what I'd been through, I needed it more than ever.

I stepped out of the elevator and caught sight of Jackie sitting at her desk. She glanced up and grinned, then hurried around her desk to give me a hug. "Shelby! You had us all so worried. I'm so glad you're okay."

"Thanks. Me too."

"When Joe told me he wanted to go prospecting with you, I thought he was nuts, but I'm sure glad he was there to help find you. I'm even more grateful that Chris and Josh had so much faith in your dog. That made all the difference to Joe." She was thinking *and Ramos*, but she figured I already knew that.

"Yeah, isn't it crazy how things turn out? When we got Coco, and he turned out to be a search-and-rescue dog, I never thought I'd be the one he needed to rescue."

She nodded, thinking life was strange that way. "Then there was the poker tournament you won. I have to admit that when I'd heard you'd beaten Sonny out of ten million dollars..." She shook her head. "It did my heart good." She leaned toward me and lowered her voice. "And he's still alive, which is a miracle, if you ask me. How did you do it?"

"Oh... it wasn't just me. Uncle Joey just needed time to think it through." It didn't sound like she knew anything about the Debt Collector, so I wasn't about to mention him. "So it all worked out in the end."

"Yes, thankfully, it did. I just hope we never hear from Sonny again."

"Now that's something I don't think you'll have to worry about... so are Stewart and Ian already here?"

She shook her head. "Not yet, but why don't you head down to Joe's office? He'll want to talk to you before they get here."

"Okay."

I stepped to the end of the hallway and gave a quick knock before opening the door. Both Uncle Joey and Ramos jumped to their feet and hurried over to give me a hug. Ramos was closer, so he got to me first. His hug was tight, but heartfelt and sweet.

Uncle Joey hugged me tightly as well. He pulled away, but still held onto my upper arms. "Let me look at you."

He examined my face, taking in my scraped cheek, cut lip, and stitched chin. "You look pretty good for falling into a hole. How do you feel?"

"Good... really good." For some stupid reason, my eyes filled with tears. "A little weepy though, sorry."

His lips pressed together, and he pulled me in for another hug. "Of all the times you've been in trouble Shelby, this one got to me the most. I guess it's because you just disappeared, and I didn't know if we'd ever find you."

Unable to speak, I nodded against his chest. He let out a breath and straightened, letting me go and wiping his eyes.

"I want to hear what happened to you up there, but first we have to deal with Stewart and Ian."

His phone rang, and he picked it up. "Yes? ... Good. Put them in the conference room, and we'll be right there." He caught my gaze. "I don't trust them, and I think your disappearance played right into their hands."

"Why?"

He shrugged. "I think they wanted us to leave so they could go back to that cave. When I spoke with them before you got lost, they told me they thought that cave held real promise, but now they're not telling me anything. I'm not sure I can believe anything they say."

I nodded. "Makes sense to me. They didn't want to share the gold, so telling you it's not there fits right in with their plans."

"So, if that is the lost mine, I want you to catch them in the lie. I won't let them get away with double-crossing me."

"Uh... right. But..." I hesitated, unsure what to tell him. "I can do that."

Uncle Joey noticed my hesitation, and his eyes narrowed. "But what?"

"I'll tell you after we see what they have to say."

I was asking him to trust me, and he didn't hesitate. "Okay."

On the way down the hall, I stopped at my office door. "I'm going to leave my bag in here." Uncle Joey nodded and continued down the hall. Ramos held the door open and waited for me. I sent him a grateful smile and realized that he'd blocked his thoughts. I couldn't pick up a thing. A prickle of panic stabbed through me. Why would he do that?

Reaching inside my bag, I grabbed Jeremiah's journal to give back to Stewart. Next, I pushed the bag into the bottom drawer of my desk and rejoined Ramos in the hall. "Is everything okay?"

His brows drew together. "Of course. Why?"

"Uh..." I shrugged. "I just... wondered." I couldn't exactly tell him it bothered me that I couldn't hear his thoughts.

He shook his head and took a breath. "I'll tell you later."

I swallowed. "Okay." Crap. What did that mean? Was he going to tell me he couldn't be around me anymore? Or that he cared too much, and he had to move on? Would our time together come to an end because I was married and unavailable? Was it taking too much of a toll on him?

By the time we got to the conference room, my heart was breaking, and I was a mess. I couldn't lose Ramos... I just couldn't. But I couldn't lose Chris and what we had together either. What had I done? Was I the biggest idiot that ever lived?

"Shelby?" Uncle Joey's brows drew together. "Everything okay?"

"Oh... sure." I glanced around the room and realized everyone was sitting down but me. I hurried to my chair beside Uncle Joey and pasted a pleasant smile on my face. "Hey guys. Here's Jeremiah's journal." I handed it to Stewart. "Sorry I didn't get it back to you sooner, but I was... you know... lost."

Stewart's eyes widened. In the excitement, he'd forgotten all about it. "Thanks Shelby. We're glad to see you're okay. You had us worried."

"Yeah. It was... pretty horrible. I thought I was going to die in that hole. I was really lucky."

He nodded. "You have an amazing dog. I was impressed with your son, too. He kept a cool head and did everything right."

"Thanks. Yeah. He's great." Tears filled my eyes again, and I quickly blinked them away. What the freak was wrong with me?

"So tell us what you've found," Uncle Joey said. "We're hoping for some good news."

"I think I've got some for you. After all the excitement, we went back to the cave, only this time we were better prepared." Stewart blamed himself that we'd gotten so turned around the first time. It was the excitement that did it, but that was no excuse.

"We took a metal detector, along with more flashlights and ropes." He paused. His gaze shifted between me and Uncle Joey while excitement danced in his eyes. "We found some gold. So far, it's only been a few small rocks, and nothing like Jeremiah described in his journal. But I think it shows promise. In order to really know what's there, we've got to shore up the entrance and do some digging."

I met Uncle Joey's surprised gaze before turning to Stewart. "Wow, that's amazing. So you're sure it was mined in the past?"

"Yes. We think there might have been a collapse in that part of the cave because of the mining they'd been doing. If we can dig it out, we're hoping that's where we'll find the gold. We've already staked a claim there, so now we just need to get the ball rolling."

Uncle Joey nodded, his eyes glazing over with gold-fever excitement. "So what are you proposing?"

"We need a mining crew to shore up the entrance and passages that lead to the part of the cave that collapsed. Then we can start digging out the rocks there and see if we find anything."

Ian jumped in. "It looks good, but it's not a sure thing. The metal detector gave us some hope that we're onto something, but, like Stewart said, it could be a little, or it could be a lot. We won't know until we get into it."

"That's where we need you." Stewart broke in, taking over. "We'll need more investment money to get things off the ground. I know it's a risk, but I think it's worth it." Stewart was convinced that skeleton belonged to Jeremiah Taft, and somewhere in that cave was the motherlode of gold Taft had found all those years ago.

Uncle Joey was thinking that this wasn't what he'd expected. They weren't trying to pull one over on him after all, and now he had the option of going into the mining business. Was it worth it? He glanced my way. What did I think? It was mostly my idea, and partly my money, so what did I want?

I sent him a nod and focused on Ian and Stewart. They were so eager to find the gold that it surprised me. Had I been like that? If I hadn't fallen in that hole, would I be ready to join their scheme? "We'd like some time to think about it."

Stewart blinked. He had not expected me to say that. "Oh... of course." He glanced at Ian. "We'd like to know soon though."

"Have you spent all the money Uncle Joey gave you?"

"No." He was thinking they'd spent about half, most of it on their debts, but it would run out quickly once they started mining.

"How about this... there's not a lot of time left before winter sets in. Why don't you do what you can with the funds you already have? Once you run out, we can decide if you've found anything worth pursuing."

Uncle Joey smiled, thinking that sounded reasonable. "I think that's an excellent plan, Shelby." He glanced at the men. "Are we in agreement?"

They both nodded, and Uncle Joey stood, offering them his hand. "Good. Then we'll expect another report in a few weeks."

After shaking hands all around, they left, only slightly disappointed.

I'd picked up that Stewart had wanted a bigger commitment from us, at least a couple million dollars, but, with the stakes so high, he could understand my caution. Still, once he found the motherlode, he was sure we'd back him, so that's what he needed to concentrate on now.

I knew that wasn't going to happen, but that didn't mean there wasn't gold in that cave. Apparently, they'd found a few rocks with gold in them, so maybe there was more? But I wasn't going to back it now, or ever. Not when I knew where the real mine was. Of course, did I know where it was? I'd been there, but could I find my way back?

"Well, Shelby," Uncle Joey said. "That was an excellent plan you came up with." He was proud of me, especially since I'd been so gung ho about backing this project in the first place. I was showing some real restraint.

"Thanks, but I have a confession to make."

His brows rose. "What's that?"

I glanced between him and Ramos. "Come to my office, and I'll tell you."

This time, I sat behind the desk, with Ramos and Uncle Joey taking the chairs in front of me. The chairs in my office weren't quite as nice as those in Uncle Joey's, but they worked just as well.

Both of them studied me with speculation, wondering what I was up to. I couldn't help the big grin that flashed over my face. Reaching down, I slid the bottom drawer of my desk open and pulled out my bag. I'd chosen this bag because it was big, ugly, and zipped along the top.

Taking a deep breath, I reached in and pulled out a rock made of shiny, white quartz and crisscrossed with heavy, golden veins. It was my favorite, and I set it on top of my desk. Next, I pulled two more stunning rocks out of the bag and set them beside the first. They were all about the same size and filled with beautiful, yellow gold.

Both Ramos and Uncle Joey gasped. Uncle Joey swore under his breath, and Ramos sat there with his mouth open. They both shifted to the edge of their seats and leaned forward to get a better look.

"That's pure gold," Uncle Joey blurted.

"Damn," Ramos said. His gaze caught mine before falling back to the rocks. "Can I..."

"Sure. This one's mine." I touched the first rock. "But those are for each of you."

Uncle Joey took the rock closest to him and held it reverently. At first he was surprised at how heavy it was, but then he shook his head, knowing it only made sense. Ramos took his and held it under the light, marveling at the rock's beauty. He'd never seen anything like it.

I watched them with a smile on my face, giving them time to absorb what they held in their hands. After a moment of complete awe, they set the rocks back on my desk and looked at me. Uncle Joey spoke first. "Tell us everything."

I began with the scent of mint that I'd picked up after Stewart let me take Jeremiah's journal. "I smelled it on the way to that ridge, so I thought we were on the right track, but it disappeared somewhere along the way.

"I didn't smell it again until I got lost. I feel so stupid, because I didn't even realize I'd gotten turned around. When I couldn't see Ramos anywhere, I panicked. Instead of staying put, I went back to the trees, but now I don't think it was even the same trees."

I met Ramos's gaze. "I called your name several times, but when I didn't get a response, I decided to try a different direction."

I shook my head. "That's when I smelled the same minty scent as before. I followed it, hoping Jeremiah was leading me back to camp. Boy was I wrong. I was looking up at that big tree in the clearing when I fell into the hole. It knocked the breath right out of me, and roughed me up a bit, but I was fine. I just couldn't get back out.

"That's when I realized it was more than just a hole. I turned on my flashlight and stepped into a small cavern. I found Jeremiah's bones there, along with a pouch full of gold. There was gold everywhere I looked. It was..." I shook my head. "Breathtaking."

"I thought there might be another way out, so I followed a tunnel as far as I could, only to find it blocked by a bunch of rocks. It must have happened while Jeremiah was in there, and that's why he couldn't get out. It's probably why no one else ever found the cave again."

Uncle Joey turned to Ramos. "Do you know where it is? If we went back, could you find it again?"

Ramos shrugged. "I'm not sure. I wasn't paying much attention, but I think I know the general direction, so I might be able to find it."

Uncle Joey glanced my way. Why didn't I tell them about the gold when they found me? They could have marked the general vicinity on the map they'd brought. Now it might be lost forever.

"I know what you're thinking, but I was traumatized. And... there was something else."

"What?" Uncle Joey asked.

"I think it may have been the burial place of an ancient Indian Chief." I told them about the second cavern I'd found and the petroglyphs on the walls. "A stone box with the top knocked off was filled with bones and gold. I got some weird vibes from it, so I pushed the stone back on top of the box.

"As soon as I did, the beating sound I'd been hearing in my head stopped. So I think I did the right thing, but I didn't dare go back in that cavern."

Uncle Joey's brows drew together. "So... you think the cave is cursed? Was that the reason you didn't say anything?"

"Well... when you say it like that, it seems silly, but..." I shrugged. "I just wasn't ready to talk about it... until now. I mean... I took those three rocks out, and nothing bad happened to me, so maybe it's okay."

Ramos nodded. He could understand my hesitation, especially if I heard dead people. Or did I just smell them? He was a little confused.

I shook my head. "I'm confused too. All I know is that when I entered the cavern with the petroglyphs, I heard a beating sound—like a heart. Once I stepped closer to the stone box, it got louder and louder until I could hardly stand it. After I pushed the stone lid back over the box, it stopped.

"I got out of there as fast as I could. To be honest, it freaked me out. Then, on top of that, I had to spend two nights down there with Jeremiah's bones. I'm surprised I'm not a nervous wreck."

"You did fine, Shelby." Uncle Joey leaned forward. "You're here... and these rocks are amazing. Now I understand why you didn't want to finance Stewart's excavation." He sat back and folded his hands together. "And now that I think about it, you did the right thing by not telling anyone."

He was thinking that now we wouldn't have to share our find with Stewart, so I'd done well, even if we never found it again.

Ramos glanced my way. "But what about Josh? He was using a GPS tracker during our search. He probably knows exactly where you were."

Ramos was thinking about his drive home with Josh. He'd been impressed with Josh's clear-headed focus during the search, and Josh had even opened up to him a little on the drive home.

Ramos wondered if I knew how much Josh wanted a car of his own. He thought Josh could handle it. Hell, Josh was more responsible than any kid he'd ever known at that age, so he hoped I'd consider it, because he was tempted to give the kid a car if I didn't.

My brows rose, and I sent Ramos a smile, pleased that he thought Josh was a great kid, since I happened to agree.

"Is that right, Shelby?" Uncle Joey asked. "Would Josh know?"

I nodded. "Yeah... he could probably figure it out, but I'm not ready to involve him in this."

"I agree. Maybe someday we can go back there, but, for now, I think we should put these rocks in my safe."

"Really? But my rock looks so pretty on my desk next to my paperweight from the newspaper. It kind of makes up for not having my poker trophy, you know?"

"That's right. What happened to it?"

"I think I left it in the car, or in Sonny's office. I don't know for sure."

"That's too bad." Uncle Joey was thinking he could ask Sonny to send it to us, but he didn't want to talk to the bastard.

"I might be able to help with that," Ramos said. "But it means you'll have to take a ride with me on my bike."

My eyes widened. "Uh... really? Well... sure. I can do that." I didn't want to sound too eager, but who was I kidding? Both of them smirked.

Ramos quickly blocked his thoughts, but I was beginning to understand why now. He didn't want me to know what he'd done, but it was a little late for that. "So how did you get it?"

"You'll see. Now stop eavesdropping."

I couldn't help the smile that sprang to my lips. "Okay... okay. Let's go already."

"I'll put these away." Uncle Joey picked up all three of the golden rocks, impressed by how heavy they were, and we followed him out of my office. He turned right toward his office, and we turned left down the hall.

"We'll be back in a minute." Ramos told Jackie.

I sent her a big smile. She shook her head, but couldn't help smiling back. I just looked too darn happy for her to be a spoil-sport about Ramos.

In the elevator, Ramos pushed the button for the parking level.

"So where are we going?"

Ramos shook his head, knowing he couldn't keep a secret from me, no matter how hard he tried. "I wanted to surprise you, but you're not going to let me."

"Nope, I'm not."

"I was hoping to have it sitting on your desk when you came in today, but it didn't get here soon enough, so now we've got to pick it up from Manetto's place."

At my raised brows, he continued. "I tracked it down and had my contact ship it there." He checked his phone, bringing up the text alert. "It says it was delivered an hour ago."

We stepped into the parking garage. Ramos clicked his key fob to open the trunk of his car. My helmet sat inside, and he handed it over. A few minutes later, I swung my leg over the seat of his bike and settled in behind him.

I held onto him tightly, and we roared out of the parking garage. Butterflies danced in my stomach, and my breath caught in my lungs. With a big grin on my face, and the wind in my hair, I settled in to enjoy the ride.

With everything I'd gone through lately, being on the back of a motorcycle behind Ramos was good for my soul, and, after feeling so scared and helpless, I'd never again take it for granted.

Sure, bad things happened, even though I'd tried to make sure they didn't. All the planning in the world wouldn't change that. There were just too many things I couldn't control or predict... even with the advantage of my mind reading skills.

But there was also a lot of good that happened too, and I wouldn't trade those times for anything.

So... maybe it was time to admit that my life was never going to go the way I planned it, but maybe that was just the way it was supposed to be.

Thank you for reading **High Stakes Crime: A Shelby Nichols Adventure**. I am currently hard at work on Shelby's next adventure and promise to do my best for another thrilling ride!

If you enjoyed this book, please consider leaving a review on Amazon. It's a great way to thank an author and keep her writing! **High Stakes Crime** is also available on Kindle and Audible!

Want to know more about Ella St. John? Get **Angel Falls: Sand and Shadows Book 1** and find out how Ella, the nurse Shelby meets in Ghostly Serenade, ended up in Las Vegas with Aiden Creed. It is available in ebook, paperback, hardback, and audible. Don't miss this exciting adventure!

Ramos has his own book! **Devil in a Black Suit,** a book about Ramos and his mysterious past from his point of view is available in paperback, ebook, and audible formats. Get your copy today!

NEWSLETTER SIGNUP For news, updates, and special offers, please sign up for my newsletter on my website: www.colleenhelme.com. To thank you for subscribing you will receive a FREE ebook.

SHELBY NICHOLS CONSULTING Don't miss Shelby's blog posts about her everyday life! Be sure to visit shelbynicholsconsulting.com.

ABOUT THE AUTHOR

USA TODAY AND WALL STREET JOURNAL BESTSLLING AUTHOR

Colleen Helme is the author of the bestselling Shelby Nichols Adventure Series, a wildly entertaining and highly humorous series about Shelby Nichols, a woman with the ability to read minds.

She is also the author of the Sand and Shadow Series, a spin-off from the Shelby Nichols Series featuring Ella St. John, a woman with a special 'healing' touch. Between writing about these two friends, Colleen has her hands full, but is enjoying every minute of it, especially when they appear in books together.

When not writing, Colleen spends most of her time thinking about new ways to get her characters in and out of trouble. She loves to connect with readers and admits that fans of her books keep her writing.

Connect with Colleen at www.colleenhelme.com

Printed in Great Britain
by Amazon

25049366R00182